A CHOICE OF NIGHTMARES

"A page-turning adventure from a novelist with a style the rest of us can only wish for." —Charlie Stella

"Kostoff's debut novel takes a disturbing look at the drug trade and the destruction it wreaks, not only on users but on suppliers as well." —*Publishers Weekly*

"A noir thriller that delivers with vivid writing, smart plotting, and a deeper-than-usual insight into its flawed central character."
—*Kirkus Reviews*

THE LONG FALL

"...there is some genuine suspense and dark humor here." —*Booklist*

"...craftily written noir thriller... Kostoff's narrative goes down nice and easy..." —*Publishers Weekly*

"...reminded me of the best of Elmore Leonard." —James Hockings

LATE RAIN

"Kostoff ... returns to crime fiction with a promising series debut starring a principled cop who is beginning to heal himself."
—Sue O'Brien, *Booklist*

WORDS TO DIE FOR

"In this one, his display of razor-sharp prose and compelling narrative drive is at its height... Kostoff here adapts the noir tradition to a soul-searching examination of postmodern trends in recent American social history." —William M. Ramsey

"Dark humor and revulsion mingle uneasily throughout, especially as the narrative rolls to its chaotic final outcome. It's a compelling and fast-moving novel, combining a well-tuned mystery plot with scathing satire." —Amazon reader

"Kostoff manages to generate interest and intrigue throughout and tops it all off with a fascinating ending." —W. A. Burt

Lynn Kostoff Bibliography

A Choice of Nightmares (1991)
The Long Fall (2003)
Late Rain (2010)
Words to Die For (2014)
The Length of Days (2025)

THE LENGTH OF DAYS

LYNN KOSTOFF

Stark House Press • Eureka California

THE LENGTH OF DAYS

Published by Stark House Press
1315 H Street
Eureka, CA 95501
griffinskye3@sbcglobal.net
www.starkhousepress.com

THE LENGTH OF DAYS
Published by permission of the author and copyright © 2025 by Lynn Kostoff

All rights reserved under International and Pan-American Copyright
Conventions.

ISBN: 979-8-88601-151-7

Cover and text design by Mark Shepard, shepgraphics.com
Proofreading by Bill Kelly

PUBLISHER'S NOTE:
This is a work of fiction, though it takes place in a mix of real and imagined
places. Names, characters, places and incidents are a wild mix of fact and
fiction; any resemblance to actual persons, living or dead, events or locales,
may not be all that coincidental.
Without limiting the rights under copyright reserved above, no part of this
publication may be reproduced, stored, or introduced into a retrieval system
or transmitted in any form or by any means (electronic, mechanical,
photocopying, recording or otherwise) without the prior written permission
of both the copyright owner and the above publisher of the book.

First Stark House Press Edition: July 2025

For Melanie and Jeremy

And in memory of Janet and Lewis Kostoff

"I returned, and saw under the sun, that the race
is not to the swift, not the battle to the strong,
neither yet bread to the wise, nor yet riches to men
of understanding, nor yet favour to men of
skill; but time and chance happeneth to them all."
ECCLESIASTES 9.11

"There's a difference between Destiny and Fate.
It's important not to confuse the two.
Destiny is a wet dream.
It's Fate you have to look out for.
Fate measures the length of your days.
The length of your days measures you."
—John Sloane, owner and proprietor,
the Colorado Bar, Tu Do Street, Saigon

PART ONE

SLOTS

THE LENGTH OF DAYS — ONE

Wednesdays and Saturdays, Samuel Fulton runs the Presidents. It started as a simple routine but is now edging its way into ritual, gaining emotional and psychological weight with each run, Samuel leaving his townhouse at Bayview Manor late in the afternoon and taking Hanover Avenue until it intersects with Fremont Street in northwest Magnolia Beach, Samuel then driving three blocks and pulling into the lot of the Parnassus Diner where he eventually takes a window seat and orders black coffee as a preamble to the unvarying order of a cheeseburger platter, Samuel, in the interim, paging through *The Magnolia Beach Monitor* and trying to acclimate himself to what he has yet to see as or call home since his wife Glenda and he moved there fourteen months ago.

It's a Wednesday, so his waitress is Shirley. Saturdays, it's Jena.

Shirley's in her early forties, at least thirty years his junior, with two ex-husbands in the wind and three grown children, only one of whom stays in touch beyond birthdays and holidays. She has a kindly smile, a smoker's cough, sun-cured South Carolina skin, and pale blue eyes fanning into laugh lines. She's dating the owner of Tommy's Towing Service but claims it's not serious.

Shirley pours his coffee. "Any change?" she asks. That, too, has become part of the ritual. It's followed by Samuel shaking his head no and then thanking her for asking.

Fifteen minutes later, Shirley brings his cheeseburger platter. Samuel sets aside his newspaper. He spreads a napkin across his lap and turns down a refill on the coffee. He eats slowly, with measured bites, and when he's done, he slips the tip beneath his plate, takes his bill to the front register, and pays up. Before leaving, he turns the knob on a squat metal canister, and a wooden toothpick drops into a curved slot. Samuel tucks the toothpick in the corner of his mouth and leaves.

Outside, February still can't make up its mind if it's late winter or early spring, the days continually seesawing between freeze and bud, and Samuel Fulton stands for a moment in the parking lot and looks at an uneasy skyline full of mismatched light and mottled gray cloudbanks. Right then, he misses the Midwest and the clear demarcation of seasons, days that squarely fit the calendar.

For the next twenty minutes, Samuel drives his Taurus through northwest Magnolia Beach. On Saturdays, he plays the car radio. Wednesdays, he likes the silence. This quadrant of the city is blue-collar and old-school middle class, its neighborhoods as high as upward mobility can or will ever take its inhabitants.

Near Delray's Small Engine Repair, a middle-aged couple is walking a brown and white dog. They wave as Samuel passes, and he lifts his hand a little late in a delayed reaction. He has not gotten used to the South's habit of waving at strangers. He can understand and appreciate the sentiment behind the gesture, but as a Midwesterner who'd used his waves for people he knew, the whole thing still feels a little too indiscriminate.

Samuel slows as he drives past St. Matthew's Lutheran Church. He looks at the large red doors fronting the church. He knows what will happen when those red doors open on this particular Ash Wednesday evening. He can already feel the rector's fingers on his forehead and then hear the words that accompany the sign of the cross: *Remember that you are dust, and to dust you shall return.*

Samuel, however, doesn't wait for those doors to open. At seventy-one, he knows all too well that dust is a truth that he and most of the residents at the Bayview Manor complex wake up to and put to bed each day.

As Samuel gets back on Fremont, the sky suddenly collapses under the weight of the clouds, and he hits the lights and wipers on the Taurus. The rain arrives at a sharp slant, growing hard and insistent. Within two blocks, he has the defroster on high. The wipers move like a set of arms thrown up over and over in surprise or surrender.

He thinks about turning around and heading back to the Bayview complex, but Madison's coming up on his left, and Samuel taps the blinker and begins to run the Presidents, following Madison to Roosevelt and Roosevelt to Jackson and Jackson to Washington and Washington to Harrison and Harrison to Taylor and Taylor to Jefferson. The neighborhood is World War II vintage, a mix of one- and two-story homes, most wood or asbestos-sided and bounded by tree-lined sidewalks fronting the network of streets running in strict right-angled grids.

There's a run of thunder off to the west, and by the time Samuel makes Jefferson, it feels as if he's driven into an eight-hundred-and-twenty-seven-mile-long memory, one that's been in place for close to fifty years.

THE LENGTH OF DAYS

Right now, for all intents and purposes, he could have been back in Ryland, Ohio, newly married, flush with plans and promises, and about to turn onto Alexander Street and into the driveway of the first home his wife Glenda and he had owned.

519 Alexander or 805 Jefferson. A white wood house that fit either address.

Samuel glances down at the dash. The *Service Engine Soon* light surfaces and flickers and then holds. He slows, then pulls in next to the curb.

The Taurus's engine shudders and cuts off.

The front door of the white house bursts open. A young woman in a black bra and red panties starts running at a diagonal across the front lawn. She's carrying a pair of high-heeled shoes in her left hand.

A tall man wearing khakis and a pale blue shirt chases after her.

The woman looks back over her shoulder. She slips and falls and gets up again. She's lost one of the shoes she'd been carrying.

The rain begins to pick up again, thin silvery sheets that the wind turns inside out.

The woman is running toward Samuel and the Taurus. She's yelling something, but Samuel can't make out the words.

The man closes in, catching up and grabbing a fistful of hair. The woman tries to break free, but finally can't. The man starts dragging her back toward the house.

Samuel hits the horn on the Taurus once, then twice more. The man pauses, surprised.

Samuel scrambles for his Tracfone, but in his haste, drops it. He's not sure if it's on the floor or between the console separating the driver and passenger seats.

The man has reversed course. He's now dragging the young woman toward the Taurus.

Behind him, the front door of the house opens again. Two more women come running out.

The man looks over his shoulder. Samuel keeps searching for the Tracfone, but his fingers feel like they belong to someone else.

The two women are fast. They make the sidewalk, then street, and disappear behind a rippling curtain of rain.

Early evening breaks under the weight of the weather. Samuel continues to scramble for the phone.

When he looks up, the man and the young woman are standing just outside the passenger door.

The man's hand is still wrapped in the woman's hair. He tenses and keeps his arm rigid, pushing her face against the passenger window. The woman's features are flattened and mashed on the glass and at the same time are obscenely animated by the rain running around them.

Samuel's hand bumps into the phone. He grabs and lifts it and punches in 9-1-1.

The man, younger than Samuel originally thought, begins tapping on the passenger window. He then lifts his index finger, moving it left to right and right to left, metronome style, signaling Samuel to put down the phone.

The operator comes on, apologizing for the delay because of the volume of weather-related calls, and asks Samuel the nature of his emergency.

Before Samuel can reply, the young man places a hand on either side of the young woman's head, and then with an abrupt twist, like someone trying to break a stubborn seal on a jar, he snaps her neck.

The young man lifts his hands, and the woman disappears.

Samuel can't believe what he's just witnessed. The taking of a life should have been more concrete and horrific. Instead, it feels dreamlike, soft at the edges, like something the rain delivered.

The Tracfone drops Samuel's call to 9-1-1.

The young man tries the front and rear doors, and when he finds them locked, he begins tapping on the passenger window.

Samuel keys the ignition. It clicks and grinds. The *Service Engine Soon* light comes back on.

The tapping stops.

Samuel looks over. There's a pair of hands, palms open, wiping at the glass, clearing rain, and then a face appears.

The ignition catches. Samuel drops the Taurus into *Drive* and hits the gas.

It's not until he's made the corner of Jefferson and Taylor and taken a hard left that Samuel, corralling his panic and confusion, suddenly realizes the man got a better look at Samuel than Samuel did at him.

THE LENGTH OF DAYS – TWO

The call comes through a few minutes after the WTKW van leaves the Cornelius Street Animal Shelter. Nelson Cavanaugh, the station manager, tells them to get over to 805 Jefferson ASAP.

Dave Preston, the driver, keys the GPS. Paul, the cameraman, rolls up the passenger side window. Pam Graves, riding shotgun, readjusts her seatbelt.

"Finally, a real story," Paul says, "after a very long afternoon of gnomes and winsome canines."

Dave runs a stop sign. "I thought Lionel was okay."

"It's more than a house fire," Paul says. "You heard Cavanaugh. Word is, this one's different. We're not simply talking Wall of Flames. Raging Inferno. Details at 11:00."

Dave slows, then runs another stop sign.

"Think she can handle it?" Paul says.

"What? Who?" Dave glances over.

Paul points over his shoulder and toward the back seat.

They're talking as if Pam is not there. It's something she's gotten used to.

Or almost used to.

"This one's definitely outside her job description," Paul says. "It's more Rebecca Tower's venue."

"Where is she anyway? She still on maternity leave?"

Paul nods yes. "You ever meet her husband?" Paul shakes his head. "El Wiener."

"I heard there was a paternity pool," Dave says. "In-house."

"They went with Vegas Odds. No shortage of contenders." Paul taps the passenger side window. "El Wiener was a longshot. Me, I put fifty bucks on Mr. Weatherman, Frank Berlin. He's never been able to keep it zipped."

Pam looks out her window. They're on Branch Street now. The world outside is a clean blur that's moving like stretch of film on fast forward.

"ETA," Dave says. "Eight minutes. Ten tops."

"Back to my point. What if this turns out to be an exclusive? Little Miss Sunshine there in the back seat? I have my doubts."

"I can hear you, you know," Pam says.

Paul shrugs. "No offense, but you're not Rebecca Tower."

"I never claimed I was." Pam works on gathering herself. "And I didn't ask for this one."

"Hey, that's why they call it news and the way it breaks." Paul just manages to choke off the *Sweetheart*. He'd been in just enough in-house sessions of workplace harassment to know how far he could push it.

Branch Street disappears. A left onto Fremont and another stretch of traffic-laden potholes and working-class homes that run together like a footnote to something more important.

No, that's not right. A footnote, that's how Paul Westbrook, the cameraman, would see it. Pam Graves knows better. She was born in Magnolia Beach. She's lived here, except for four years of undergraduate school, her entire life. It's home. For Paul Westbrook, Magnolia Beach is a stutter-step opportunity. He's passing through, fueled on his ambition and self-regard, to something bigger. Everything in front of his camera eventually translates to another line on his resume.

Or almost everything. He reserves a scorched-earth scorn for Pam Graves and the stories she regularly covers.

Human Interest Stories. Second and third tier news. Filler and Fluff. A sentimental bromide for the usual shitstorm of bad news occupying the other slots.

Pam Grave's the face who puts the best face on things. She covers bake sales, pageants, festivals, charities, and grand openings. She does uplifting segments on people beating the odds on an alphabet of diseases. She profiles veterans and veterinarians, elementary school teachers and high school coaches, directors of youth programs, ministers, and good neighbors.

She conducts apple-pie interviews with members of the Tourist Bureau and Chamber of Commerce.

This afternoon she'd done her bi-weekly segment of *Rescue Me!* at the Cornelius Street Animal Shelter highlighting a Lab named Lionel, a Collie-mix named Lucy, and a Jack Russell named Jack. Earlier in the day she visited Harold and Genevieve Olmstead at their home in Northwest Magnolia Beach where they introduced Pam and Paul Westbrook's camera to two hundred and thirty-seven hand-painted gnomes of varying sizes occupying their front and back yards.

Tomorrow morning she was scheduled to meet Sandy Harrison, the owner and director of High Steppin', to discuss her ballroom dancing program for special needs kids.

THE LENGTH OF DAYS

Pam Graves understands that what's coming up at 805 Jefferson is something that doesn't fit her job description. Rebecca Tower is the lead investigative reporter for WTKW, yes, and not her, and that's okay with Pam. She doesn't want to be Rebecca Tower, but Rebecca Tower, marooned in week thirty of a difficult pregnancy, isn't available, and Pam Graves is.

"Here we go," Dave Preston says, turning onto Jefferson. The sky above the 800 block is charcoal and smoke-choked, the street itself choked in police cars, fire engines, EMS vehicles, and competing local news vans, and crowds of neighbors and onlookers.

"Shit," Paul Westbrook says, "there goes anything approaching an exclusive."

"I got us here as fast as I could." Dave pulls the WTKW van to the curb and shuts it off. They're a good three blocks away from the scene of the fire.

Dave Preston stays in the van. Paul and Pam work their way down the street. Paul discusses establishing shots. They keep hearing conflicting reports about injuries and body counts. The numbers, though, in each case sound a little too high for a single-dwelling residence.

"Exactly what the hell is going on here?" Paul says. There's a lot of crime scene tape. Too much.

Pam Graves points to the northwest. "Over there. An opening two houses over. The far corner of the lot."

It's the equivalent of a back door or end run. They move down the driveway and cut underneath four large magnolias. They cross into the next lot and follow the yellow crime scene tape until it runs out in the neighboring backyard.

Where they run into a patrolman who stops them.

Pam reaches over and touches Paul Westbrook's forearm. "Give me a second, okay?"

Pam Graves walks over to the patrolman and leans in. He tilts his head, meeting her, then looks away for a moment. Another moment of hesitation. He looks down at his shoes. Finally, he holds up five fingers.

Pam leans closer and asks him another question. He shakes his head twice. Pam reaches over and touches his shoulder. He looks at her and then away and eventually answers her.

Pam Graves waves Paul over. They start across the yard.

"What the hell was that?" Paul asks.

"Get ready. We have five minutes at the scene. That's all."

"How'd you get us in?"

"A favor. He knows my family. His name is Leo Williams. I used to babysit his daughter."

They follow the tree line, a mix of magnolias, pecans, and dogwoods, the leaves of their eastern face scorched and curdled from the fire. Pam and Westbrook move into a clearing. The grass beneath their feet is black and damp from the spray of firehoses and rain earlier in the afternoon.

"Oh shit," Paul Westbrook says. His words are drained of their customary cynicism and filled instead with the blunt horror of a nightmare.

Pam looks over her shoulder and then away. She keys the mike, and Westbrook nods and begins filming.

The one look had been enough. It had been an unobstructed view into the equivalent of a small corner of Hell.

The fire has eaten the house, its two stories collapsing and leaving only a small portion of the front roof canted streetward. Firefighters are still moving in and out of the spiraling smoke. The scattered contents of the house look like deformed versions of themselves. Among them are charred bodies and exposed bones. Someone is shouting out numbers and calling for more body bags.

Pam Graves looks at the camera and delivers the details at hand and more, delivering what Paul Westbrook thought they'd missed out on: something approximating an exclusive. Pam had asked Leo Williams why, given the heavy rains earlier in the day, the house had burned as completely as it had. He told her one of the fire marshals, a friend of his, had said from all early signs, the fire had been deliberately set. Something was off-kilter because the earlier rains should have slowed the burn, but they hadn't.

Pam kept the details straight and clean, leaving out Leo Williams's name and the fire marshal's rank, substituting the usual informed sources close to the scene, but sometime along the way the wind had shifted, and all those details and facts Pam Graves has thought she'd been delivering have gotten away from her, and she starts crying.

She can't help it or stop.

A shift in the wind and someone calling out a number—eight and counting—and suddenly she's crying and choking on her words, but she's determined to continue, telling herself she can do the job, despite what the wind has delivered: the insistent odor of burnt flesh.

The odor riding wave after wave of the wind coming in from the east. She's never smelled anything like it. It's two synonyms beyond

THE LENGTH OF DAYS

appalling and occupies its own space.

There's the smell of burnt flesh and the sound of her words and the voice of someone calling for more body bags and Paul Westbrook's camera is rolling and time is running out, the five-minute favor that she'd managed to garner, and right then, with her voice breaking, Pam Graves goes on to finish the segment while caught up in a second wave of tears.

THE LENGTH OF DAYS — THREE

Nguyen Duc Xuan starts each day by invoking a name and then repeating it over and over until he comes to inhabit it.

Until the name and breath are one.

Until Nguyen Duc Xuan once again becomes Johnny Doc Nowell.

Then Johnny Doc Nowell smokes a cigarette. The first of eleven, no more, no less each day.

He moves to the east window of his heavily-mortgaged house on Danvers Lane and looks out into the late winter light and across the marsh and inlet to what he's come to see, at least until today, as his Greatest Folly.

It's the scene that greets him every day. Close to three-quarters of a mile of oceanfront property that was to be the exclusive future home of a high-end gated community named West Wind Estates. A community that had become stalled in its tracks after no more than a couple tentative steps in 2008 and the arrival of Collateralized Debt Obligations and Credit Default Swaps. Until then it had been a sure thing that Johnny Doc and a number of other investors had put Big Money into. Until Big Money suddenly wasn't anymore.

Despite a vow not to, he checks his watch for the fourth time in the last twenty minutes and then pulls down his shirtsleeve to cover it.

He's waiting, still waiting, for a callback from his attorney, Raychard Balen.

Johnny Doc Nowell is more worried than afraid and more afraid than hopeful about the report from Balen.

The sawgrass in the marsh and inlet still holds a brittle winter brown, a faint green ring at its roots a pale promise of spring. It's low tide, and there are egrets and herons fishing for their supper among the exposed oyster-shell atolls.

February is eating the last of the light.

"I'm here," Johnny Doc says when his cellphone rings through.

"805 Jefferson, a fire," Raychard Balen says, "you got some dead girls on your hands. Maybe a couple more alive but in the wind. I'm still checking on details, but I don't think there are any innocent bystanders on this one."

"Have you talked to the Bowen Brothers?"

"I have a call into Nathaniel Laine, their Suit, but I haven't heard back from any of them."

"I expect that will shortly change."

"Right now, I recommend staying away from the Full Moon. It will take the police some time to tie you to 805 Jefferson, but a Massage Parlor is going to be automatically on their radar."

"I'll talk to Bishop and Nina. They'll keep things running at the Moon."

"Tell them to scale things back until we know exactly what we're looking at," Balen says. "Maybe shut it down for a while. Claim that it's for repairs or renovations, and leave it at that."

Johnny Doc doesn't say anything.

"You hear anything I just said? Those weren't a troop of Girl Scouts that got incinerated at Jefferson. Right now, you don't want anything that will draw attention to you, however indirectly."

"Okay, okay, I'll talk to Bishop."

"Now we're getting somewhere. Please tell me something else," Balen says, "and let me sleep the peace of the Just tonight. You're not still fucking his wife, Nina, are you?"

"That's over," Johnny Doc says. "Not that it's your business."

"I'm your lawyer, and your ass is potentially on the line. Of course it's my business. I want to keep your checks clearing."

The tide is starting to rise. Johnny Doc watches the last of the light disappear on the remains of the West Wind Estates site. He doesn't want to think of the dead bodies at 805 Jefferson. He doesn't want to think about shutting down, however temporarily, the Full Moon Massage Parlor.

Time and money have become synonymous.

"Next step?" he asks.

"I have a cop on retainer," Raychard Balen says, "and a short leash."

"Can you trust him?"

"He has a price tag," Balen says, "and he doesn't have a history of overreaching. He'll get you results if there are any to be gotten."

"Okay," Johnny Doc Nowell says.

"Keep a low profile until we get a better feel for things," Balen says. "Let's remember we're dealing with the Bowen Brothers, and on a good day, that's the equivalent of meeting the first cousins of Satan."

THE LENGTH OF DAYS — FOUR

The Bayview Assisted Living Center and its sister subdivision, Bayview Manor, are in southwest Magnolia Beach, near the airport, on thirty-one acres. The Center has four wings radiating at clock hands of 10, 2, 4, and 8 from a central hub housing dining rooms, entertainment centers, lounges, computer lab, library, arts and craft rooms, and a non-denominational chapel. The grounds are pristine, full of branching pathways that eschew right angles but are obligingly dotted with strategically placed wooden benches. There's a man-made lake. Tennis courts. Putting greens. The Bayview has a six minibus fleet with regular routes throughout Magnolia Beach. The Bayview's Mission Statement, duplicated on its website and brochures, promises everything just short of eternal life.

Each of the four wings is surrounded by a semi-circle of townhouses and condos collectively known as Bayview Manor. Samuel Fulton lives in a townhouse off B-Wing.

A townhouse that he'd shared with his wife, Glenda, before the Transient Ischemic Event and the three strokes that followed.

His wife, who now resides in C-Wing of Bayview.

In the meantime, he has to decide what to do about Weldon Trulane III. Samuel is not exactly sure if Weldon is a guest, a roommate, a squatter, or some unwieldy combination of all three.

Right now, Weldon is in the living room with the television turned to an afternoon talk show.

He moves past Weldon into the kitchen. Samuel pours himself a glass of iced tea and looks out the back window at the long slow slope of green grass leading to Bayview's western parking lot. The end of the afternoon shadows is already running through the trees.

It happened fast. That's what he'd told Detective Townes. Samuel had driven straight to the police station after he'd witnessed the murder. On the way there, he had been passed by a string of fire trucks, EMS vehicles, and police cruisers, all speeding and running lights, their sirens a long syncopated wail.

At the station he talked to an officer Olson who called Detective Townes, and Samuel had given his statement, and that statement had ultimately added up to those paltry three words.

THE LENGTH OF DAYS	**21**

It happened fast.

He'd tried, but finally had been unable to summon up anything more than a blur of details: A blue shirt. Rain. A woman with black hair yelling something he couldn't understand. His misplaced Tracfone. The man's fingers—long and manicured, Samuel could remember that—on the dark-haired woman's neck and then the snap. A snap he hadn't actually heard but which was still real, he was sure. The rain smearing the windows and windshield of the Taurus. The *Check Engine* light blinking. Two women running from the house and disappearing. A set of hands wiping away the rain on the passenger side window of the Taurus.

Detective Townes kept circling back to the man Samuel had seen. Samuel tried. And tried again. The harder he tried, however, the more the man eluded him, Samuel trying to explain to Detective Townes, "I saw him, but it wasn't like I *saw* him." Samuel finally adding, *It happened fast.*

Detective Townes had looked at him for a long moment and then had thanked him and given Samuel his card. Samuel had driven back to Bayview Manor. He hadn't been able to shake the feeling that he had not so much witnessed a murder as a murder had somehow witnessed him.

"Hey Samuel," Weldon Trulane calls out from the living room. "The local's almost on."

Four and a half weeks ago, as Samuel was shortcutting across the grounds to his townhouse, he ran into a short, wiry man throwing a barrage of bright white stones at the entrance to D-Wing. It turned out the man had pirated the stones from one of the flowerbeds. His aim was horribly off, skewing toward the parking lot. The man was simultaneously cursing and crying. He eventually depleted the pile of stones at his feet and turned toward Samuel as if noting him for the first time.

Samuel had asked him if he was all right.

The man took off his glasses, wiped them down, and put them back on. "Which Wing are you in?"

Samuel lifted his hand and pointed over his shoulder. "No Wing. One of the townhouses."

The man nodded twice. "Any liquor there?"

"Just beer," Samuel had said.

"My friend, there is no such thing as just beer," he said. "Let's go."

It didn't take long to run through Samuel's supply, and he ended up going out for reinforcements, stopping along the way at Dave's Deli for sandwiches and chips and slaw.

When he got back, Weldon was going through Samuel's DVD and CD collections.

"No Porn?" he said. "Disappointed in you, friend. No Professor Longhair either. Man can't say he's lived until he's listened to the Professor."

Weldon had taken one of the new beers and waved off the sandwiches. He dropped onto the couch and surveyed the inside of the townhouse. "No offense, Samuel, but I think anybody taking a look at you and the place would come away with the definite impression that you're a quintessential Top-40 kind of guy on all levels."

Samuel lowered himself into a chair and looked at the sandwich on his plate. "What impression you think someone might have of you?"

"That I'm misunderstood. Perhaps on a quasi-tragic level." He toasted Samuel with his beer.

"Is that why you were throwing all those white stones at D-Wing?"

Weldon took a long swallow of beer and tilted his head. "You know what they call D-Wing, don't you?"

"It's for the Terminals," Samuel said after a while.

"Death's Anteroom," Weldon said. "That's what they call it. Check-ins and Check-outs are synonyms." He looked down and away. "A good friend is residing there."

"I'm sorry to hear that."

"Duly noted," Weldon Trulane had said. "Now how about another beer?"

When Weldon Trulane III eventually worked his way through the evening's beer supply and passed out on the couch, Samuel hunted down a blanket and covered him and then went on to bed.

Weldon had shown up the next day around suppertime. He continued to show up, usually a little earlier each afternoon, until the time when Weldon woke up hungover on the couch and when he showed up in the afternoon had shrunk to flashpoint and then disappeared altogether, and somehow Weldon Trulane III had taken up residence in the townhouse without Samuel ever exactly figuring out how.

Why seemed tied to a sister in east Magnolia Beach who had kicked him out of the family home. *Why* was also tied to Weldon's spending habits, all of which were firmly in the profligate camp.

At bottom, *why* probably had more to do with Samuel himself though and the hole in the center of his days after his wife Glenda, his one and true and only love for over forty-nine years of marriage, had ended up

THE LENGTH OF DAYS

in Bayview's C-Wing.

"Hey Samuel," Weldon calls from the living room. "Didn't you hear me? The local's starting."

Samuel leaves the kitchen, cuts across the living room, and drops into his recliner. Ben Brandt, the head anchor for WTKW, opens with a lead story about a fire earlier in the afternoon.

When Brandt mentions the address, Samuel sits up straighter. He can't quite believe what he's just heard. He feels his blood jump, and he lowers his head for a moment. When he lifts it again, he's looking at the house at 805 Jefferson or what would have been the house if it hadn't burned to the ground.

Weldon Trulane III points at the scorch and rubble. "All too familiar. A visual metaphor. Reminds me of the way my life and luck have been tending of late."

Samuel ignores him. The segment shifts to a young woman in a dark blue WTKW windbreaker. She's a small woman, maybe 5' 3", with light brown hair and a dribble of freckles across the bridge of her nose. Samuel can't remember her name until she identifies herself—Pam Graves—but he immediately recognizes her from the bi-weekly segment of *Rescue Me!* filmed at the Cornelius Street Animal Shelter.

"Jesus," Weldon Trulane says, "Did you hear that? Eight bodies and counting."

They watch Pam Graves, wreathed in smoke and backdropped by the muted voices of the EMS and fire rescue people, slowly start to break down on-camera. A hitch in her voice. One that grew more pronounced. A recurring tic in the corner of her mouth. Her eyes welling and then spilling over.

"Damn, I need another beer," Weldon says and heads for the kitchen.

Samuel watches Pam Graves struggle to finish her segment. He knows what she's feeling.

Bushwhacked and stranded in the moment.

It's the same feeling Samuel Fulton has each time he steps into room C-10 in C-Wing and sits down across from his wife Glenda.

THE LENGTH OF DAYS — FIVE

Until this evening, Pam Graves believed she understood her place in the world. It wasn't something she had to discover or figure out; it had been shown to her over and over, starting with her entrance into the world itself when she appeared two minutes after her twin brother's birth.

If something like Fate governed a life, Pam Graves had been marked by hers at that point and then marked again and again over the next twenty-six years.

Over and over, Pam Graves was the perpetual runner-up, the close but no cigar, the silver medalist, the six of one and half dozen of another, the B+ in the shadow of the A, the better and more but not the best or most, her place in the world doubling as a place-marker.

Until this evening.

Right now, driving down Atlantic Avenue in the coastal town she'd always seen as home, Pam Graves feels unmoored.

The feeling won't leave her alone. Or maybe it's left her too alone.

The evening holds no safe harbors. She's been driving around Magnolia Beach for the last one and a half hours. The car's interior is running a few degrees this side of cold. She's turned the heater off because the air flow smells burnt.

The evening feels like it's running on an endless loop. She'd hoped to be snagged by the familiar. That was the point of the drive. The plan was to circle through the everyday landmarks of her childhood, teen, and later years and let their accumulated weight ground her again.

It hasn't worked though. The drive has failed to deliver what she'd hoped. Her breath burns high in her chest. Her fingers too tight on the wheel. The world outside her windshield refuses to focus, alternately intruding and retreating as she moves through it.

She's made one stop: Saint Andrew's Episcopal Church, just in time for the close of Ash Wednesday's services. Her family had been lukewarm Methodists, but Daren Lowe, her significant other, was raised as an old-school Episcopalian but only attended, if he remembered to attend at all, a few times a year. Pam, however, had liked the ritual of Mass and continued to attend on her own.

She can still feel the ghost of the priest's fingers on her forehead. His

THE LENGTH OF DAYS 25

words the fine print on what she'd witnessed and smelled at 805 Jefferson Street.

Her second stop and Pam finds herself in the driveway of her parents' house. It's a split-level in a thicket of split-levels in a subdivision near the Magnolia Beach regional airport.

Her dad answers at the first knock. It's as if he's been patiently waiting for her to appear.

"Welcome, Marked Woman," he says. He smiles and points at her forehead.

They move into the kitchen. Her dad opens the refrigerator and takes out a brown paper bag and sets it on the single plate at the table.

"I've already eaten, and your mother is working late." He sits down across from Pam. "It's a Dave's Double-Decker Club. Dill pickle side and a bag of chips."

The bag has a line drawing caricature of her father's head with Dave's Deli haloing it.

"Your mother's going to be sorry she missed you," he says.

Pam nods and takes a bite of the sandwich. She can't bring herself to tell her father that The Second Wave, her mother's bookstore, had been closed when she drove by it earlier.

It isn't the first time she can't bring herself to tell him.

Pam waits for her father to change the subject as he inevitably will and does when he reaches over and snags a potato chip from her plate and then asks how her fiancé is doing.

Technically, Daren Lowe inhabits the borderline of fiancé territory, but Pam gives her standard response. "Well, you know, Daren is Daren."

"I drove by The Lowe Tide on the way home," her father says, "and the lot was packed."

"Wednesdays are BOGO Craft Beer Night."

Her father smiles and shakes his head. "That article in *Southern Focus* changed things for Daren. No argument there. Like I said, the lot was packed."

The Lowe Tide had been a longstanding off-the-radar bar and grill frequented by locals. Nine months ago it had been "discovered" and profiled *in Southern Focus* magazine and subsequently had become the new off-the-map designation for tourists who wanted to experience its "gritty and eccentric charms".

"Last time I heard Dave's Deli is doing all right too," Pam says.

"No complaints. After all, everybody loves sandwiches." Her father snags another chip.

No Complaints could double as her father's mantra. He is one of the most even-tempered men Pam has ever known. He has the equilibrium of a gyroscope. The smile he offers the world is genuine.

She finishes her sandwich. She tries to remember how her day started. She remembers all too well how it ended.

As if on cue, her cellphone rings. Pam checks caller ID, but she already knows who's calling: the station manager at WTKW, Nelson Cavanaugh. She's been avoiding the call all evening.

After the on-camera breakdown at 805 Jefferson, Pam expects to be fired. When the wind shifted, she lost all objectivity and presence. She can still hear people calling for more body bags.

"Pam," Nelson Cavanaugh asks, "you there? I've been trying to get ahold of you."

She says she's sorry.

"What's that?"

"I said I'm sorry, Nelson." She hears her voice getting away from her. "I needed to step up, and I didn't." She lets out a breath. "Or maybe it was couldn't."

"Hold it, okay?" Nelson says. "Your segment. I thought you'd heard. The segment's gone viral. You're national news, Pam."

THE LENGTH OF DAYS – SIX

While Johnny Doc Nowell gets around to talk about what he needed, Patrolman Carl Adkin is thinking about Slots.

Slots, their form and function, the way you drop into one and then hide in plain sight.

You let the world take you at face value, and then you find and go on to occupy a certain type of freedom as well as a backhanded clarity that comes from being underestimated.

That's where real power resides.

Patrolman Carl Adkin knows how he's perceived by the majority of his peers, the people he's paid to protect and serve, and at least some of the criminals who cross his path. To them, he is nothing more than a bundle of clichés. The small-town high school linebacker who couldn't cut it in college. Who then joined the Marines, serving neither honorably or dishonorably, and after marshalling out, returned home and married his high school honey, moving through a string of abbreviated minimum wage jobs before a career shift to the Magnolia Beach Police Department, his life and career unfolding along bland and predictable lines, his wife dropping three kids within five and a half years, two boys, one a little shit, one a mama's boy, and a daughter who's a Cinderella in-training. Carl mowed the lawn, paid taxes, went deer hunting and bass fishing, and punched the clock each Sunday at First Methodist on Sagmore where he worshipped a God who had created a universe which conveniently ran on principles that were conveniently similar to the ones Carl himself operated on.

Carl understood there were Slots the world provided and all you had to do was step into yours.

Things then fit.

And when things fit, what you wanted became what you were, and what you were became what you did.

There were times, though, when you were dislodged from or couldn't find your Slot, and then you ended up like Johnny Doc Nowell, a man who was seriously afraid but didn't yet realize he was.

They're in Johnny Doc's office, Johnny Doc behind a small metal desk, Carl, off the books, on his lunch break.

"Raychard Balen," Johnny Doc says, "tells me you get results."

"Raychard Balen, attorney at law, has the ethics of a tapeworm, but yes, I'll get what you need done." Carl waits, then adds, "Within reason and for the right price." Which as far as Carl is concerned are synonyms.

Johnny Doc leans back in his chair. "I was under the impression Raychard Balen and you were friends."

"A favor here or there doesn't make you a friend," Carl says. "Maybe, on occasion, an accomplice, but not a friend."

"Okay, then," Johnny Doc says, "you need to understand this is the Bowen Brothers we're dealing with." He opens a desk drawer and takes out an ashtray and a pack of Marlboro Reds. Before lighting up, he counts the number of butts in the ashtray.

"The fourteen girls at 805 Jefferson weren't mine," Johnny Doc says. "They belonged to Don and Danny Bowen. I was providing a safe house until the brothers decided where they were going to move them. I am, I was, the equivalent of an absentee landlord. The fire changed everything."

"A response," Carl says, "okay. What are we talking here?"

"A gesture," Johnny Doc says. "Something clear and to the point that would hold off the Bowens until I can work something out."

"You need a Gesture, fine," Carl says. "Who exactly is it aimed at?"

"Franklin Rawlings, Gary Lidd, and one yet to be determined."

"Rawlings is white-bread predictable, but Gary Lidd?" Carl says. "Seriously? Gary worked for you? Gary's the kind would fuck up trying to flush a toilet."

"Gary was temporary. Some fill-in help, that's all," Johnny Doc says. "Franklin was the one overseeing the house."

Carl watches Johnny Doc Nowell's hands shake.

"We're talking a Gesture," Johnny Doc repeats. "Something reassuring. Let the Bowens know I'm on top of things." Johnny Doc knits his fingers. "Also, a bonus if you bring in the two girls who are AWOL."

Johnny Doc opens the middle drawer of the desk. He rummages for a pen, tests it out on his palm, then takes an index card, writes down a figure, and slides the card across the table.

Carl Adkin picks it up. Looks at it.

"Sufficient?" Johnny Doc asks.

"Consider me motivated," Carl says.

That established, Carl runs the rest of his shift and turns in the blue and white and checks out. He skips the locker room and the ritual of changing back into civilian clothes.

He's off-duty but still inhabits the uniform.

THE LENGTH OF DAYS

He times it so that he runs into Homicide Detective Jackson Towne in the parking lot. That, in itself, is lucky since Towne is notorious for arriving late and cutting out early on his shifts.

Towne manages to be both ambitious and lazy. Having a brother who works in the mayor's office helps on either count.

Towne's unlocking his Escalade when Adkin catches up and asks if there are any new developments on the house fire and bodies from Jefferson Street.

Towne tilts his head left, then right, cracking his neck and loosening his shoulders, then shrugs. "One witness, but he was too rattled to see anything helpful. I got a couple teams looking at the teeth. Maybe they'll scare up a few names, give us something to go on. Until then, well, it's just an 'until then'."

"I hear you," Adkin says. He tells Towne good night and to fly right and then crosses the lot to his Jeep Cherokee. He calls his wife and says he'll be late for supper, then hits a Stop-and-Go for gas and an energy drink. He has one, maybe two, stops to make.

One thing Carl knows about Franklin Rawlings: he had no imagination whatsoever. He was the King of Literal. And that made him easy to track.

So Carl starts with the obvious, driving to south Magnolia Beach and stopping at the Roundtable Apartments, originally a mom and pop motel that had not so much been converted as devolved into its present state.

Ken, the day manager, is still on. He runs five foot six in cowboy boots and has maintained a malt shop pompadour for as long as Carl has known him. Two bottom teeth are MIA and the rest stained the color of a watery soda. He's wearing a gray University of South Carolina sweatshirt with the sleeves scissored off at the shoulder.

Ken leans against the front counter and pretends to think about the question.

"Gary Lidd doesn't live here," he says.

"I know that, Ken. I asked if you'd seen him."

He frowns. "I guess that would depend on when."

"I hear the music," Carl says, "but I'm not in the mood for a dance."

"Okay, okay," Ken says, holding up his right hand cross-guard style. "I haven't seen Gary around, and it's been two, maybe three, days since I saw Rawlings." He points over Carl's shoulder to a parking lot checkerboarded with broken asphalt and potholes. "That's Rawlings's apartment over there, D-5, but his car's not there."

Carl leans over and taps the countertop. "That wasn't too difficult, was it?"

Ken leans closer too. "Always good to see you, Officer Carl. You're always near the top of my Christmas card list."

Carl shakes his head and walks back to the Cherokee. If you're hunting the King of the Literal and he's not at his apartment, you move to the next obvious choice.

He drives to northeast Magnolia Beach where the property values are only marginally higher than its southern counterpoint. Carl has been hearing rumors over that last year that northeast Magnolia Beach is headed for some major league rehab and gentrification, but Carl figures 2008's economic debacles have left those rumors hollow.

1527 Dunbar is a single story with asbestos siding and a chimney canted thirty degrees off center. The lawn is small and square, still holding its winter-brown. The front of the house is lined with half-hearted azaleas, and there's a heavyset middle-aged woman in a faded housedress and scuffed bedroom slippers standing on the porch smoking a cigarette.

Before Carl can ask, she points inside, the flesh on her bicep shivering with the movement.

Franklin Rawlings is in the kitchen, sitting at the table with a glass of milk, a half-eaten sandwich, and a newspaper folded open to the crosswords. He has a short yellow pencil tucked behind his left ear.

"Don't get up," Carl says.

Franklin takes a sip of milk. "I'm not in hiding."

"Good to know, Frank."

"If you don't mind, I prefer Franklin."

"Roger that, Frank."

Rawlings sighs and goes back to the sandwich. He chews as if he's counting each considered bite.

Carl sits down across from him. The table-top is sticky. "Lots of dead girls, Frank."

"I wasn't there," Rawlings says. "I want that established upfront."

"Am I smelling Alibi here?"

Rawlings slowly lets out his breath. "We're talking an eleven letter word for setting things straight. Alibi has five letters. I'm trying to provide you with an explanation, Officer Adkin."

"Okay, I'm listening."

"You ever try to calculate menstrual cycles?" Franklin momentarily shuts his eyes. "I'm overseeing a house with fourteen women. It's a

THE LENGTH OF DAYS 31

three-quarters moon, pushing full. Four start their periods. I thought I had things covered. The next thing I know, the power of suggestion, there are five more bleeding. All of sudden, it's like every one of them is clamoring for Midol and tampons, and we're in short supply of each." Franklin scratches at his jawline. "And dark chocolate. I have a house full of women, and I'm looking at a three-quarters moon and no Midol, tampons, or dark chocolate to speak of on the premises."

He holds up both index fingers and then takes out his wallet. He begins thumbing through it and eventually plucks out a rectangular piece of paper and slides it across the table.

"Note the time and date," he says. "I was making a run."

Carl studies the receipt. It's from one of the pharmacy chains on Old Market Boulevard. It appears Franklin Rawlings is in the clear.

"So I should be talking to Gary Lidd?" Carl says.

"Gary or Eric."

"Not familiar with an Eric." Carl leans over and drops a hand on Franklin's shoulder. "How about a last name?"

Franklin eyes Carl's hand. "He has one, but I don't know it."

Carl begins to squeeze Rawlings's shoulder, gradually notching up the pressure. "You sure about that?"

Rawlings eventually lays out what he knows. Eric no-last-name dropped by 805 Jefferson at least two or three times a week. He knew Gary Lidd, but Rawlings said they didn't act like they were friends. Eric and Gary would smoke some dope, and then Eric would disappear into one of the upstairs bedrooms with one or more of the girls.

Carl asks if there's anything else.

Franklin finishes his milk and sets the glass down next to the sandwich. "The one time I asked Gary about Eric, Gary told me that Eric said he worked for the Bowen Brothers and that he was sort of like their agent, you know, and checking up on things."

Carl works through that one again. Johnny Doc Nowell had not said anything about an Eric who worked for the Bowens. He asks Franklin if this Eric had been at the house the day of the fire.

"I don't know," he says. "He wasn't while I was there. Maybe later though, when I was making the pharmacy run."

"Then it appears I need to talk to Gary," Carl says. "You wouldn't have any idea where he might be?"

Franklin picks up the sandwich, and it's halfway to his mouth when he stops, considers, and then takes a bite. "Maybe one thing," he says.

Maybe one thing turns out to be Magnolia Beach General Hospital.

Carl consoles himself that it's at least on the way home. The energy drink has long bypassed whatever juice it had provided, and the end of shift and his extracurricular activities for Johnny Doc Nowell have left him both exhausted and ravenous.

At the hospital, he waves to and badges the woman manning the check-in desk and heads for the elevators where he punches the button for the fifth floor. He talks to the nurse manning the station.

Crystal Beade is in Room 512. Carl slips inside and closes the door.

Crystal is marooned in the middle stage of her last trimester. It's her second round of premature labor. She's in her mid-twenties, small-breasted with a hugely distended abdomen, sharp chin, a mottled complexion, faded blue eyes, and overly teased hair holding the color and texture of worn corduroy.

"Ms. Beade," Carl says, "you don't know me, but…"

"You're wrong there," she says, interrupting him. "I know you." She slowly raises her hands to her abdomen, cradling it.

"You do?"

She nods. "High school."

"Sorry, I can't place you."

"Not me. I was in the sixth grade. Part of the background scenery," Crystal says. "I'm talking about my sister. Deanna. You dated her."

"Right," Carl says. "Deanna. I remember. We only dated for a while."

"Meaning once," Crystal says. "That's how it usually worked."

She had that right, Carl thinks. Deanna Beade was a punchboard. Everybody knew that.

"How's she doing?" he asks.

Crystal closes her eyes for a moment. "She's thirty-four and divorced and an alkie with a liver the size of Kansas. She's got two kids and works as a maid at the Breezeway Motel when she remembers to show up."

A short knock and the door opening, a thin nurse with a brisk smile coming in to take Crystal's temperature and blood pressure.

"Pressure's a little high," she says, glancing over at Carl, and then waiting a moment before asking, "Everything all right here?"

Adkin juggles a smile and a nod, and the nurse leaves.

"A wasted trip," Crystal says. "That's all this is. I've seen the news. I know why you're here."

"Gary had certain responsibilities," Carl says. "They did not include a house fire and twelve dead bodies. Including a front lawn murder." He stops and lifts his hands, palms out. "There are consequences, and they

THE LENGTH OF DAYS

aren't going away." Carl drops another pause, pressing for effect. "No reason you have to join the party."

"He's the father of this child," Crystal says.

"Hey, you're talking Gary Lidd," Carl says. "At best, he's a little friction and a teaspoon of semen."

"I'm telling you," Crystal says, "I haven't seen him, and I don't know where he is."

Carl tilts his head and looks at the ceiling and starts softly whistling. It's been an afternoon of attitudes, and he's ready to close it out.

Crystal sits up a little further in bed. "You heard what I said."

"That I did," Carl says. "I wish I could say the same."

THE LENGTH OF DAYS – SEVEN

Johnny Doc Nowell hits the signal on the black Dodge Ram 4x4 and turns right into the parking lot of Pinewood Bowling. The lot is empty, the painted parking spaces faded and smudged. He crosses the lot at a diagonal and drives slowly along the north side of the building and parks in back near a set of rear doors. A large black bowling ball is painted on the left door and appears to be moving toward the right door which holds a set of pins with human faces and worried expressions.

Pinewood Bowling was the first of Johnny Doc's properties to go into foreclosure.

The Bank of the South has been a little lax in its follow-up practices, putting a thick and unwieldy chain on the front doors but not bothering to change the locks on the back. Johnny Doc still has the keys.

The inside of the Pinewood is twilight-dark and has the damp-cardboard smell of a building that's been closed up for a long time. Johnny Doc slowly walks the width of the building in his street shoes, the answering echo sounding as if he's been followed.

He turns and walks back, detouring to a spot behind the concession and drink counter. There's a small tin ashtray on the otherwise empty shelves behind him. He sets the ashtray in front of him and lights a cigarette.

Johnny Doc smokes eleven cigarettes a day. No more. No less. It's a practice he's borrowed from an American expatriate in 1975 Saigon. His name was John Sloane, and Johnny Doc, thirteen years old at the time, used to run errands for him and others at the Colorado Bar. Sloane explained that eleven cigarettes a day was the closest thing to a philosophy of life he'd found. *Remember, nobody dies from ten cigarettes a day*, he said. Why eleven then? Johnny Doc had asked. *Because the eleventh one tempts but doesn't mock Fate, and it's important you understand and respect the difference between the two.*

Johnny Doc takes out his cellphone and checks the time. It's still early for his off-the-books meet with his lawyer, Raychard Balen, to discuss some very fragile and tenuous negotiations with the Bowen Brothers.

Most people knew Don and Danny Bowen from their commercials

THE LENGTH OF DAYS 35

tied to three enterprises: On The Clock, a chain of Temp Services; Floor To Ceiling, a maid and housekeeping service; Earth Angels, a caregiving franchise.

Enterprises which involved moving large numbers of people among its various branches.

Enterprises which worked as shell corporations for D&DB's larger ventures: a network of massage parlors covering the Southeast and flanking the North-South I-95 corridor.

Don and Danny Bowen enjoyed hiding in plain sight. They were in each of their commercials, having crafted public personae as regular guys, maybe a little slow on the uptake but good at heart. They were in their early forties and always appeared in satiny bowling shirts and polyester slacks. They were twins and enjoyed a running series of bad jokes based on that.

Don and Danny's private personae were another story. They were Genghis Kahns with a Southern accent. Stalins on a half-shell.

At bottom, Don and Danny Bowen moved bodies. Lots of bodies. Those bodies eventually intersected with other bodies. The bodies they intersected with had cash and credit cards.

The Bowen brothers knew the price of a body to a penny.

They also knew math, in particular, multiplication tables and therefore the price of twelve dead and burned bodies, plus two that still remained among the living and on the loose.

There'd been a phone call from Charlotte to verify the amount and another to set the terms of repayment.

The dead women at 805 Jefferson had not belonged to Johnny Doc Nowell. The dead and burned bodies had originally been *In Transit*. Johnny Doc was simply collecting rent until they were moved. He had been responsible for them until then.

Don and Danny Bowen expected restitution.

Johnny Doc Newell though had a problem with cash flow. Basically, it didn't.

The current voice-piece for the Bowens, one Nathaniel Laine, laid out a date and the repayment terms.

Johnny Doc had gone into stall and delay. He mentioned the two missing girls. The media spotlight on twelve burned bodies and the front yard homicide. He brought up Gary Lidd who was still in the wind. He suggested that Gary had answers to some pressing questions. Those questions and the answers to them required a little more time and a little room to maneuver. Johnny Doc explained he was personally checking into the whole thing. He mentioned trying to locate a third party who'd claimed to be an agent working for the Bowens. He promised to keep Laine, and subsequently, the Bowens, in the loop.

A little more time.

Johnny Doc floated just enough promises to gain a reprieve. A short one, though, carrying some long consequences.

THE LENGTH OF DAYS – EIGHT

Pam Graves doesn't say much during the course of a long lunch at The Tradewinds, a high-end restaurant jutting over the Atlantic that's on its third incarnation courtesy of Hurricane Hugo in 1989 and Hurricane Floyd in 1999 and a fire that left it DOA in 2003. The east, west, and south walls are glassed-in floor-to-ceiling, and the sky and ocean outside them are cloud-and-wind streaked in late February light.

Seated at the private table along with Pam are Andrew Findley, president of the Tourist Bureau, Kristen Miller, the mayor of Magnolia Beach, Ben Trumbull, chair of the Chamber of Commerce, Nelson Cavanaugh, WTKW's station manager, Marie LeClair, owner of WTKW, Billy Raymond, Chief of Police, and the guest of honor, Madison Hopewell, the lead investigative reporter for the Doorway Cable News Network.

Madison's on the ground in Magnolia Beach because of dead girls. Twelve of them at last count.

Madison Hopewell has presence. She burns with it. Fills the room with it. She is the sun around which everyone at the table orbits. She intimidates and charms. People fear and want to please her in equal measure.

So, at the conclusion of lunch, as they are crossing the parking lot, Pam Graves is not prepared for the moment when Madison Hopewell leans in and says quietly, "Ride with me."

Her car and driver are waiting. Madison Hopewell and Pam climb into the back seat. The driver is a thin twenty-something with a careful ponytail and red lacquered nails. She studies Madison from the rearview mirror, then turns her head and delivers a wide smile.

"I'm a fan, Ms. Hopewell. My boyfriend and me, we never miss you on Doorway. My favorite was when you did that report on infiltrating that cult in South Dakota. My boyfriend, he liked the way you handled yourself when you interviewed that cartel guy."

"Thank you," Madison says, leaning forward to read the license below the dash and adding, "Katy. I'm glad to hear that."

"I bet you're here because of the fire and those dead girls." Katy shifts her gaze to Pam. "Hey, you're the one that cried."

"Katy," Madison says, "I need to talk with Ms. Graves. How about you take us downtown to the Colonial? That's where I'm staying."

Katy puts the car in gear. Pam grows increasingly uncomfortable when she senses Madison studying her. Despite her best efforts, her face flushes.

"Your real one?" Madison says. "Your name, I mean."

"Excuse me, but Pam Graves has always been my name."

Madison shakes her head. "You were born lucky then. You have one you can grow into. I had to change mine. There's a difference."

"I'm not sure I understand. Grow into it?"

"Pam Graves," Madison says. "Listen to it." She reaches over and touches Pam's shoulder. "A nice mix of innocence and gravitas. It fits." She studies her again, and Pam feels another blush building. "When you outgrow it, you'll be Pamela Graves. By that time, you'll have shed the innocence and added authority to the gravitas." She waits a moment before adding, "You won't have to live inside your name. You'll be your name."

Pam looks down at the floorboards, then, momentarily, out the window. She's not sure what to say.

"Margaret Hordeski," Madison says. "That's how I started. I dropped and left it behind along with my first husband the first chance I got."

Katy pulls up to a red light. They're on Atlantic Avenue. To the left is the Full Moon Massage Parlor. "You might want to check that place out, Ms. Madison. Lots of rumors about who visits and what goes on there."

"Thanks for the tip."

Pam can hear the impatience running Madison's words even if Katy can't. In the next breath, Katy asks if Madison would like to visit the scene of the fire. "I know a shortcut," she adds.

Madison waves the offer off. "Tomorrow, maybe. Just the Colonial for now."

Pam watches a couple jaywalk Atlantic. They're holding hands and wearing matching hats.

"I did a little research and checked up on you," Madison says. "I was betting Theatre."

Pam frowns. "Again, I'm sorry, but I don't follow."

"Theatre," Madison repeats. "Either your major in college or you had experience. Summer Stock. Community Theatre. Along those lines." Madison aims a smile at Pam. "Like everyone else in the country, I saw the segment at the fire. That was quite a performance. Nicely timed too. It's paid off big-time for you."

THE LENGTH OF DAYS

Pam waits a moment before answering. "But it wasn't a performance, Ms. Hopewell."

"Hey, between us." Madison touches Pam's shoulder again. "You were convincing. It's like faking an orgasm. Nobody else has to know."

"I told you the truth. It wasn't a performance." Pam tells her about the shift in the wind and the sudden smell of burnt flesh. The drifting smoke and the posture of bones spread among the rubble. Someone calling out for more body bags. And finally about choking back tears but unable to stop them as the world turned itself inside out and it felt like she'd lost her place there and any claims she could make on it,

"I wish it had never happened," Pam says. "I wasn't even supposed to be there."

Madison Hopewell shakes her head. "But you were there. That can't be undone. You need to own your ambition, Ms. Graves."

"I'm not even sure I know what that means."

"Oh, I think you do," Madison Hopewell says, "and if you don't, you will soon enough."

THE LENGTH OF DAYS — NINE

Samuel Fulton did not start remembering any of his dreams until he'd cleared his seventieth birthday, and then his nights had taken on an abiding and fundamental confusion, one characterized by dense clusters and thickened layers of intransigent details that seemed to have little or no connection to the seven decades he'd previously seen as his life.

Samuel believes the appearance of those dreams has less to do with age as with the equally unexpected appearance of what the young doctor in the Emergency Room had referred to as the Transient Ischemic Event and the three strokes which followed that robbed his wife of her speech and mobility.

His dreams lately have been as disorienting and disturbing as the letter that Samuel had discovered when he was packing some of his wife's things for her move from their townhouse to C-Wing of the Bayview Assisted Living Center.

The letter, more than anything else, that turned everything in his life inside out.

A letter, with the month and day—October 17th—but no year, which had gone on to rewire their shared history and upend everything he'd thought as inviolate.

C-Wing has dual tracks based on need. The east corridors are for the Chronics, the west for the Acutes. Samuel crosses the lobby to a semicircular work station where he's given a visitor's pass by a young woman in brown horn-rimmed glasses.

Samuel heads toward the west corridor. There's a short, dark-haired man running a buffing machine near the double doors. He shuts it off when he spots Samuel and walks over and shakes his hand.

"Mr. Sam."

"How's it going, Arturo?"

"No complaints. Paycheck to paycheck like everybody else in the country." He steps back and opens one of the doors. "You tell Mrs. Sam hello for me."

Samuel thanks him and heads down the corridor. He's surrounded by soft confectionary Muzak. He stops for a moment at the door to C-10, takes a breath, and then steps inside.

THE LENGTH OF DAYS 41

Glenda is out of bed and in her wheelchair. At some point, her nurse had stationed her facing the window. She's jacketed in a white terry cloth robe. On her feet are a pair of white cross-trainers, a superfluous substitute for slippers since the stroke has left her legs useless. The curtains are pulled back, and she's looking into the heart of a late-February afternoon.

Samuel calls out her name. No response. The same when he rests his hand on her shoulder and leans in and kisses her forehead.

The room's décor is a standoff between efficiency and comfort. A motorized hospital bed. Lemon-sherbet walls. Thin carpeting for ease of movement with the wheelchair. Faux samplers with faux needlepoint palmettos, seashells, and pelicans. A television that usually remains off. A small corner desk holding a pile of paperbacks and a lamp and a pencil holder and wooden globe. A bathroom tucked in the opposite corner. A compact recliner.

The stroke has shaved years off Glenda's features, erasing lines and smoothening wrinkles. The pale gray eyes don't generate or reflect much light at all, and it's that light Samuel had always counted on and fell in love with. He can still remember all too easily the first time he'd seen her, when Glenda McGuire, a mid-year transfer student, had stepped into his sixth grade world history class and where through the simple luck of the alphabet came to be seated in the row of desks next to him, her soft-edged profile and middle of the back blue-black hair coming to occupy his peripheral vision and most of his hormone-fueled thoughts during Mr. Nelson's lecture on the Ottoman Empire.

They've been married over forty-nine years.

Each afternoon, Samuel reads to Glenda for a half hour. It's a continuation of the routine she'd followed when she'd worked as a teacher. Glenda would come home, pour herself a generous glass of wine, and retreat to an overstuffed chair in the living room and read for thirty minutes. Then she'd get up and start working on supper.

Samuel picks up the paperback at the top of the pile. The novel's entitled *Dead and Butter*, a sequel to *Biscuits and Bullets*, about a mother-daughter duo who in addition to having some serious generational differences—the mother's an 80's Yuppie and the daughter running to Goths-R-Us—find themselves having to help solve any number of crimes while simultaneously running a small-town bakery and catering operation outside Asheville, North Carolina.

Samuel had once asked Glenda why she liked the books, pointing out the obvious, that they seemed patently out of touch with reality, and

Glenda had tipped the glass of wine in his direction and told him that after a day of dealing with close to thirty fourth graders, patently unreal was just what the doctor ordered.

The thing is, Samuel has to be careful how he stacks the books on the dresser. He has a hard time keeping them straight. *Dead and Butter* doesn't seem any different from *Biscuits and Bullets*, and Samuel has the feeling that *Dead and Butter* will not significantly differ from the next one in the series, *Doughnuts and Death Threats*, or any of the others down the line like *Pastries and Pistols* or *Turnovers and Tourniquets*.

This afternoon, Samuel is simply working through the pages, long ago having abandoned any suspension of disbelief in the constant mother-daughter bickering or the PG blood-splattered twists in the plots, concentrating instead on the sound of the words themselves, Samuel keeping his voice low and even, as if he could return and replace all the words his wife had lost after the stroke.

He reads two chapters and stops. He closes the book and replaces it on the stack. He takes Glenda's hand, and together they look out into an abbreviated afternoon, and for a while, they sit in a silence that feels as if it's not defined by the absence of words.

THE LENGTH OF DAYS — TEN

Arturo Morales puts in three hours of housecleaning overtime at C-Wing in the Bayview Assisted Living Center. Before signing out, he uses the restroom and washes up. He says goodnight to the security guard after asking about his family. Outside the evening still holds a damp February chill. Arturo crosses the parking lot to his car, a twenty-one-year-old Chevy Impala with shocks that are a twelve-year memory and whose original paint job has retreated to a cloudy blue.

He opens the trunk and takes out a canvas grocery bag and then walks to the northeast corner of the lot and stands next to a white Honda Civic.

Arturo is waiting for a Certified Nursing Assistant named Kevin Minot. Kevin's in his mid-thirties with thinning hair, a medium-sized overbite, and a waxy complexion. Until six months ago when she unexpectedly died, he had lived with his mother.

Kevin's old school when it comes to Porn. He likes VHS tapes. No DVDs or internet streaming for him.

Luckily for Kevin, Arturo has a cousin who worked B&E's. One of his jobs was cleaning out a Steamy Nites video store a week before it went Chapter-11. His cousin moved the bounty to a Store-It in south Magnolia Beach.

Arturo's cousin owed him a favor concerning a Charter Arms .38 that had been in circulation longer than it should have been, and the Charter Arms was tied to a number of jobs that could in turn be tied to Arturo's cousin if it landed in the wrong cop's hands.

Arturo had made sure it didn't.

Which is how Arturo has come to be holding a grocery bag full of pornography and standing next to Kevin Minot's white Honda Civic on a chilly February evening.

Kevin shows up fifteen minutes later. He's still in his CNA uniform. Arturo gives him the bag. Kevin hands over an amber prescription bottle holding thirty Oxycodone.

As a CNA, Kevin can give out meds. With the Chronics and Acutes at Bayview, he will occasionally palm an Oxy and replace it with an over-the-counter decongestant, usually Claritin, that's a close match. Kevin's careful and takes his time. He usually contacts Arturo when he's harvested at least two dozen Oxys.

They tell each other good night. Kevin puts the bag in his trunk. Arturo walks back to his Impala.

Arturo drives to south Magnolia Beach for a late supper at Casa Lucinda's. He orders two burritos and a Corona and takes his time finishing all three.

It's not God or politics that holds the world together. Arturo understands it's favors, small favors, one after another, all connected, an intricate latticework of small favors as fundamental and complex as strands of DNA.

After Casa Lucinda's, Arturo takes Lamar Street until it crosses Wide Circle and then follows Case Street until he reaches what at one time had been a thriving neighborhood park before the gangbangers had turned it into their own piece of scorched-earth Armageddon.

He pulls to the curb next to a swing set without swings. The sky's clear and parading skeins of stars and a milky half-moon.

Arturo Morales waits longer than he likes before Wayne Summer taps on the driver's side window of the Impala.

Wayne has a half-hearted buzz-cut above an extra-wide forehead below which is a pair of brown eyes crowding the bridge of a nose that looks like it belongs on someone else's face.

Arturo rolls down the window. He holds up the amber prescription bottle. He shakes it, and at the rattle, Wayne's body becomes a tuning fork.

Wayne pulls out a handful of crumpled bills just as the blue and white pulls up behind Arturo. The cop is out in a blink, gun drawn.

"Hands on the roof," he tells Wayne. He tells Arturo to keep his hands at the 10 and 2 positions on the wheel.

"We were just talking, Officer," Arturo says. "We're friends, catching up, that's all."

"I'm thinking I must have interrupted a friendly drug transaction then."

"Please, Officer," Wayne says.

"No please, friend," the cop says. "We're not in the vicinity of Please anymore."

He tells Arturo to take the keys from the ignition and toss them on the sidewalk. Then he cuffs Wayne and does the same to Arturo.

"I'm willing to entertain some alternatives here," the cop says.

"No wax in these ears," Wayne says.

"Hey, wait a minute," Arturo says.

THE LENGTH OF DAYS

"First come, first serve," the cop says and puts Arturo in the back of the blue and white.

Over the next twenty minutes, Arturo watches Wayne nod his head, then nod, then nod again before turning and jogging across what's left of the park.

Arturo watches Officer Carl Adkin walk back to the blue and white. Adkin opens the rear door and unlocks the cuffs that Arturo holds up.

"It appears Wayne has elected to join the family," Adkin says. "You delivered and did good, Arturo."

"I'm not sure how helpful Wayne is going to be," Arturo says.

"Hey, I'm not looking for a brain surgeon. A snitch just needs to be scared or desperate. Preferably both."

"Do you mind?" Arturo holds up an index finger and the amber prescription bottle.

Adkin shrugs. "Sure. Okay."

Arturo dry-palms an Oxy. He wants to get back home and put a couple beers and some ESPN behind the evening.

He tosses the prescription bottle to Carl Adkin. Carl shakes it and smiles. "The new coin of the realm. I can already see the snitches lining up, ready to trade."

Arturo waits a moment before asking, "We're okay here then?"

"Absolutely," Adkin says. "Mission accomplished. Have a good evening."

Right, Arturo thinks. Mission accomplished until the next time the phone rings, and Carl Adkin needs another favor.

Arturo gives Adkin the smile and wave he expects to see and leaves. On the way home, he changes his mind about home and stops at a convenience store and buys two tall boys.

Then he drives to Houston Street and parks facing a block of burned buildings, nothing more than widespread char and rubble.

Arturo cracks a tall boy and leans back in the seat. He pops the extra Oxy tab he'd palmed back at the park without Adkin noticing and sends it to join the first that's already begun to loosen the tightness in his neck and shoulders and pull up a small smile.

The smile stays in place the longer he looks at the rubble.

Arturo can see it. What all that rubble will one day be replaced with. It becomes a little more clear each time he visits.

First, there are the jobs, the housekeeping and orderly work at C-Wing, the freelance roofing and landscaping, and the part-time weekend job at Gerald's Tires patching flats and rotating tires and doing ad hoc oil changes.

Then there are the favors. What need dictates. Where it leads and how far. Price tags and bottom lines. What you look at and away from. What you give up and in to.

Arturo reaches over for the second tall boy and pulls the tab. The Oxy is smoothening everything out that needs smoothening.

He looks across the street at the burnt-out lot. He starts smiling again.

He can see it. All the rubble cleared away. New asphalt. Bright halogen lights. A modular home on blocks that doubles as an office. The perimeters of the lot defined by bright multi-colored pennants. Then the shiny rows of cars. And of course, the sign, large and strategically placed.

Arturo Morales's Used Cars.

No, not that.

A. M. Used Cars.

No, wrong word. Not Used.

He tips back the beer and closes his eyes for a moment.

Pre-Owned. That's it. That's what they say now. Not Used. Pre-Owned.

Arturo knows cars. They're something basic. He likes that. You want to get from Point A to Point B, you need a car.

A.M.'s Pre-Owned Cars.

There are days though, and maybe this is one of them, when jobs and favors have come to carry the same weight as *used* and *pre-owned*. Arturo has always wanted to believe there should be a bigger difference between them. And that the difference should matter.

But try putting *Used* or *Pre-owned* in front of something that's important to you and then see what's what.

Something important. Like your life or your dreams.

THE LENGTH OF DAYS — ELEVEN

It takes a while, but it's small things, like iron filings gravitating toward a magnet, which finally account for Pam Graves's slowly growing unease after she's rung the doorbell at 1723 Newberry and finds it broken.

She knocks, hesitantly at first, then harder, and eventually Leo Williams opens the door. He's out of uniform.

Rather than inviting her in, Leo steps out onto the small concrete pad fronting the door. Before the door closes, Pam gets a quick glimpse inside. The day's overcast, heavy with clouds, but the drapes are closed, and there are no lights on, and the dining room table is a sprawl of dirty dishes.

Leo Williams is facing the street and not quite making eye contact by just looking over Pam's head. He's wearing a wrinkled blue shirt under a gray cardigan missing two buttons. His khakis are faded and stained at the knees as if he's been kneeling in wet grass. On his feet are a pair of battered brown corduroy slippers.

"Is this a good time, Mr. Williams?" Pam wishes she had tried to call first. She'd trusted to chance on the visit.

"Good time?" Leo William frowns slightly, as if he's trying to parse out a difficult and slippery concept in another language.

Pam's been hunting down leads for Madison Hopewell. She's hoping that Leo Williams, the patrolman who had given Pam and the cameraman Paul Westbrook a five-minute favor at the scene of the fire and the tip about probable origin, might be good for another favor.

Now, she's not so sure. Leo Williams, out of uniform, doesn't resemble the man she knew when she babysat for his wife Joanne and him close to a decade ago. Then, Leo, his wife, and their seven-year-old daughter Angela seemed to fit the same mold as every other family Pam knew.

Leo Williams now resembles a man whose life has outrun him. He's become the kind of man who lives in a house with a broken doorbell.

"I'm sorry to bother you," Pam says.

"You still haven't told me why you're here," he says.

She decides to go with a hybrid of a lie and the truth. "I just wanted to thank you for granting access at the fire and answering my questions."

"You already thanked me," he says slowly, then stops, waiting for her to go on.

Pam's not sure she can or wants to. Once again, she feels as if the world she thought she knew has been turned inside out. Leo Williams out of his uniform and her memories of the house and family don't match up, and she says the first thing that comes to mind.

"I hope Mrs. Williams and Angela are doing fine."

He keeps his gaze aimed over her head. "My wife's in ICU and won't be leaving it," he says, "and Angela's run away three times now. She's living with my sister in Birmingham until she can get herself and things straightened out." He abruptly stops speaking as if he's run out of his daily ration of words.

Then just as abruptly Leo Williams gives her an unreadable smile and asks, "Your family? How are they?"

Pam momentarily chokes on answering. His tone is the verbal equivalent of someone about to turn over a rock and expose what's beneath.

"It was nice seeing you again, Mr. Williams. I have to go now." Pam starts to leave, but he grabs her arm.

"I really have to go now, Mr. Williams."

He drops his hand from her arm and resurrects the unnerving off-center smile. "Don't you want to know?"

For a moment, Pam's afraid he's talking about her family.

"The name you're after," he says, "it's Samuel Fulton. He lives in a townhouse in Bayview Manor."

Before Pam can thank him, Leo Williams is through the door and shutting it quietly behind him.

THE LENGTH OF DAYS – TWELVE

Twice a month, while on Patrol, Carl Adkin stops by the Laughing Zebra Mini-Mart on his lunch break. The owner and operator is Jimmy LaSalle Sr. who won the Laughing Zebra in a high-stakes poker game hosted by an equally high stakes real estate broker from Mt. Pleasant, South Carolina. The Zebra is in a newly transitional neighborhood in south Magnolia Beach. Five years ago, it was the equivalent of a demilitarized zone.

When Carl enters, Jimmy Sr. is manning the register. He's sporting a feathered mound of silver-gray hair and an open-collared sports shirt unbuttoned to mid-chest where a St. Michael medal is lost in a thicket of silver chest hair and 70's nostalgia.

Jimmy Sr. give his customary greeting. "Your money's no good here, Officer. At the Laughing Zebra, heroes will always have a free lunch."

Carl gives him his bimonthly nod and thanks. "I'll have the regular then."

Carl slides into a booth with a view streetside of an ABC State Store, its façade painted white and punctuated by a large red dot and barred windows. A steady stream of midday customers moves in and out of the front doors. Next to the ABC Store is a large one-story discount furniture outlet.

Jimmy Sr. brings over a Styrofoam container and a large Mountain Dew in a wide-mouthed plastic cup and sets both in front of Carl.

"A little bit of news," he says. "My boy, Jimmy Jr., he got himself engaged. Nice girl, originally from Darlington, and works over at the Target on Walnut and Fifth."

"That's great," Carl says. "Won't be long till you're telling me you're a grandfather."

Jimmy Sr. nods, then looks over Carl's head and out the window. "You think, two and a half years, you'd be able to put it out of your head and behind you, but there are times, mostly nights, when the what ifs won't leave you alone."

Carl takes a hit of the Dew. "Everything turned out all right, Jimmy."

"That's the thing of it," he says, "and it should be enough. But the all right isn't. Or not quite. The What Ifs won't leave the All Rights alone."

"Jimmy Jr. is still above ground and doing fine. Phil Davies isn't either one. Relax and enjoy your life, Jimmy. You deserve it."

"I don't know what I'd of done if I'd lost Jimmy Jr. I mean I lost his mother to the cancer six months before Phil Davies walked in here." Jimmy abruptly stops talking, shakes his head, and points at the Styrofoam container in front of Carl. "Go on, eat your lunch. I talk too much. That's how you know you're getting old, the talking too much." He turns and heads back to the front counter.

Lunch is a sausage dog with fried onions and peppers on a hoagie bun, a bent dill pickle, and a pile of nacho fries.

Carl's sitting about ten feet away from where he shot Phil Davies two and a half years ago.

The shooting was Roadmap Science. Little League Physics. Carl had stepped into the Laughing Zebra intending to buy a soda. Jimmy Jr. was behind the counter. Next to him was a twitching piece of protoplasm named Phil Davies. He was holding a .22 pistol against Jimmy's left temple. With his back partially turned, Davies hadn't immediately noticed Carl's entrance.

It came down to the simple element of surprise. Carl was less surprised than Davies, that's all. Phil Davies's shot went wide. Carl's didn't.

The local and regional papers called him a hero. For a while, Carl had pretended to believe it.

Another blue and white pulls in next to Carl's, and Truman Cooke slowly unpacks himself from behind the wheel. He looks up and spots Carl at the window seat. He nods and smiles.

Truman orders two chili dogs all the way and a medium orange soda and waits while Jimmy Sr. fixes them before joining Carl at the table.

They ask about each other's families, bring each other up to date. As far as Carl's concerned, Truman's a brother, closer to him than the two he shares by blood and biology. They've known each other since first grade. They rode bikes together, hung out in Carl's treehouse, watched the same TV shows, rooted for the same pro teams, drank their first beers together, double-dated with their high school sweethearts, played on the same all-state football team, Truman an offensive lineman and Carl a running back, both joining the Marines after graduation, then marrying their high school sweethearts after mustering out, followed by two years as UPS drivers before deciding to enter the police academy and now eleven years on the job, they are still married to the same women and have three kids, Carl two boys and a girl, Truman two girls and a boy.

"Denisha and Linda cooking up something this weekend," Truman

THE LENGTH OF DAYS

says.

Carl nods. "Okay by me, as long as it includes some NBA action and cold beer."

"I hear you, Friend." Truman starts in on the second chili dog.

Carl's finished his sausage dog and is leaning back in the booth. "You know what I miss, Truman? The day you could smoke a cigarette with a clear conscience after a meal."

Truman waits a moment before saying, "Something I been meaning to talk to you about."

Carl holds up his hand. "I told you, no hurry about getting back on that loan. Glad to help out."

Truman starts rubbing his jaw and squinting.

"What?" Carl asks.

"Friend," Truman says, "I been hearing things and not of a reassuring nature. Your name and Johnny Doc Nowell's came up a couple times."

"Hey," Carl says. "You know how that plays. Snitch Logic. Cop Gossip. You can't take either to the bank."

"I keep hearing things," Truman says. "Can't help but to worry."

Carl shrugs and holds up both hands.

"So things are straight?" Truman asks.

"You ever heard of a ruler?" Carl says. "Draw a line. That's me."

Truman finishes his hot dog, nods, and says, "That's good to hear."

THE LENGTH OF DAYS — THIRTEEN

Arturo Morales is buffing the central corridor of D-Wing at Bayview Manor. He guides the machine left to right and back again, and it moves across the floor in a quiet hum. He feels the vibration, moving like a low-watt electrical charge, move through his wrists and forearms. It's been twenty-five days since he's had a day off.

He keeps thinking about that empty lot on Houston Street. He tries to summon up the image of row after row of used cars under the halogen lights, a bright rainbow of pennants waving in a soft wind, Arturo himself in a new suit, crisp white shirt, and bolo tie and moving among his inventory, but there are times, and tonight is one of them, when no matter how hard he tries, it feels as if he's looking at his dreams through the wrong end of a telescope.

Working D-Wing tonight doesn't help matters.

D-Wing is what's left when nothing else is. It's as if everyone housed there is looking over the edge of their lives, and the steady hum of the buffing machine is not loud enough to drown out the chorus of wheeze, scream, curse, plead, cry, and moan that soundtrack the hallway.

Down at its end, Mr. Weldon Trulane backs out of room D-21. "Hey, newsflash, Sweetcakes," he shouts. "I haven't been drinking, and I understand the concept of Visiting Hours."

Turning on his heel, he starts toward Arturo, pausing only enough to say, "You need to pass on to Nurse Ratched there, that we've already read the book and seen the movie."

Arturo doesn't know a Nurse Ratched. It's Nurse Givens and Nurse Gordon on duty tonight on D-Wing.

It's not the first time, though, that Arturo has been caught off guard by Weldon Trulane's anger or off-kilter kindness. He is known around Bayview as the loosest of the loose cannons.

Arturo feels his phone vibrate in the left front pocket of his uniform. He looks around, then shuts off the buffing machine, and checks his messages. The latest is from Carl Adkin.

"A couple things here, Arturo. You hear anything, get right back to me. Anything on the two girls still AWOL, a nice finder's fee there. Second, anything on a batch of free-range semiautomatics, mixed caliber, making the rounds. Next, you see Gary Lidd, get back ASAP. Last,

THE LENGTH OF DAYS

haven't seen much of my new Snitch Wayne Summer. You see him, tell him I've been asking about him and expecting a meet. He was a no-show at the last one, and I am currently not harboring kind thoughts about him."

Favors. Favors within Favors.

Arturo finishes buffing the hallway. He stores the machine in the utility closet. He eats an apple in the break room. He fights to keep his eyes open, but doesn't take the quarter-tab of Dexedrine he keeps for shifts like this because he needs the sleep when he gets back to his room.

Arturo spends the rest of his shift as a temporary orderly, helping out Nurse Givens and Nurse Gordon when Kenny, the regularly orderly, has to go home early.

It's 11:20 when Arturo finally clocks out. The night air still has a late-winter bite. His breath streams white as he cuts across the grounds to the parking lot. The cold air doesn't touch his exhaustion. Right now, he just wants to get back to his room at the Drake Hotel, crack open a couple beers, watch some World Soccer highlights, and sleep for a decade or two.

Parked next to his Impala is a silver Lexus with the engine running and its parking lights on.

Arturo unlocks the Impala and is about to slide under the wheel when the passenger side window of the Lexus powers down, and a voice with a long reach says, "Hello, Arturo."

Felina Fuentes. She's even more beautiful than he remembers, and Arturo knows there's nothing wrong with his memory.

Before he can respond, a hand appears. "Been a while, Arturo." On the third finger, there's an oversized gold ring whose face is perimetered in parallel lines of diamond chips and at whose center is a line of small right-angled rubies that form an *L*.

"Hello Luis," Arturo says.

"How about some late supper on Felina and me?" Luis asks. "We can catch up."

"Not tonight," Arturo says. "Busy shift. I'm tired."

"We're only in town for a couple days. Tonight would be better." From the angle of his lean, half of Luis's face is in shadow.

"Not for me," Arturo says. "Maybe another time."

"Please, Arturo," Felina says quietly.

They end up at a nearby Denny's at a window seat with a view of the Good-As-Nu Tire Outlet and a Everything's-A-Dollar on Fountain

Avenue. One of the halogen lights in the Everything's-A-Dollar lot is strobing erratically.

Luis and Felina sit side by side across from Arturo. They're conspicuously overdressed, given the rest of the clientele, Luis in a light gray suit, pink shirt, and pale blue tie, Felina in a black dress with a string of pearls looped above some PG cleavage.

Luis Sorbano makes a show of taking out a pair of wire-rimmed glasses and studying the menu as if it were an exotic wine list. Felina glances at Arturo, then away.

When the waitress appears, Luis insists that Arturo order a Grand Slam, Luis going for a three-egg omelet and home fries for himself, and Felina turning everything down except a coffee with cream.

Luis raises his eyebrows. "Women. What can you say?"

A History, Arturo guesses that's what the three of them had or have. For two and a half years though, it had just been Felina and him. They had met at a mutual friend's daughter's Quinceanera, Arturo twenty-one at the time and doing roofing and ad hoc construction jobs and living in Burlington, North Carolina, Felina nineteen and working as a receptionist at an Urgent Care Clinic and thinking about starting tech school, a whole future starting to take shape between them, Arturo two months from asking Felina to marry him when Luis Sorbano walked into the Urgent Care with a sinus infection.

Felina turned Luis Sorbano down the first four times he asked her out.

Things changed after the fifth, Luis pulling a classic end run and meeting with Felina's parents and respectfully presenting his bona fides, which in Luis's case turned out to be the fact that he just opened a sports bar called Wings, Beers, and Burgers in Greensboro. Then Luis had appended the magic word: *Franchises.*

Suddenly Felina was not answering Arturo's phone calls or answering the door.

She married Luis Sorbano six weeks later.

Arturo left Burlington, moved to Charlotte, later to Magnolia Beach.

He hadn't seen Felina in eight years. Hadn't thought about her for at least a day and a half.

Now, a booth at Denny's. Her reflection in the window. Felina having grown into her beauty. It's as if that full beauty had been waiting for her, and she now fully inhabits it.

Across the street, the halogen light in the parking lot of Everything's-A-Dollar slowly strobes its way to extinction.

THE LENGTH OF DAYS

Luis Sorbano cuts his omelet into quarters, then forks each quarter into small squares. Felina sips her coffee. Arturo waits.

"Food's getting cold," Luis says, pointing at Arturo's plate.

"Why?" Arturo asks.

"Why's your food getting cold?" Luis Sorbano shakes his head. "You don't eat it, that's what happens."

"This meeting. Why?"

"Old Arturo here has never been much for foreplay, has he?" Luis leans over, dipping his shoulder into Felina's. "Don't you agree, Dear?"

"Connie Fuentes," Felina says, looking at Arturo. "My niece."

"Listen and learn," Luis says. "There's some people can't do either. Case in point: Connie."

"She's fifteen," Felina says.

And gone, Arturo discovers. Connie and her best friend Julia Ramos taking off, doing the runaway number, four months ago now, eluding the police and the private investigators Luis and Felina hired, two fifteen-year-olds in the wind, off the grid, on the move, severing all contact with their family and friends, disappearing into the world.

"Three months," Felina repeats.

"Willful as only a teenage girl can be," Luis says. "That's how she ended up staying with us in the first place. Felina's brother and her own mother couldn't make her listen. We took her in, gave her a fresh start, and this is how she repays us."

Felina lifts and then sets down her coffee cup. "We need you to help find her."

"I don't understand," Arturo says. He's momentarily distracted by her expression.

"Connie is in Magnolia Beach," Felina says. "And hiding. I'm sure of it."

"Why not the police then?"

"We just want her back," Luis answers. "And then we can get her the help she needs. It's a family matter. We want to keep it at that."

"Why are you so sure she's here?"

"The girls and the fire," Felina says. "The news reports said they could identify four out of the twelve through dental records. One of them was Julie Ramos. She and Connie were inseparable. And Connie wasn't one of the other eight."

Luis Sorbano finishes his omelet and pushes the plate away. "You know Magnolia Beach. You live here. You know where to look and who to ask, and we're ready and able to reimburse you for that help." Luis lifts his left hand and ticks off each finger, appending a thousand dollars to each.

Felina excuses herself and leaves the booth for the restroom. Arturo and Luis watch her go.

"Times Three," Luis says.

"What? You're telling me $15,000?"

Luis Sorbano nods. "Felina and Family. You know how it goes. That's how Connie ended up staying with us in the first place."

Luis holds his right-hand palm out. "I know what's next. You want to know why I started out at $5,000 and then kicked it up."

Arturo nods. Luis looks over his shoulder in the direction of the bathroom. "As always, the why is Felina and always will be. You find Connie, but I want to be the one to deliver her to Felina. I need to re-establish myself in her eyes."

Luis runs his fingers through his hair. He waits a moment before adding, "Time, Amigo, it can do things, like take the luster off, especially when it comes to men and women." He shakes his head. "I need to be the one to deliver her. That's why times three. A hero, me returning Connie, what I'll see again in Felina's eyes."

Felina returns from the restroom. Luis stands, and she slides into the booth and sits. She looks over at Arturo. "Please," she says.

Right then, Arturo's time-travelling ten and a half years back to the Quinceanera in Burlington, North Carolina where he'd asked a young woman to dance, and when he'd learned her name, he had asked about Rosa's Cantina, and when she tilted her head at him, puzzled, he'd told her about Marty Robbins and "El Paso" and a young outlaw in love who against all logic and common sense both killed for and later returned to his true love and inevitable doom, taking bullet after bullet from the posse chasing him, only to end up in his love's arms, the final refrain doubling as his fate: *One little kiss, Felina, and goodbye.*

THE LENGTH OF DAYS — FOURTEEN

They set up along the curb fronting the Full Moon Massage Parlor on Atlantic. Dave Preston driving the white WTKW van. Paul Westbrook handling the camera. Madison Hopewell in a dark blue dress with a large white button holding a 12+2 pinned just above her left breast. Pam Graves the vestigial conscience of the group.

Earlier she'd pointed out that the Full Moon and Bishop Conover, the manager, and his common-law wife Nina had no clear or overt connection with the twelve dead and two missing girls, and Madison Hopewell had shaken her head and given her the kind of smile an elementary school teacher gives to a well-intentioned but struggling student.

Pam now steps aside as Paul Westbrook starts shooting and Madison begins her delivery, dropping into some high-octane self-righteousness and segueing into the billion-plus dollar a year engine running sex trafficking. The psychological, emotional, and physical cost to its victims. Massage parlors providing both camouflage and convenient venue for sex traffickers. The blurred legal lines between legitimate massage parlors and sex-for-money. The standard issue claim of a victimless crime and the equally standard issue degradation of the exploited. Morality ultimately an afterthought or at best collateral damage.

But Madison Hopewell then admitting, all those facts and statistics, all those sordid and lucrative situations, are ultimately too abstract and dull-edged. A context is what's needed. A necessary frame.

So today Madison Hopewell brings things a little closer to home. She talks about how beach towns in particular often provided some of the richest hunting grounds for sex traffickers. Beach towns were conveniently anonymous and tempting locales for runaways to lose themselves. Beach towns were also the perfect vehicle for tourists and adventurous teens to let their guard down and cut loose a little.

Beach towns were porous on any number of levels.

Romeos and Florence Nightingales were common fixtures in beach towns. Both had their own particular skill sets and usually worked together. Romeos ran on seductive charms, the bad boys promising good times, and Nightingales on a comforting empathy, the sisterly friends who stepped in before it was too late and rescued you from the dark charms of the Romeos.

Throw in some lost, malcontented, or adventurous teenage girls and you were in business.

A low cost and very lucrative business.

After the shoot, Madison Hopewell taps Pam on the shoulder and points north a block to the Breakers Inn and Happy Hour. Paul Westbrook and Dave Preston are already on their way there.

Then someone calls out Madison Hopewell's name.

They watch a figure crossing the lot of the Full Moon on a diagonal, his stride a passive-aggressive mix of easy and purposeful. He's tall and lanky and wearing a white shirt, jeans, and cowboy boots. His hair is shoulder-length and deep black.

He's joined shortly after by a short woman in a peasant blouse, jeans, and rope sandals. She wears a ring on each finger of her right hand and on her left arm a pile-up of brightly colored bracelets.

"Let's call this a repeat request," Bishop Conover says, trying on a smile. "It's not too late to kill the story."

Madison toes the line and swath of grass between lot and sidewalk. "We've already discussed this. Public Domain, Mr. Conover. We never stepped foot on your property."

Bishop Conover crosses his arms across his chest. "Let's be reasonable. Public Domain or not, that shot was deceptive and unfair. I'm a legitimate businessman. Your audience is going to draw the wrong conclusions."

"I did a segment on the often horrendous and exploitive consequences for the victims of sex trafficking. Fourteen of them in this case." Madison drops her hands to hips. "My segment was at bottom a PSA."

"I'm politely calling bullshit on that PSA, Ms. Hopewell. Your whole angle and the button you're wearing, the Full Moon as backdrop, you know the whole thing will ultimately come across as accusatory. I'm asking you again to please kill the story." He leans in a little closer. "Or at least move it to a different location."

Madison glances over at Pam and then aims another smile at Bishop Conover. "I never mentioned you or your establishment by name. Not once."

Conover drops his arms. Pam notices him involuntarily clenching and unclenching his left hand. A vein in his neck bulges and retreats with each squeeze and release.

The woman steps in and holds up both hands, palms out. "Excuse my husband. He can get a little prickly this time of day."

THE LENGTH OF DAYS

"I noticed," Madison Hopewell says.

Nina Conover's smile never wavers. "A different perspective," she says. "You know, there's a school of thought that maintains sex work is ultimately empowering. It's liberating and honest. Women owning their bodies and breaking society's hypocritical bonds."

"It's hard for most people to see giving hand and blow jobs for money to sad and desperate men as empowering," Madison says.

Bishop Conover goes back to clenching and unclenching his left hand. He points at Madison and Pam with his right.

"You two," he says after a moment. "Cunts all the way." He abruptly stops, turns, and starts back across the lot.

"Ladies," Nina Conover says, "I hope you know what you're doing."

"What was that?" Pam asks Madison. They watch Nina Conover leave.

"Sometimes you need to stir things up," Madison says, "and then step back and see what happens. Most of the time, something will."

That's what Pam Graves is afraid of.

THE LENGTH OF DAYS — FIFTEEN

At ten, Johnny Doc drives to the old downtown district of Magnolia Beach. He parks in the lot behind the home office of the Bank of the South.

The receptionist is in her early twenties. She's overdressed and overearnest, her smile hiding the not so quiet desperation of the newly hired in a tight job market. She asks if he has an appointment. Johnny Doc nods yes.

Rhodes Woodbury is the Vice President of the bank. He has a low-tide hairline, the smile of a politician, the eyes of an umpire, and a widescreen waistline. His suit is light gray and his shirt and tie a half shade under flamboyant.

"Johnny," he says, taking both of Johnny's hands between his own.

Johnny Doc nods and sits in a chair directly in front of the desk. Over the next few minutes, he watches Rhodes Woodbury pretend to study files and shuffle papers. Then Rhodes stops and leans back in his chair and a moment later drops the smile and raises his eyebrows.

"I need a loan," Johnny Doc says.

"Exactly how much are we talking about?" he says, drawing out each word.

"In the neighborhood of 900,000."

"Ouch," Rhodes says. "The times being what they are."

"Exactly," Johnny Doc says. "The times being what they are."

"I assume you're referring to the bailouts," Rhodes says. "We've petitioned and applied, but we're not Goldman Sachs." He shakes his head. "We're at the back of the back of the back of the line at best."

"We've known each other a long time," Johnny Doc says.

Rhodes nods slowly. "A fact."

"I need some help here."

Rhodes delivers another display of headshaking. "Welcome to 2009. We're all working without a net now."

Johnny Doc leans forward in his chair. "I need some help, Rhodes."

"Nothing wrong with my hearing, friend. Maybe something with yours. You might want to get that checked."

"What else, Rhodes? Don't give me 2009 or the calendar. I know what year it is. What I want to know is what else."

THE LENGTH OF DAYS   61

Rhodes Woodbury gets up and crosses the office to a corner station holding a fresh pot of coffee. He pours two cups, then points at two bowls holding sugar packets and thimble-sized containers of cream. Johnny Doc shakes his head no to each. Rhodes returns to his desk and hands Johnny Doc his coffee. Before sitting down, he takes off his sports jacket and drapes it across the back of his chair. He's wearing a pair of dark blue wide-banded suspenders over a pale blue shirt bisected by a tie filled with a competing welter of blue and green lines. The light from the east window of the office runs through what's left of his hairline, illuminating a pink swath of scalp.

"Okay, then," Rhodes says, settling back in his chair. He takes two hits on the coffee, then says, "Rumors. *What else* is rumors." He takes another sip. "None of them remotely in the territory of comfortable."

Johnny Doc doesn't say anything.

He waits, and eventually Rhodes says, "I know the house is yours. 805 Jefferson. That's between us." Rhodes runs two fingers across his upper lip. "But there's still the dead girls, the missing ones, and a lot of media coverage. The Bank of the South can't afford blowback right now. Neither can I."

"I have low visibility on the Jefferson Street property."

"But not on the Full Moon Massage Parlor."

"There are no direct ties to the Full Moon and 805 Jefferson."

"Rumors are still rumors and can carry the weight of facts at times."

A double-blind. That's what Johnny Doc's lawyer, Raychard Balen, set up for the property at 805 Jefferson. The first step was setting up a Land Trust. The Land Trust is then tied to an Irrevocable Living Trust that in turn titles ownership of the property. That title needs a trustee. By law, the trustee as beneficiary cannot reveal the name of the property owner.

The usual Land Trust arrangement is to have the attorney set up as trustee. The tax bill comes to him, and he forwards it to the original owner for payment.

Raychard Balen had added an extra layer of protection and anonymity for Johnny Doc. Instead of Balen acting as trustee, he named Jack Doyle, an old drunk and damaged vet residing in the Firestone Assisted Living Center in South Magnolia Beach. Jack Doyle had no family. He gave Raychard Balen Power of Attorney over his affairs. In another recursive move, he also named Balen as beneficiary. In this case, the left hand and right hand each pulled its own sleight of hand.

The arrangement bought Johnny Doc time. It would take no small amount of digging before he could be identified as the owner of 805 Jefferson.

What that left him with, in the meantime, was what he owed the Bowen Brothers as restitution for the twelve dead and two missing girls.

Johnny Doc lays it all out for Rhodes and then takes a long moment and studies him. "This careful side is something new in you, Rhodes. You used to be Slash-and-burn and Take-no-prisoners."

Rhodes Woodbury starts to lift his coffee cup, gets it halfway to his mouth, then stops and sets it back down. "Survival of the fittest. It works in both directions. Sometimes its terms change, and you have to change with them."

"I know a little something about survival of the fittest. That's why I'm here."

"You're not hearing me. I can't help you," Rhodes says. "Not at present. It's a new jungle out there, friend."

"You had no trouble helping me before."

"Before was Before."

Johnny Doc looks down at the floor, gathering himself. "How's Karen?" he asks.

Rhodes goes into exaggerated headshaking. "That's where you want to take this?"

"I don't want to," Johnny Doc says.

"You're threatening me with that now?" Rhodes says. "You going to call my wife and tell her about my extracurricular activities at the Full Moon?"

Rhodes Woodbury had a Free Pass, courtesy of Johnny Doc by way of Bishop Conover, manager of the Full Moon. Rhodes had pretty much worked his way through the Full Moon's roster a couple times.

"No," Johnny Doc says. "I am not going to call Karen."

Rhodes leans back in his chair and smiles. "That's a wise move. You see, Karen has her own version of survival of the fittest. Some days it's called 'Looking the other way.' On others, 'Ask no questions.' On others yet, 'Don't rock the boat.'" Rhodes holds up both hands and smiles. "Next week we're looking at twenty-seven years of wedded bliss."

"I wasn't planning on calling Karen," Johnny Doc says.

"Once again, glad to hear that."

"Actually, I was thinking of someone else," Johnny Doc says. "Maybe, Carlisle Anderson."

Rhodes Woodbury doesn't say anything.

THE LENGTH OF DAYS

"Maybe we understand each other now," Johnny Doc says. Carlisle Anderson is a former Baptist minister and current President of the Bank of the South's Magnolia Beach branches. He's also Rhodes Woodbury's father-in-law. The Baptist in him is not a fan of Survival of the Fittest. As a father, he is, however, a big fan of his daughter, wedding vows, and the Sixth Commandment.

"Maybe we can start over," Johnny Doc says. He lays out what he needs

"No way I can go 9 on the loan," Rhodes says, "phone call or not. Not with your credit and investment history. You're barely solvent after the West Winds Estate debacle. I can't pull a rabbit out of a hat when there's no hat."

"I still have Beachwear and More and Nu- Nails. They've been assessed at 950,000. I can put them up as collateral."

"You need to understand we'll need to leave the Full Moon out of this at this stage." Rhodes Woodbury leans forward and steeples his fingers. "You also need to remember 950,000 is early 2006 money." He pulls over a file and starts thumbing. He eventually stops, runs his index finger down a page, and then sits back. "We're looking at a 15% drop, minimum, currently. That leaves the properties in the neighborhood of 800,000 and change."

"I need some help here," Johnny Doc says again. He's been running numbers in his head and sees where this is starting to go and more than likely end up.

April 1975 and March 2009. Johnny Doc standing in the shadow each threw. He wants to believe he can still tell the difference between desperation and hope.

The twelve dead and two missing girls at 805 Jefferson had been what they call First Generation. Meaning, they were prime, mostly young runaways and illegals with years of earning powers in front of them. They had been in transit. Johnny Doc had provided and guaranteed a safe house until the Bowen Brothers indicated destination.

"Okay," Rhodes Woodbury says. "Here's what you're looking at. The 2009 assessment on the properties comes in at 807,500. That's a 15% drop from 2006. I can do the standard Collateral Coverage Ratio and the standard Discounted Collateral Value at 20% which lands at 646,000. That's the top end of what I can do. The very top end."

Johnny Doc does the math. He'd still have to come up with just over 250,000 dollars, rabbits and hats notwithstanding.

"How are we going to package the loan?" Rhodes Woodbury asks.

"Don't say Personal. That won't cut it. And as we established, the Full Moon is off the table for now."

"Anything you can fold the loan into?"

A very slow nod. "Maybe, a couple things," he says. "There's a new assisted living center proposal on West Lancaster. Maybe that. Or a new waste disposal franchise. Maybe split the difference between the two." He looks over at Johnny Doc. "Whichever option we try to run with, it's going to take some time."

Johnny Doc points out that the line between some time and no time is rapidly shrinking.

THE LENGTH OF DAYS—SIXTEEN

The Lowe Tide is buried in a working-class neighborhood on Baylor Street in North Magnolia Beach. Looking at its façade, a hybrid of asbestos shingles, red brick faded to pink, and yellow pine tongue-and-groove, most people would mistake it at first glance as abandoned. The locals know better. The Lowe Tide opened in 1969 and billed itself as a private club. It was owned and run by Mason Lowe as a bulwark against any possible patronage by Blacks, Jews, Feminists, Out-of-the-closet Gays, Liberals, Snowbirds or any combination thereof.

In addition to The Lowe Tide, Mason Lowe owned two lucrative and longstanding furniture outlets, one in Myrtle Beach, the other in Mt. Pleasant. Mason died at 89 and had been married four times, each bride's age in inverse proportion to his own. He had been counting on a male heir, but the closest he came to one was his nephew, Daren Lowe. At the time of Mason's death, Daren was a junior at Coker College in Hartsville, South Carolina and a half-hearted History major and puppy-dog boyfriend of one Susan Duncan. Susan Duncan was also the roommate of Pam Graves at Coker. Susan Duncan came from old Georgetown, South Carolina money and eventually decided she was owed more out of life than puppy-dog romance and half-hearted ambition and dumped Daren Lowe for one Malcom Fairns from Charleston, South Carolina whose family had deep pockets and equally deep political ties.

When Susan Duncan dumped him, Daren Lowe went full-bore heartbroken and looked around for a willing ear and confidante. He found one in Pam Graves who listened patiently to the renditions of his side of things concerning the relationship and then kept listening and kept listening.

It was what Pam Graves did.

She eventually ended up sleeping with Daren Lowe during spring break of their junior year. She could not say exactly why. It was just the way things in her world tended.

Shortly after, Mason Lowe died and bequeathed Daren a very healthy trust fund and the deed to The Lowe Tide. Daren dropped out of Coker and returned to Magnolia Beach where he began a mix-signaled long-distance relationship with Pam Graves. She went on to finish her senior year and started an entry-level at WTKW in Magnolia Beach and continued a face-to-face version of their long-distance mix-signaled relationship.

Which is how Pam Graves comes to be sitting at the south end of the L-shaped bar at The Lowe Tide on a Friday night an hour before last call.

On the other side of the bar, Daren's tending and winks at her. Pam's nursing her second glass of wine. Looking around at the crowd, she wonders if Mason Lowe is literally spinning in his grave, given how the tenor of the clientele has changed since his nephew took over.

Most of the original clientele were dead or in nursing homes, and now it's wall-to-wall Hipsters, all designer tattoos and bite-sized ideology, the men sporting carefully groomed stubble passing for beards, the women sporting multi-colored yoga pants and retro shades of lipstick. There's still a sprinkling of locals in the mix, mostly service and construction workers, a few shrimpers, and a contingent of students from the local tech school and community college.

Until last year, when The Lowe Tide had ended up in a feature article in *Southern Focus* magazine and a subsequent profile on the regional PBS affiliate, the local clientele had been The Tide's mainstay. Daren Lowe, cushioned by his uncle's trust fund, had been content at being a half-hearted entrepreneur whose profit margin perpetually had a foot on either side of the red and black.

The *Southern Focus* and PBS coverage changed all that. Daren Lowe had become a success in spite of himself. The new crowd was taken by The Tide's "authenticity" and "idiosyncratic" charms. Those charms consisted of an unvarying four item menu—half-pound chili cheeseburger, Shrimp Po'Boys, blackened fish tacos, and homemade Low Country pimento cheese sandwiches on Texas Toast—thrift store table and chairs, a schizophrenic jukebox selection, and an array of tee-shirts for sale boasting silkscreened slogans like *How Lowe Can You Go? Lowe and Behold, It's On The Lowe-Down, I'm Feeling Lowe Today, Don't Get High, Get Lowe,* and one simply denoting *The Lowe Tide, Where Else?*

The establishment's crowning charm, however, was Daren Lowe's practice on Wednesday nights of taking a polaroid photo of new patrons and presenting it to them and then letting them tape, thumbtack, or staple the photo anywhere on The Tide's walls and eventually ceilings. The cumulative effect of sitting among hundreds and hundreds of layered faces and lives literally surrounding you from the walls and

THE LENGTH OF DAYS

ceiling was akin to the overwhelming mystery and pathos that arose from viewing prehistoric cave paintings for the first time.

From behind the bar, Daren holds up a bottle of white wine and points it at Pam's glass, but Pam waves off the offer. Given her mood, she's tempted by a third glass but decides to continue to nurse her way through the second.

The day had been like too many other days. Each lead on the twelve dead women that Pam pursued sooner or later dead-ended or simply disappeared. Part of the problem was Magnolia Beach itself. Too much of a beach town was built on transience. Nothing held. Most of Pam Graves's days ran on innuendo that segued into gossip that bled into rumors that, however initially promising, never went anywhere.

In the meantime, there were twelve dead women and two more on the loose and no sign of anything resembling a motive or closure.

Then Madison Hopewell decided to up the ante.

Yesterday, Madison Hopewell and Pam had visited Samuel Fulton at the Bayview townhouse. Madison pushed him hard to see if he could remember more of what he'd witnessed. They went over the sequence of events three times from different angles, but Samuel hadn't been able to contribute anything new. Rain. A man snapping a woman's neck outside the passenger window of his Taurus. Two young girls running across the yard and away. Another figure on the doorstep of the house waving his arms.

Pam had thanked him and was preparing to leave when Madison Hopewell leaned over and touched her arm and said, *I have an idea.*

Pam protested, but Madison persisted and in the end convinced Samuel Fulton to appear on camera and assert that he'd overcome his initial confusion and shock, and now he could in fact recognize the man who'd snapped the woman's neck should he ever see him again in a police lineup or on the street.

A Bull's-Eye, Pam had thought, that's what Madison Hopewell had painted on Samuel Fulton's forehead. Her anger had quickly melted into guilt though when Pam had to admit to herself that Samuel Fulton had more than likely agreed to the scenario to please, not Madison Hopewell, but her. A good man, he wanted to help and, along the way, thank Pam for the small kindnesses to his wife Glenda on Pam's visits to Glenda's room at Bayview.

Madison Hopewell had shut down any official blowback from the ruse with a couple of long lunches with the chief of police and the police commissioner. In order to placate the Tourist Bureau and

68　　　　　　　　　　　　　　　　　　　　**LYNN KOSTOFF**

Chamber of Commerce contingent, she'd also developed the practice in many of her shoots of highlighting some of the positive attributes and local highlights of Magnolia Beach as contrasting segue to the tragic events at 805 Jefferson Street.

Pam lifts her bag and sets it on the bar and takes out her notebook. Five pages in are four names: Julie Ramos. Ronnie Caldwell. LaShonda Greene. Tina Chow. She looks at the names, studying them. They are the equivalent of keys without locks. They lead nowhere. Open nothing.

She takes out a pen. Thinks about locks without keys. She begins writing.

Every so often, she takes out her phone and runs a Google search. Then she goes back to writing and keeps count.

Somewhere along the way, she reaches for her wine glass and discovers it's been refilled. At the other end of the bar, Daren Lowe aims an index finger and winks. He's wearing a pair of beat-up athletic shoes, jeans without a belt, and a red T-shirt with *Take The Lowe Road* lettered in white.

Pam keys her phone and searches one more time. She finds what she needs and goes back to her notebook. When she's done, she leans back and closes her eyes. She remembers a dream from three nights ago that she's spent two days trying to forget.

She reads over what she's written, testing each syllable. Then it's last call and sudden overhead lights that bring the polaroids covering the walls and ceiling into sharp relief. Pam signals Daren that she's headed for the addition to The Lowe Tide that doubles as Daren's apartment. She's looking forward to a shower.

The addition was originally tacked onto The Lowe Tide as an after-hours place for Mason Lowe and his cronies to hold marathon high-stakes poker games. It's a little over 900 square feet, and Daren, true to his take-everything-at-face-value and path-of-least-resistance worldview, has furnished it with a hybrid aesthetic of anonymous budget motel rooms and student dorms. The only concession to vanity or personal taste is a sixty-inch widescreen and an oversized throne-like recliner.

By the time Pam's finished with her shower, Daren has closed The Tide for the night. He's poured each of them a nightcap.

"I like that," he says, pointing at Pam, "the towel look. There's something sexy about a woman who's wrapped herself in a towel."

"You've seen too many movies."

"Everyone's seen too many movies." He points at Pam's bag on the

THE LENGTH OF DAYS

counter. "Your notebook. What were you so intent on? I saw you scribbling until last call."

"Names," Pam says. "They needed names."

Daren hits his beer and frowns. "They, who?"

"The dead girls," Pam says. "They were only able to identify four of them through dental records. The rest they couldn't. Eight dead girls without a name. They at least deserved that. A name. I gave each of them one."

"And that makes a difference?"

"Maybe a little. I hope so. It felt right."

Twenty minutes later, their drinks finished, her towel on the floor and Daren's clothes dropped step by step to the bed, Pam Graves has opened her legs, and Daren Lowe has entered her, and in their movements, there but not quite in sync, Pam Graves starts to hear the girls' names, all twelve of them now, in the spaces between her breaths, and she reaches up, cupping her hand on the back of Daren's neck, trying to slow him down, and starts to whisper the names, but Daren, cresting toward early orgasm, buries his face in her neck, and what Pam Graves is left with instead are strangled syllables, wet and distorted, as Daren Lowe empties himself inside her.

THE LENGTH OF DAYS—SEVENTEEN

If you spent time in a Viet Cong reeducation camp, the odds are you'd have no trouble handling a phone call from a Suit in Charlotte, North Carolina.

But as Johnny Doc Newell stands at the east window of his home and watches the Inlet slowly swell with high tide, the voice, something about the voice of the lawyer, one Nathaniel Laine, throws him momentarily off balance, and Johnny Doc feels whatever advantage or edge he'd managed to gain so far over Laine begin to slip away, and he closes his eyes for a moment on the rising tide and the world attached to it.

A kind of vertigo, right then.

Because Nathaniel Laine's voice has come to take on the measured cadences of Colonel Le Van Thu, and Johnny Doc is simultaneously in the reeducation camp northeast of Saigon and at the east window of his home in Magnolia Beach, South Carolina.

The languages, geography, and situations are completely different, but the cadence, smooth, implacable, and insistent, of the voices isn't.

And maybe, Johnny Doc thinks, the situations aren't all that different. A reeducation is a reeducation is a reeducation.

Nathaniel Laine is asking about updates and deadlines and promises. He keeps bringing up the fact that Johnny Doc was responsible for the girls at the safe house because they were in transit. He was getting paid to take care of them until they were moved.

At the same time, Colonel Le Van Thu is asking if Johnny Doc can name his sins.

Johnny Doc tells each of them what he wants to hear.

And Colonel Le Van Thu goes on to explain to Johnny Doc that to repair, you must first break down; to restore, you must then take away; to fill, you must empty; then, finally, you are free of sin and of incorrect thoughts that lead to incorrect actions, and you have erased the decadent and corrupt *I* and regained the pathway to the true and inviolate *We*.

Johnny Doc continues to try to buy time with Laine and the Bowen Brothers. He tells Laine he has someone—a cop—working behind the scenes on the particulars of the house fire. As shaky as the details are, Johnny Doc insinuates that Gary Lidd, the stoner who'd been overseeing

THE LENGTH OF DAYS

the safe house and girls the day of the fire, might in fact be more than he appears, that Gary might or might not have ties to one of the Bowen Brothers' rivals, and that Johnny Doc and the cop need more time to get to the bottom of things. He also brings up the troublesome matter of someone named Eric hanging around the house and claiming to be an agent for the Bowen Brothers.

And as Johnny Doc looks over the Inlet at an egret gliding across the late morning sky like a slow white star falling, he hears himself tell Colonel Le Van Thu, "I am empty. Truly empty now."

The Colonel nods and says, "When the body cleanses itself, the mind follows."

Days upon days without food. Isolated in a four foot by six foot 'classroom.' Kept awake for three days running. Living under the constant glare of blinding lights. No sense of night or day or of time passing at all. One long moment of unending light while his body hungered and consumed itself. Passing out and being kicked awake. Water rationed out in drops. Then the door opening and Colonel Le Van Thu appearing once again and asking Johnny Doc to name his sins. The Colonel holding a bowl of rice and fish heads as eventual reward. Johnny Doc doing the North Vietnamese catechism and naming the sins of the ego and then cupping his fingers to shovel the rice and fish heads over and over, barely taking the time to chew.

Colonel Le Van Thu smiling the whole time. Waiting until Johnny Doc finished to ask, "Are you emptied of self, now?"

Johnny Doc nodding and replying, "I am truly empty."

The Colonel saying, "Not quite, but soon you will be."

Johnny Doc feeling it then, a hot liquid tearing and teaming in his bowels, coming to understand too late, much too late, that the bowl of rice and fish heads the Colonel had handed him had been laced with laxatives.

The Colonel standing in the door of the room and watching, Johnny Doc crying and shitting himself over and over until there was nothing beyond the smell and endless waves of cramps.

The Colonel saying, "Inside is outside and outside is inside, no more false dichotomies. What you smell is the self. Do you understand now?"

Johnny Doc crying and nodding and choking on tears.

"Good," the Colonel saying just before leaving the doorway.

And Nathaniel Laine with his steadily unfolding inflections and measured cadences saying, "My clients have limited reserves of patience. You need to understand that you're approaching the end of Stage One.

Your lawyer, Rachard Balen, should have made that clear to you. You need to deliver on your promises."

THE LENGTH OF DAYS — EIGHTEEN

Early evening and Arturo Morales takes the Chevy down Branch until it intersects with Holbrook Street. He drives three blocks east and parks across from the 4-Star Laundromat. The sky is cloud-dense and the wind brisk. Near the front door, three girls huddle like herons, shifting from foot to foot, their legs lengthened and thinned by the tight miniskirts no larger than dishtowels riding their hips and upper thighs.

Arturo gets out of the car and crosses the street. The girls watch him approach and fall into what passes for seductive poses running the gamut from wide-eyed innocent to I've-seen-and-done-everything. The girls are anywhere from mid-teens to mid-twenties, but the eyeliner-mascara-lipstick combos level the playing field, erasing and adding years so that they all inhabit one indiscriminate age.

Arturo steps up, and the smallest of the three shakes her head and waves him off. "Count me out, Mister. Me, I don't fuck Mexican."

The girl next to her laughs. "She's new, Lover. Give her another week or so and then see what she says." She tilts her head and adds, "I don't mind traveling South of the Border."

Arturo takes the photo of Connie Fuentes out of his shirt pocket and shows it to the girls, asking each to take a close look and tell him if any of them has seen her.

The third girl, black-haired, thin-armed, and high-heeled, leans close and says, "Give me five minutes, Honey, and I'll make you forget her name."

An Afro American man in an Oklahoma City Thunder jersey and baggy jeans steps out of the front door of the 4-Star. "You browsing or buying?"

"Hey Too-Tall," Arturo says.

"Whoa," he says. "My Man Arturo got the itch?" He points at the redhead. "My advice, try Monica. She know where and how to scratch."

Arturo waves off the offer and then shows Too-Tall Connie Fuentes's photo and explains who she is. Too-Tall asks how long.

"Around three, four months," Arturo says, "but around here, probably anywhere from three, four weeks."

Too-Tall shakes his head no. "Not on my watch." He points toward the door. "Too-Wide in. We can ask him."

Too-Tall and Too-Wide are brothers, and as far as their names and truth in advertising go, Too-Tall isn't and Too-Wide is.

Too-Wide has set up an open-air makeshift office just inside the door of the 4-Star. The office consists of a folding card table backed by a heavy wooden church pew that's been sawn in half to accommodate the three hundred plus pounds he carries around. Too-Wide has just started another of his endless rounds of solitaire. At his left elbow are five cellphones and at the other, a two-liter bottle of Mountain Dew and an ashtray half full of Newport butts.

Arturo supposes that there are people who occasionally actually frequent the 4-Star to do their laundry, but they are decidedly in the minority. The usual clientele are there for dope, sports bets, quick high-end loans, information, guns, and a small stable of girls, most of whom are runaways that appear and disappear on a regular basis.

Arturo hands the photo of Connie Fuentes to Too-Wide who studies it for approximately half a minute before handing it back.

Arturo listens to the rumble and labored rhythm of Too-Wide's breathing, and then he takes out his wallet and places two tens on the card table.

"Word is," Too-Wide says, "and no guarantee here because we're talking white men, this weed-head name of Wayne, he coming by the 4 Star with friends flashing pictures some girls. May be one match yours."

"Wayne?" Arturo says. "You mean Wayne Summer?" Wayne Summer who'd become patrolman Carl Adkin's newly-hatched snitch after Arturo had set him up in a park-side dope deal late last month.

Too-Wide nods.

"Wayne's friends," Arturo asks, "they have a name?"

"Indeed." Too-Wide sits back and waits.

Arturo dredges up another ten and a five. "Tapping me out, Too-Wide."

"One name of Gary."

"How about a last name, Too-Wide?"

"You know the 4 Star not a last name kind of place. We like to keep things straight and simple here." Too-Wide tips a Newport out of the pack and taps it twice on his wrist.

"The other friend then?"

"Can't say one way or other. Never actually seen him. He's the one drive the van, a green one, Ford, and older than your momma." Too-Wide leans back and hits the Newport and jets smoke from both nostrils.

THE LENGTH OF DAYS

"Might be I heard a green van be seen at the Horizon more than once lately too."

Arturo thanks him and starts to leave when Too-Wide says, "One more thing. You never say why you looking for that girl. Man asks questions got to have a point to them in there somewhere."

Arturo decides on the spot to give Too-Wide half the truth, which is probably what Too-Wide expects anyway. He makes no mention of Luis Sorbano and the bounty. "The girl has been missing for three, going on four months. She's related to a woman I love."

Too-Wide stamps out the Newport and slowly nods twice. "In the name of Love. I hear that. I always figure you for a fool, Arturo."

The Horizon Inn is on the corner of East Tenth Street and La Mar Avenue, and on the drive there, Arturo Morales reluctantly admits to himself that he might have in fact told Too-Wide the whole truth rather than its half-sister. He's uncomfortable admitting that. But he can't help being moth-driven to the light of its movie-ready storyline: he finds and rescues Connie. Felina sees him for the man he is and confesses she's always loved him. She leaves her husband, Luis Sorbano. Felina and Arturo go on to make a life together, happy and in love until the final credits roll.

The Horizon Inn is located in the equivalent of a stretch of no-man's-land where Magnolia Beach proper begins to shade into its southern counterpart. The Horizon itself is dark and brown-bricked with two small barred windows on either side of a narrow metal front door. There's no sign announcing the building's name. You either know the Horizon or you don't.

The clientele reflects that dynamic. There's a mix of age ranges, races, locals and tourists, and old and new and no money. It's a place run on Need, and you left any moral or ethical considerations at the door.

Arturo takes a stool at the far end of the bar. He orders a beer and chaser and sets out the photo of Connie Fuentes. The bartender notices but makes no comment.

Arturo waits, and it's not until he's deep into his third round before the bartender takes out his cell and keys a text.

A few minutes later, Arturo senses someone standing behind him. He eventually takes a stool next to Arturo and orders a scotch and soda, light on the latter and top-shelf on the former.

He studies Connie's photo without picking it up.

"Let's say I do," he says to Arturo's unasked question. "My name's Eric by the way."

All-American. Looking at the guy, Arturo is struck by how this Eric fits it. Pale blue oxford shirt. Pressed khakis. Around five foot eleven. Wide-chested. Thin sandy-blonde hair with sharp razor-cut lines. Eyes two shades darker than the shirt. This Eric inhabited a kind of retro version of handsome, his features like the lines of a classic car. His posture and smile suggested a confidence that passed through entitlement and eventually rested in a barely concealed arrogance. A man for whom all things were accessible. A man who was the obverse of everything that defined Arturo's life.

Arturo gives his name, and Eric nods as if he'd already figured it out. He then signals the bartender to set up another round for each of them and picks up the photo, cupping it in his palm and studying it.

He eventually hands it back to Arturo. "So you like the young ones, friend."

Arturo nods, letting things ride. "Do you know her?"

"I just might." Eric takes a sip of his scotch and soda and closes his eyes for a moment. "I know a lot of others like her too," he says.

"Her," Arturo says. "She's the one I want. The only one."

"It appears you know your mind." Eric turns and moves off the barstool. "Excuse me a moment while I make a call or two."

While Eric's gone, Arturo mentally runs through an estimate of his cash reserves. He's hoping he has enough left from Luis Sorbano's stake to open the doors leading to Connie Fuentes.

Eric returns and slides onto his barstool. "I talked to a friend who said if you're my friend, he'll be your friend too." Eric smiles. "But I'll have to make the introductions."

And introductions, of course, have a price tag. Arturo watches Eric write his on a bar napkin. Arturo agrees.

"My friend who soon will be your friend will bring his van around with the girl," Eric says and finishes off his drink. "If she's the one you're looking for, you'll have to discuss terms with him."

Arturo asks where.

Eric's smile is easy and wide. "Just a short walk," he says. "The north corner of the parking lot behind the Horizon. Fifteen minutes. My friend's name is Gary. He'll be driving a green van."

Arturo starts to take out his wallet, but Eric touches his forearm. "Just add my Intro to the tab. Michael, the bartender, will see that I get it." He claps Arturo on the back and walks away.

Fifteen minutes later, Arturo has left the Horizon and is moving across the lot on a diagonal toward a row of dumpsters along a stretch

THE LENGTH OF DAYS

of chain-link fence. A van, squat as a loaf of bread, is trailing exhaust and parked nearby.

Perhaps it was the last round of drinks or Arturo underestimating his new friend Eric or maybe something else entirely, but whatever the case, Arturo is a half-step behind himself, and he knows he's made a mistake when the van's headlights flare, and the van hangs a left and starts moving slowly toward him. The driver flashes his lights twice.

A small distraction but enough of one.

A rush of footsteps from behind.

And then a voice.

Leave her alone. She's not yours.

Followed by what more than likely is a piece of pipe or a short-handled wooden bat connecting with his kidneys, once, twice, three times, and pain becomes the engine of the universe as the stars pinwheel across the sky and blank out in an abrupt eclipse.

THE LENGTH OF DAYS — NINETEEN

Wednesday 1:37 a.m.

Tonight, the world, maybe the whole universe, feels much too quiet. Samuel Fulton misses his wife's voice. Everything that the damage to the Wernicke and Broca areas in the right sector of her brain has taken away.

But what he's missing most right now runs even deeper.

His life.

He wants it back.

Samuel has come to believe—or fear—he missed it the first time around. A love letter, one that he hadn't written, that Samuel found secreted in the bottom drawer of Glenda's jewelry box had shown him that.

He thought he'd had a life. One that he could call his own. He had shown up for every day of it. And was proud of that.

Maybe that was the problem. Maybe he'd confused proud with happy. Maybe he'd confused happy for the truth.

At bottom, though, Samuel Fulton tells himself he had never believed in or worried about Maybe.

Happy would do that to you. Happy always trumped Maybe.

So did Love.

And it had been easy to love Glenda née McGuire.

Maybe too easy.

But forty-nine years of marriage. A life together. A lifetime together. That should have made a difference.

That's why he had not been ready to discover a love letter that he hadn't written, one that his wife had saved and obviously never thought he'd find.

There should not have been room in those forty-nine years for something like that.

But even now, with the letter open in front of him, Samuel cannot make the words hold to the page, the sentences breaking apart after a month and day—October 17—but no year, so that all he is left with tonight is the quiet and *Dearest Glenda* and *just consider* and *certain feelings can't* and *know it's difficult* and *trust your* and *more than you*

THE LENGTH OF DAYS 79

can ever and *please* before the closing *yours forever* and a single handwritten initial, something resembling a hasty capital *C* or a poorly constructed *G* or maybe a badly misshapen *B*

Wednesday 1:37 a.m.

In his living room, Johnny Doc Nowell awakes on the couch. Across the room, Turner Classic Movies is on, the volume a little too high, and Johnny Doc can't find the remote.

As he moves around the room, Johnny Doc realizes he's carrying the Taurus Ultra-lite, that he'd fallen asleep holding it as he'd done on other nights, the other nights collapsing into this one, concentrating and distilling concern into worry, worry into alarm, alarm into panic, and panic into fear, a fear that's raw and unadulterated because Johnny Doc Nowell understands, more than understands, that he's running out of time.

Nathaniel Laine, the Suit and mouthpiece for the Bowen Brothers, has been calling again about a meet to discuss restitution for the twelve dead and two missing girls.

Johnny Doc is running out of stall and delay tactics. The loan from Rhodes Woodbury at The Bank of the South continues to be slow in coming. Without the loan, he'd been hoping he could serve up Gary Lidd who had been working as overseer at the house on 805 Jefferson. Either Lidd or the Eric-with-no-last-name that nobody had been able to identify. Johnny Doc was hoping that either one would do as a scapegoat.

He'd fallen asleep earlier watching *Houseboat*.

The plot had been inconsequential and painfully predictable, but none of the mattered to Johnny Doc. What mattered is Sophia Loren and Archibald Alec Leach.

Archibald Alec Leach who reinvented himself as Cary Grant. No, Johnny Doc thinks, not reinvented. *Perfected.*

Cary Grant everything a young Nguyen Duc Xuan, fresh from the Viet Cong reeducation camps, needed to remeasure himself for a life in a new world. Remeasure and aspire to and inhabit.

Dashing. Charming. Debonair. Worldly. Suave. Sophisticated.

Someone at home in the world and his skin.

In America, you turn on the television and discover who you hope to be.

Cary Grant was never just in his movies. He was always simultaneously inside and outside of whatever the camera framed. He was always wholly Cary Grant, and the characters he played shared his DNA.

Cary Grant remade himself so perfectly that he could never again be anything or anyone other than himself.

A kind of ingrown transcendence there. A homemade salvation.

In his search for the remote, Johnny Doc comes across an overflowing ashtray.

He counts the butts.

Twelve.

His panic and fear double-up.

He remembers John Sloane leaning on the bar at the Colorado in Saigon and telling him, *Nobody dies from ten cigarettes a day. Smoke eleven. No more no less. Eleven tempts but doesn't mock Fate, and it's important that you understand and respect the difference between the two.*

Johnny Doc finds himself thinking of the dead girls.

Sees them locked in the room off the kitchen at 805 Jefferson.

He wonders what their last words were.

The ratio of pleas to curses.

Johnny Doc suspects that is what the world is run on.

He keeps looking for the remote.

He glances over at the television. The twelve girls are real now. They've moved in. They won't be ignored.

Neither will Robert Preston who is inhabiting a universe that violates natural law.

One in which ordinary people arbitrarily break into song and dance.

For some reason that he's never been able to explain or understand, Johnny Doc is disturbed on something approaching the molecular level by the dynamics of a Musical. He's left with a confusing mix of the creepy and the absurd.

Johnny Doc is chained to 1:37 a.m. and a widescreen television holding *The Music Man* with Robert Preston as Professor Harold Hill, a con man whose redemption is engineered by a near-spinster librarian named Marian, and Johnny Doc can't find the remote anywhere, and he's still holding the Taurus Ultra-lite, and he's scared because there are twelve dead girls following him around the living room, all of them on fire and marching in step with Professor Harold Hill and his new squeeze and the ranks of red-suited band members moving down Main Street of River City, Iowa, and it feels right now like it all will go on forever.

THE LENGTH OF DAYS

Wednesday 1:37 a.m.

Carl Adkin has gotten out of bed and begun patrolling his house. It's a ranch on Chestnut Lane in Delmar Woods, a late 1970's subdivision in western Magnolia Beach with generous lots by current 2009 standards, the neighborhood equally divided among ranch and split-levels and Tudors.

Carl moves room by room. His wife, Linda, is a big fan of nightlights, every available open socket seemingly occupied by one, and as Carl starts down the hallway off the master bedroom, he's reminded of parallel lines of landing lights at an airport runway seen from a window seat of a plane beginning to make its final approach and descent.

The house is quiet. It had been quiet too when he first woke up, so he can't say for sure why he's doing what he's doing.

The first door he opens is to his oldest son's room. The air's close and leavened with testosterone. Carl Jr. is fifteen going on twenty-five, his body on the fast-track to manhood, his beard almost as heavy as his father's. His wide body almost fills the single twin bed, and he sleeps on his stomach, covers twisted, arms akimbo, head turned to the side like a swimmer about to take a breath before the next stroke.

Down and across the hall is his second son's room. Richard—not Dick or Rich or Richie or Rick—is thirteen and a mystery. He's polite and distant. He wears a quiet confidence that's unnerving. It's as if he knows something nobody else does. Richard smiles easily, but Carl can't remember him outright laughing. He sleeps on his back, his head squarely in the center of his pillow, the covers crossing his chest like a crease, his arms outside them with his hands palm-down.

Next is the bathroom. He's already checked the one off the master bedroom when he first got up. All he finds in this one is the sound of a steady drip from the faucet he's never been able to fix and an overflowing wastebasket that should have been emptied three days ago.

Then it's his daughter's bedroom. Savannah is the easy one, eight years old and a daddy's girl, eager to please and easy to please, sweetness incarnate, no fine print to her love. She sleeps with the covers pulled to her neck like a Disney princess in training.

Carl moves to the end of the hallway. Nothing. The house is resolutely quiet. He tells himself he should just turn around and return to the master bedroom and his marriage bed and his wife Linda who will be sleeping deep in the covers. His wife who always sleeps through the night. His wife whose body he has touched, tasted, and entered for almost half his life. The woman he loves because she has never once surprised him.

Carl steps out of the hallway into the living room. It's dominated by a large picture window overlooking a front lawn coated in light from a three-quarters moon. He looks around at the furniture and wide-screen television. Everything's in place. And that's okay. More than okay.

There's nothing extraordinary here, Carl thinks. This house and neighborhood and Linda and his two sons and daughter. Himself too. The extraordinary is overrated. Nobody wants to admit that, but it is. You want happiness? Look for the obvious and ordinary. No surprises. Or at least small, manageable ones.

Slots.

Carl came up with the idea of Slots during dead times on Patrol. Nothing like one of those lightbulbs-going-off-over-his-head moments. Instead, something self-evident. Right there in front of him. All he had to do is take the time to look.

At bottom, what's a Slot? Something that needs filled. Something waiting to be filled.

A day is a slot. So is a life. Carl likes the idea, the comfort and shape of it, that the world is full of slots, and all you have to do is find yours and inhabit it to be content and for things to make sense.

You find your Slot and fill it, and then it goes on and fills you. You know who you are.

And Carl does. He's a cop, husband, and father. He may do a little freelance work for people like Johnny Doc Nowell, maybe providing some helpful info or applying a little pressure in the right places, but he keeps his greed in check and focused. He doesn't overreach.

A bonus. That's how Carl sees the envelope filled with straight cash that Johnny Doc and the others pass on. A little bonus that lets Carl buy for his wife and children what a cop's salary would prohibit.

Linda's been talking about a new refrigerator, one of the monster stainless-steel ones that look like something out of a sci-fi flick. Carl Jr. dropping none too subtle hints about an ATV. Richard, Carl has no idea what he wants but figures a couple fresh C-notes ought to take care of. Savannah has been begging Carl about bankrolling a play date with a dozen of her classmates at one of those theme kid restaurants that serve up bad pizza and video games and waiters dressed up like cartoon characters.

Carl's hoping if he can put the lid back on Johnny Doc's current batch

THE LENGTH OF DAYS   **83**

of trouble, then Johnny Doc will be good for picking up the full tab.

All those dead girls have Johnny Doc Nowell running scared. He's moved beyond worried. Carl can smell the fear on him every time they meet, and if anything, the odor is getting stronger.

Right now, Johnny Doc needs two things. One is finding Gary Lidd, an overseer at the safe house who took off after the fire, and the second is finding the two girls on the loose before the authorities and media do.

Carl is thinking he can squeeze the bonus from Johnny Doc if he can deliver Gary or the two missing girls. Carl knows how to play fear.

Carl stands at the picture window in the middle of his living room. The moon burns an icy white, turning the lawn, street, and neighborhood into the equivalent of a photographic negative.

Carl breathes it all in. Everything fits and is in place.

He still can't say for sure what woke him or why he's still up and awake.

Carl finally settles on Pork Chops. Normally, he has a strong stomach, but tonight, it must have been that extra pork chop at supper.

A little indigestion. Nothing more than that.

Wednesday 1:37 a.m.

Arturo Morales is in the closet-sized bathroom of his efficiency on the fourth floor of the Drake Hotel in southeast Magnolia Beach. He's standing over the toilet, weaving slightly and wincing, while he pisses blood. His kidneys are a long ache.

The bathroom mirror is at his back. When he turns, Arturo is treated to a reflection whose left temple and cheek appear to have been vigorously sandpapered, courtesy of the asphalt in the back lot of the Horizon Inn.

He moves to the kitchen and the refrigerator where he takes out three bottles of beer and then sets them on the table and opens them one by one.

The living room is eleven feet from the kitchen table. The bedroom is the inside of the living room sofa when it's opened and pulled out. The sofa is ten feet from the bathroom. Besides the calendar nailed to the wall next to the refrigerator and to the right of the hot plate, Arturo has a radio and portable television. His closet is a stack of cardboard boxes. Add a standing lamp and you can call it home.

Arturo drains the first beer in two long swallows, then sits back in the folding chair and waits for it to shake hands with the pain running his kidneys.

He takes a little more time with the second beer. The pain is easing off just enough for him to find some refuge thinking about the vacant lot on Houston Street.

The warehouse originally on it burned down eighteen months ago. It was for sale for a year and in foreclosure for the last six months. Right now, no investor in his right mind is interested in southeast Magnolia Beach, particularly after what 2008 had birthed. Arturo has been counting on that. The Bank of the South holds the lien on the property and is more than ready to unload it.

Arturo figures if he can collect the 15,000 dollars for delivering Connie Fuentes to Luis Sorbano, then that in combination with what he's saved over the last ten years working two and three jobs at a time will put his name on the deed and eventually set the stage for A.M. MOTORS.

Arturo is patient. He understands its truth. It's both simple and long. He doesn't argue with it.

He tips his head back and finishes the second beer. He closes his eyes. His kidneys throb and burn.

He's about to pick up the third beer when someone knocks. Billy Jo, his next-door neighbor, steps inside. "I saw the light under the door," he says.

Or maybe She.

Arturo is never sure which one fits. Billy Jo doesn't seem to either.

"I could use a beer," Billy Jo says.

Arturo points to the refrigerator. Billy Jo brings back one for each of them.

Billy Jo sits down and pulls off his wig. "The world is full of Strange and Wonderful, Mr. Monk. The problem is telling them apart."

"My name's Arturo. You know that. Not Monk."

Billy Jo swings his or her arms wide. "But it suits you. No, it absolutely fits you." He nods. "And it's what everyone in the building calls you behind your back."

Arturo takes the photo of Connie Fuentes and slides it in Billy Jo's direction.

"Sorry, friend. Same as every time you show it," Billy Jo says. "I even have the copy you gave me taped up on my refrigerator. No sign of her though."

Billy Jo kicks off his heels. They are dark blue with four-inch spikes.

THE LENGTH OF DAYS

"I got hit on by an old man tonight. Must have been over seventy." He shakes his head. "I don't know if to be insulted or flattered."

"No offense," Arturo says, "but it's been a long day."

"No offense," Billy Jo says, "but it shows." He points toward Arturo's temple and cheek. "I thought Monks were lovers, not fighters."

Before Arturo can respond, Billy Jo's at the refrigerator and back with two more beers. He opens both and then slides one over to Arturo.

"Okay," Arturo says, "but we need to make this Last Call. I have the afternoon shift at the Bayview tomorrow."

"Ever have your heart broken, Arturo?" Billy Jo slips down the straps of his dress and then works out the layers of carefully folded handkerchiefs with which he's lined each cup of his bra.

Arturo watches Billy Jo transform from an anorexically thin, overly made-up woman to a thin pasty-skinned young man in his early twenties. When he lifts his beer, Billy Jo's bicep and the rest of the arm attached to it are the size of a broomstick.

"I imagine everybody has at one time or another," Arturo says. He has no interest or inclination to take it further. He does not want to visit any memories tied to Felina Fuentes right now.

"There was something about the eyes," Billy Jo says.

"The eyes?"

"The old man I was telling you about," Billy Jo says. "I was over at the Horizon, and he sat down on the stool next to me. He offered to buy me a beer, and before I could answer, he was running his hand along the inside of my thigh."

"Okay, okay," Arturo says. "I see where this is going."

Billy Jo laughs and salutes him with his beer. "That's exactly the same as what I said." He lets out his breath. "The old guy thought he was the original Smooth Talker." Billy Jo shakes his head. "But then I got a look at his eyes."

Billy Jo looks over his shoulder at the door. "An old man's eyes and what you see in them at closing time while he has his hand high on the inside of your thigh, Arturo, nobody's ready for that."

"I suppose not."

"No supposing," Billy Jo says, getting up from the table. He picks up and tips back his beer, then gathers his wig and high heels and heads for the door. "No supposing, whatsoever, believe me, Arturo."

Wednesday 1:37 a.m.

Pam Graves, postcoital, chases sleep, but it eludes her. She's drifting between two states and unable to inhabit either: a body whose muscles are slowly trying to unclench and relax and a mind that won't quite shut down. It's a standoff that Daren Lowe lying next to her doesn't share. He dropped into sleep five minutes after his orgasm.

Pam Graves's orgasm was approximately approximate, there and not quite there. It's something she's become accustomed to with Daren Lowe. Though she tried to coach Daren about her pleasure and needs during their lovemaking sessions and while Daren gamely ran through her requests and instructions, her orgasm is always an almost. It's like a trailer to a movie, one that gives the viewer a sense of the contours and context of the film, emphasizing its high points but doesn't give away the climax and conclusion.

So at 1:37 a.m. Pam Graves inhabits a body that won't follow itself into sleep and a mind that still chasing its own shadow, and she finds herself thinking about her dead twin, Pete, and Curtis Brooks.

She doesn't know why. She can't figure out a why.

Pam Graves feels Daren Lowe's semen drying deep on the inside of her thigh. The ceiling of the apartment is dark, a sky without constellations, and her insomnia runs outside all clocks.

Pam's twin brother, dead now six years after a star-crossed weekend home from college, their parents out of town, Pete and two of his college friends working their way through both cabinets, the medicine and the liquor, all three ending up passed out Saturday night on the living room floor, but only two waking up on Sunday morning.

A family life left with inadequate answers for too many questions, a twin brother who disappeared among various explanations for his death, an overdose either accidental or intentional, attributed to the recent breakup with a long-term girlfriend, his disillusion with college and subsequent failing grades, a religious crisis, a deep love of risk-taking and testing limits, and finally an in-your-face gesture toward his parents after years of acrimonious fights and rebellion launched in his adolescence.

Speculations that afforded no closure and trailed off finally into a heavily padded silence.

That silence, then, leaking through her insomnia into another memory. One seemingly disconnected.

THE LENGTH OF DAYS

Middle School. Curtis Brooks, the janitor. Or custodian. She can't remember which one she's supposed to use. After a while it doesn't matter because Curtis Brooks disappears. He becomes a man in a green uniform. And eventually, a green uniform, nothing more, one that runs a buffing machine and empties classroom trash cans. A ghost of a ghost.

Insomnia is a trapdoor. Pam Graves falls through the early morning hours into what she's been trying to remember.

The food court at the Magnolia Beach mall. Pam Graves is thirteen, a set of new braces on her teeth and a new set of breasts six and a half months behind her best friend Jackie Malone's. Pam Graves holding a certificate for second place in the annual middle school spelling bee, after having been edged out by her rival, Angela Devane, because she had momentarily blanked on a rule she knew as well as her home address—i before e except after c. Instead of *Bondieuserie*, she had spelled *Bondeiuserie*.

All of which lead to the food court at the Magnolia Beach mall and a thick slice of pepperoni pizza from Pizza King with her father. Food fixes, he'd said, and Pam Graves waited for him to continue, but he stopped there. She nodded and smiled and then looked across at the empty seat next to her father. Her mother had missed the spelling bee. She was also late for the consolation after-school pizza, and Pam Graves knew that late became *I'm running behind schedule*, and that eventually became *Sorry I missed it*.

She looked across the table at her father, a small man with a greeting-card worldview and a mismanaged haircut and muddy-brown eyes, a smile a little too insistent, and a waistline slowly expanding with each birthday.

In my eyes, you'll always be a Champ, he told her after ordering a second slice of pizza for each of them.

Pam Graves thanked him and looked around for her mother.

Instead, she saw a family—father, mother, a daughter, and son—who entered the food court and sat down three tables away. It took a while before she realized the father was Curtis Brooks.

The four of them were undeniably a family. Curtis Brooks, out of uniform, in a pair of neatly pressed khakis and starched white shirt and a wife and children who were television nuclear-family ready.

There was an empty chair at their table. Pam Graves couldn't admit to herself then but does now, in the heart of her insomnia, just how much she had wished she could join them.

PART TWO

**THE CITY ON THE HILL
AND
THE DEAD RAT THAT
LIVES IN THE SKY**

THE LENGTH OF DAYS – TWENTY

A faint bassline hangover is threading its way through Carl Adkin's morning as he takes the blue and white down Atlantic Avenue into old downtown Magnolia Beach.

The fact of the hangover's a surprise, a little unexpected, because Carl thought he'd kept count with the beers, but this one has managed to sneak up on him.

The origin is no mystery. Fellow Patrolman and best friend Truman Cooke and his family had come over for dinner. Carl was looking forward to pilot testing his new gas grill, a burnished sliver behemoth that he'd racked with burgers, dogs, and ribs. Carl was rock and rolling with the meat and in a good mood, a cooler of beer out on the deck and an evening with spring a couple heartbeats away, sweatshirt weather is what his wife Linda always called it, and then Truman had monkey-wrenched the whole package by bringing up the subject of money and, in particular, its source.

Carl had to keep reminding himself that Truman was Truman and his best friend. Truman saw price tags everywhere. Carl viewed things differently.

He didn't see anything wrong with giving your family what it wanted. If he had to step outside his job description once in a while to do that, well, Carl could live with that. He wasn't greedy. He was practical. He understood boundaries.

The problem was his friend Truman Cooke believed in boundaries, believed absolutely and mightily in them, always had. Even as a kid, Truman played it straight, no cutting corners when it came to subcontracting math homework out to friends and girlfriends, no casual cheating on tests to stay eligible for ball, Truman no scholar but actually proud of his C's because he earned them, something Carl could have done himself but elected not to, instead settling comfortably for B's co-authored and coaxed into being with the help of his girlfriend Linda.

Even then, Carl had understood the nature of boundaries. If you're a C at heart, you don't overstep and try to move into the world of the A's. That drew unwelcome attention. That's why he made sure Linda always threw in an extra comma splice or misspelling in the English essays she wrote for him or sabotaged a step or two when working through his quadradic equations homework.

Carl had been careful too when he moved out of the old neighborhood, a C- on its best day, and into Delmar Woods and the house on Chestnut Lane. The place was a comfortable B with a little extra credit built in, maybe a little high-end for a Patrolman's salary, but not something that drew any overscrupulous scrutiny, especially when Carl buttressed any doubt or suspicion with the lie of a great-uncle in Wisconsin and some inherited cash that let Carl and his family move comfortably into the middle of the middle class.

Truman had the same opportunities Carl had to pick up some extra coin for his family, but Truman stubbornly refused to even entertain the thought of acting on them. He, his wife Denisha, and the kids still lived in the old neighborhood. Truman still drove a secondhand rust bucket Chevy. He didn't lord his beliefs and principles over people. He simply lived them. That's what made him such a pain in the ass at times.

If Truman had one blind spot, it was Carl. They'd grown up together, tight as brothers, and had endured and ignored the standard racist remarks—Salt and Pepper had followed them through grade school and into high school and beyond—those original bonds only strengthened and deepened by the joint service in the military and police force.

Those bonds became a little strained when Truman went into his price tag routine, pointing out the obvious, that Carl's family had a lot of toys and seemed to spend indiscriminately, Truman each time giving Carl the benefit of a doubt in the end because Carl was Carl, his best friend. Just one who, like too many Americans, lived beyond his means.

That didn't keep Truman, however, from voicing some suspicions by couching them in concern.

He brought up the talk on the street, the innuendoes from certain quarters in the department, and Carl deflected both the best he could. He knew the great-uncle and inheritance scenario was wearing out, so he settled for blunt denial.

Last night, Carl had gone back to the grill and the meat, and Truman eventually dropped the hybrid rumors and talk about Johnny Doc Nowell, but without Carl noticing, the beers had added up.

Therefore, this morning, it was sunglasses and an extra hit of caffeine.

Carl continues down Atlantic Avenue, passing King of the Sea, Uncle Joe's BBQ, the Ice Cream Emporium, then closer to downtown a string of boutiques and high-end specialty shoppes, then taking a right on

THE LENGTH OF DAYS

12th Street and heading west three blocks before heading north toward Garrison Park, one of a number of small neighborhood parks the city founders had established in the years after World War II.

Carl parks the blue and white and walks along the edge of a grove of bearded oaks and between ranks of azaleas budding but short of blooming to a stretch of lawn above an irregularly-shaped duck pond. The small cadre of homeless people he expected to find isn't there. They've pulled up stakes, and that's saved him the smoke and mirrors show of evicting them, a pro forma gesture that satisfies the civilians but which ultimately changed nothing as the homeless inevitably drift back to this corner of the park. It's just one of a number of spots around the city they move to and from in nomad-like circuits.

Carl walks the perimeter, making sure campfires are out and kicking some of the trash into small piles. He's about to return to the blue and white when he spots a man sitting on the long slope facing the pond.

"Hey you," Carl says.

"Hello Officer Carl," the man says without looking back.

Carl stops. "That you, Mitch?"

He nods.

"Everyone else has left, Mitch. You need to move on too."

"I can't. I'm waiting."

"Mind telling me what for?"

"Not what. Who. Jesus. That's who I'm waiting for." Mitch points toward the east. "There's a landing strip nearby."

Carl steps over and hooks Mitch under the right armpit, lifting him to his feet. "Come on, Mitch. I don't have time for this."

Mitch looks over his shoulder. "You don't have time for Jesus?" He slowly shakes his head. "How would you feel, Officer Carl, if He said He didn't have time for you? It's not like anyone can get on the ship."

Carl sighs. "I think that one already sailed, Mitch. You know, thunderclouds, rain, two by two."

"I'm not talking that kind. I'm talking space ships." Mitch lifts his hand and traces a line across the sky from east to west with his index finger.

Carl steers him in the direction of the blue and white. He figures he can drop Mitch at one of the city shelters on Highland. He'll be safe there. Mitch might not hurt anyone, but he's been a target, an easy one, more than once in the past for people who like to put on some hurt.

"I help Him, you know," Mitch says. "Jesus, I mean. I'm like a Spirit

Guide. Or maybe better, more like a Gatekeeper. I ask the questions. They're like a test. You pass, you're pure of heart, and Jesus will take you in His spaceship to your rightful place in Heaven."

Carl figures he'll have to drive with the windows down as Mitch is a couple days past ripe. He's wearing a soiled bandana in lieu of a hat, a rumpled trench coat a size too small so that it barely clears the top of his thighs, a gray sweatshirt, a pair of jeans with questionable stains in a pattern resembling paisley print, and a pair of mismatched tennis shoes.

Despite himself, Carl can't stop himself from asking, "Hey Mitch, how come you haven't taken the big ride in that saucer?"

"The world still needs its prophets and Voices in the Wilderness." Mitch reaches up to adjust the bandana which had slipped down to the middle of his forehead. "I'm ready, but my work here isn't done."

Mitch wets the tip of his index finger and holds it up, testing the speed and direction of the wind. "Has it occurred to you, Officer Carl, that your appearance here today might in itself be a sign? Maybe you're more ready than you know."

Carl gently nudges Mitch closer to the back door of the blue and white. "We need to get going, Mitch. There's still time for you to catch some lunch at the Highland Street shelter."

"It doesn't take long," Mitch says. "The test, I mean. Three questions." He starts fumbling through the pockets of the trench coat and finally pulls out an over-creased piece of paper. "I'll read all three of them together. You take your time answering. I can only repeat them once though." Mitch looks carefully around and holds up an index finger. "I also need to whisper them."

Carl holds his breath when Mitch leans in.

Carl humors him and drops answers for all three: "Apples. The Milky Way. Alarm clocks."

When he's done, Mitch is frowning. "I'm sorry, Officer Carl. Many are called, but few you know . . ."

He turns toward the blue and white. "If it'll make you feel any better, the last one who took it missed all three." Mitch shakes his head at the memory. "Wayne got upset and wanted to take it again. Demanded it, in fact. I was forced to remind him of the eye of the needle and the fine print."

"Wait," Carl says. "You said Wayne. Wayne Summer?"

"The only and one," Mitch says. "I also told him Jesus doesn't like drugs."

THE LENGTH OF DAYS   **95**

"When and where did you see him?" Carl asks. "I've been looking for Wayne. It's important." Carl needs Wayne to connect the dots. He finds Wayne, and Wayne will lead him to Gary Lidd who was the overseer at 805 Jefferson when the fire happened, and Gary Lidd will lead to Eric-no-last-name who had been hanging out at the house and claiming to be working for the Bowen Brothers. If Carl connects enough dots, there will be a sweet bonus courtesy of Johnny Doc Nowell, and Carl's bank account needed a transfusion right now.

"When and where," Mitch says, closing his eyes and concentrating. "I'm thinking two days ago under the Rat."

"The Rat?"

Mitch nods and smiles. "Yes," he says. "I'm sure of it. I saw Wayne Summer two days ago under the Dead Rat That Lives in the Sky." Mitch slides into the back seat of the blue and white and leans back, closing his eyes again.

Carl looks up at the late morning sky. No sign of Jesus winging it in in His saucer. No signs of Dead Rats either.

His hangover starts tapping on his shoulder again.

THE LENGTH OF DAYS — TWENTY-ONE

The sky's shifting, the sun a quarter of the way to dawn, when Pam Graves pulls onto Dalton Street, heading home after spending the night at Daren Lowe's apartment. At one time, Dalton Street had been Old Money Magnolia Beach, but for the last two decades, its *noblesse* had been separated from its *oblige*, and both at best are running on fumes.

Most of the old homes Pam Graves drives past have been broken into multiple apartments or consigned to various stages of neglect. It's become a realm of delinquent and back taxes and a secondhand, shopworn respectability. There is, however, the grandeur of the live oaks lining each side of the street, their limbs thickened and lengthened by age so that they reach out in a tangled canopy.

This morning, in the soft light of a spring dawn, Dalton Street has the vague contours of a dream. Nobody's out. The world, for the moment, is holding its breath. Pam Graves pulls into the driveway of 1607. She tells herself she's home.

Home, in this case, is a carriage house that had once been part of the Williamson estate. Pam's aunt who had overseen the daily running of the estate had been left the carriage house when she retired, and Pam had been left the carriage house and the portion of the estate it sat on when her aunt died.

Pam parks and takes the flagstone pathway to the front door, unlocking it and after stepping inside, drapes her coat over the back of the living room couch, then moves past the small round table and four chairs comprising her dining room and steps into the equally small and uncluttered kitchen where she starts coffee before moving toward a hallway leading to a single bedroom and further down, the bathroom where after undressing and dropping her clothes in a hamper, she starts the shower, taking time to readjust the temperature and then stepping in, Pam emptying her mind as the water runs over her in a makeshift baptism, even though that's not what she would admit to calling it, then a few minutes later, reluctantly stepping out from under the spray when the water chills, toweling off and wrapping a thick white robe around her, and walks back barefoot to the kitchen where the coffee is ready, and after pouring a cup, Pam Graves adds cream,

THE LENGTH OF DAYS

sipping at her coffee while she starts fixing breakfast which, in this case, as on most mornings, is a bowl of oatmeal.

Her days. The way they unfurled.

She takes the bowl of oatmeal to the table. Sits down.

Simple is not the same as comfortable. Or maybe, she thinks, it's the other way around.

She picks up her spoon.

She looks at the bowl of oatmeal. Then outside the kitchen window where the yard is shrouded in a thin fog. Then looks around her home.

She sets down her spoon.

She begins searching her kitchen. For cinnamon. For strawberry jam. For honey. For something as simple as sugar. She comes back empty each time.

Something to add to the oatmeal. That's all she's looking for. That's all she needs. All she wants right now.

Comfortable is not simple.

Right now, Pam Graves's life doesn't feel like either. She's not sure why.

Edward. Last night at The Lowe Tide, she'd been nursing a glass of wine, and he'd sat next to her and introduced himself and then started hitting on her.

He was just a guy. Not someone she'd previously casually known or had much, if anything, in common with. He came across as someone who was a little too much pleased with himself and possessed a kind of bland all-purpose good looks.

She could have easily and quickly shut him down. Instead, to her surprise, she let him buy her another glass of wine.

He talked about himself and delivered the standard pickup lines as if he were reading them off a monitor.

She could have and should have shut him down at any point. But she hadn't.

She had looked around for Daren Lowe, her hybrid boyfriend and significant other and approximate fiancé, but he was pulling drafts for a line of college boys at the far end of the bar.

Pam let Edward inhabit a What If.

Until last call, Pam Graves sipped her wine and let herself drift and idly imagine a life with him or someone like him.

A different life and a different Pam Graves.

Near closing, Pam had shut him down with a *Nice meeting you, Edward.*

He frowned for a moment, as if puzzled, and then held up an index finger. He pulled a bar napkin over and wrote something on it and then slipped it in her coat pocket.

Nice meeting you too, he said and left.

Daren Lowe had then come over and topped off her wineglass.

Pam forgot about the bar napkin.

Until now.

She hunts it down.

Suddenly, her life is neither simple nor comfortable anymore.

The note is written in small and precise lettering.

You need to pay better attention, Pamela. My name's not Edward. It's Eric.

PS: let this one stand in for the rest.

112=3.92 lbs.

The numbers don't make any sense.

She boots up her computer. Starts searching.

It takes a while, but the numbers eventually yield.

The 112 is the weight of a person, in this case, more than likely a female. The 3.92 lbs. is her weight in ashes after cremation.

Or, in this case, an approximate cremation, one that occurred when you locked twelve women in a room and then burned the house down.

THE LENGTH OF DAYS – TWENTY-TWO

Mission Field Pier, on the other side of dusk, the sky full of low, dense, and clench-fisted clouds, and Samuel Fulton is at loose ends. The feeling is new and unwelcome. He'd always been a man whose life and sense of self were closely knit and tightly woven.

The Mission Field Pier stretches over the Atlantic like a geometry lesson in parallel lines. Tonight it is nearly deserted. Walking its length, Samuel passes a few die-hard fishermen casting their lines into the dark wind-driven surf. The wind itself is cold and runs in steady, overlapping gusts.

There's a private arithmetic to aging, and Samuel is doing what feels like his homework. He is seventy-one years old. He's been married forty-nine years. He worked at Ryland Iron and Steel for over fifty years. Glenda and he moved to Magnolia Beach fifteen months ago. It's been eleven months since her strokes. He's read the love letter Glenda had kept secret from him thirty-one times. In the last twenty-five years, he's cried twice that he can remember.

Something loose and loosening as Samuel Fulton feels the pilings on the pier shiver and tremble beneath him. Tonight he wants to blame his problems on geography. He misses the Midwest. He misses the weight and lived-truth of personal history, of growing up in a city that once had made things, and in making those things, made lives. He misses being a welder, of taking what's apart or broken and joining it in a smooth, nearly invisible seam.

He misses what he knows he'll never find in Magnolia Beach. It's a coastal town that feels like a separate country unto itself, only marginally connected to the rest of the state, a town that's a monument to the transient, and whose character is defined by waves of tourists and fast bucks, a false-bottomed nostalgia, and an undigestible commercial sprawl.

Samuel Fulton makes the end of the pier. He's more than a little embarrassed and uncomfortable. At loose ends, he'd come to the pier tonight because of the Voices. The Voices were part of local beach lore, part and parcel with coastal ghost stories and tales of pirates and sunken treasure and ill-starred plantation family intrigues.

According to the legend, Mission Field Pier ran into a part of the ocean where the spirits of the Dead lived, and at times, the sound of the waves carried their words if people were willing to listen.

Samuel Fulton stands at the railing and watches the waves move toward him in a steady rhythm, each crest a thin line of white, and the waves moving through that dark immensity do not sound like a whisper, no, or even a protracted stutter, or like the words that had been lost after his wife's strokes, and, feeling foolish, Samuel Fulton abruptly turns and starts back down the pier.

A set of halogens hover over each side of the stairs heading to the parking lot below. As Samuel approaches them, someone steps out of the shadows and into the pool of light.

He's a young guy, maybe early to mid-thirties, with a careful haircut except for a floppy lock of sandy-brown hair falling over his forehead. He's wearing a pale blue shirt, khakis, and deck shoes.

He makes a point of studying Samuel.

Samuel, in turn, studies him. "I know you," Samuel says after a long moment.

"Of course you do." He smiles. "I know you could call the police or yell for help, but I think you'll find it in your best interest to hear me out first." He turns and starts down the stairs.

"My best interest?"

"Yeah, but it's your wife who owns it."

A half block from the pier is the In Your Cups Coffee Shop. Samuel and the young man take a window seat. Across the street is a Seagulls Beachwear and next to it, the Sea and Shore Grill. Beyond them, further down the block, there is a crowded line of condos and motels.

The young man orders two coffees, both black. He is unfailingly polite. He then leans over and asks, "You're not carrying that piece-of-shit Tracfone, are you, Samuel? No clandestine 9-1-1 action?"

Samuel shakes his head no.

"I suppose you could say tonight was a test," the young man says. "I wanted to see if you would recognize me if we met face to face."

"I guess you have your answer," Samuel says.

"Whoa," he says, "the Senior Citizen copping an attitude, a little spit and vinegar action." He picks up his coffee, then sets it down. "I suppose from one perspective, that's admirable. From another, it could easily be construed as foolhardy and dangerous."

"Maybe you could say meeting in public is also foolhardy and dangerous," Samuel says. The coffee shop is over half-full, and it wouldn't take much to get anyone's attention.

THE LENGTH OF DAYS

101

The all-knowing smile again. "You've been hanging around Weldon Trulane too long," he says. "Some of that attitude has rubbed off." He takes a sip of coffee. "Just curious and off tonight's subject, are you two queer on each other or something?"

"Or something," Samuel says after a moment. "I'm married. Not that it's any of your business."

"My business is why we're meeting tonight," he says. "A little insurance here because I intend to remain at large." He nods twice. "I've always been fond of that phrase. It's simple and to the point but with a deep well of implications."

It's my own fault, Samuel thinks. He had choked at the police station when it came to describing the man who now sits across from him. At bottom, he disappears into his bland good looks, though upon closer inspection, Samuel notices those features are verging on overripe, like something softening and headed toward spoiled.

"Since I'm presently at large," the young man says, "I'm assuming you haven't talked to the police or media again."

Samuel looks out the window at the passing traffic and then back. "What's to prevent me from that now?"

"That's the Big Question of the evening, isn't it?"

"I have another," Samuel says. "Why? Why the young woman and snapping her neck? Why then the fire later and all those other bodies?"

"You really want to know?" He points to the condiment holder.

Samuel slides it across the table.

Samuel watches him take the salt shaker, twist off its top, and pour a small white mound on the table. He then takes out three sugar packets and tears off the top of each and empties them in a mound next to the salt.

"There's your answer," he says. "You can't tell them apart by looking. You need to taste it." The smile again. "That's the point of Life. Everything looks the same until or unless you taste it."

"You're wrong," Samuel says. "You can tell them apart if you look closely enough."

"What would be the fun then?" he asks. "Anyway, no one ever does."

"Some do."

The young man pushes the piles together and slides it to the edge of the table and glances over at Samuel before sweeping it over the edge. He then dusts off his hands and sits back in his chair.

"It's time we answer your earlier question, the one about what's preventing you from talking to the police and media this time around."

He fishes out his cellphone, fingers in his security code, and taps on the app for the camera, tapping that again to bring up the album, and then bringing up a photo of Glenda Fulton in her room at Bayview.

She's sitting in her wheelchair, and her robe and nightgown have been pulled down, exposing her breasts.

"C-Wing. Room C-10. Walked in. Walked out."

Samuel clenches his fists and starts to get out of his chair.

The young man holds up his hand, palm out. "I get it, Sammy. Chivalry isn't dead. But you need to rein it in and listen." He picks up and sets his coffee cup aside. "Forget you ever saw me. Forget this evening. Forget my looks and everything about me, and I forget Glenda Fulton and you. You have your lives back, and I remain at large."

He holds up the phone with Glenda's photo again and then abruptly shuts both down and off.

THE LENGTH OF DAYS – TWENTY-THREE

Johnny Doc Nowell had called patrolman Carl Adkin and explained what he needed. And needed as soon as possible.

Johnny Doc is running out of time.

Not the first time something like that has happened.

This time he knows what's on the horizon though.

It's not September 1972, Nguyen Duc Xuan, at thirteen, on his way to becoming Johnny Doc Nowell and living on the Saigon Streets, a runaway from the First Light Orphanage and coming to find a home of sorts on Tu Do Street at the Colorado Bar, the Colorado owned and operated by one John Sloane, American veteran and expatriate and black marketeer.

It's not September 1974, Johnny Doc Nowell running errands for John Sloane. Passing on messages. Helping Sloane open and close the Colorado. Around Saigon, Sloane is known as a *Facilitator*. He opens and closes doors. What passes through or doesn't isn't his concern. He makes things happen, and he knows when to look away and not ask questions.

It's not April 1975 and rumors running through Saigon that birth more rumors. Major Offensive. The North. Contingency Plans. Omega-City.

Johnny Doc Nowell talks to John Sloane about America. About the rumors. About evacuations.

Sloane tells him the truth behind the truth and plays B-10 on the jukebox.

You looking for a point, maybe a moral, here, Johnny Doc? Don't. There is none. You're worried about the rumors? Fine, okay. But it changes nothing. The closest thing to a point or moral is this: the Viet Cong like cold beer too. It's business, always has been and nothing else, and the Colorado Bar is open for business.

It's not April 30, 1975 when the rumors become facts, and the fall of Saigon begins in earnest, but it's no Embassy rooftop or helicopters for Johnny Doc because he's picked up running an errand for John Sloane by the North Vietnamese.

It's not the next nine years while Johnny Doc is housed in a reeducation camp overseen by Colonel Le Van Thu and then used as farm labor.

It's not 1984 when Johnny Doc Nowell manages to ride the Third Wave of Vietnamese immigration and lands in San Diego. Or the next six and a half years while he drifts around the American West and South, doing what he learned to do at the Colorado Bar. He meets people who make things happen. He runs errands. He does favors. He does not ask questions and keeps moving.

It's not 1991, when Johnny Doc moves to Palacios, Texas, a small town on the Gulf with a large Vietnamese community. He goes to work on one of the shrimp boats in the fleet owned and run by Nguyen Gia Tuan, the de facto patriarch of the community.

Johnny Doc has a plan.

He hides in plain sight. He's patient.

He's counting on a couple things.

One, that the majority of the Vietnamese community in Palacios, Texas would continue the practice that was common for many of their fellow immigrants; they carried a deep distrust of the American banking system and set up their own, usually keeping it within the community and appointing respected members to oversee and manage it.

In Palacios, Texas, Nguyen Gia Tuan is the equivalent of the Chief Officer.

For eighteen months, Johnny Doc has been waiting for Nguyen Gia Tuan to drop his guard.

In March 1993, Nguyen Gia Tuan does, and Johnny Doc Nowell quietly leaves Palacios, Texas with two red Samsonite suitcases full of cash.

It's not 1994 when Johnny Doc ends up in Magnolia Beach, South Carolina. He likes beach towns. Their transience is comforting. Once again, he hides in plain sight. He watches and waits and eventually notices a man and a woman working the boardwalk and surrounding blocks in tandem. A Romeo and a Florence Nightingale. They collect and run young girls, and they are good at it.

Johnny Doc buys the Full Moon Massage Parlor and hires Bishop Conover and his common law wife Nina to manage it. He buys the Galaxy miniature golf course. He buys a nail salon and christens it Nu-Nails. He buys a Beachwear and More franchise and a mom-and-pop motel called the Sand Dollar. He buys Pinewood Bowling with spare change.

He makes money and keeps making money. He buys a three-story house on Danvers facing the Inlet. He starts sleeping with Nina Conover.

THE LENGTH OF DAYS

He contributes to the campaign funds of any candidate who will do him the most good. He hires Raychard Balen as his lawyer. He keeps making money.

It's not 2007 when Johnny Doc Nowell does not see Collateralized Debt Obligations and Credit Default Swaps coming. No, what he sees instead is something that he has come to believe is his Destiny, a life filled with riches, respect, and power, an American Trinity housed in the opportunity to buy into a sure thing, a big money project for an exclusive gated community named West Wind Estates.

Johnny Doc goes all in.

Then it's *Welcome to 2008*.

Now, though, it's spring 2009, and Raychard Balen, his lawyer, has called with news that was unwelcome and dire.

Dire was the word that Raychard Balen had used. By the end of the call, Johnny Doc understood why.

In the meantime, Johnny Doc has put in the call to Carl Adkin.

And now Johnny Doc Nowell's left with nothing more than this moment and a view from the living room in a heavily mortgaged house that had lost most of its value as collateral.

He's left with no friends. Dwindling cash reserves. A loan from Bank of the South that still has not materialized.

The Bowen Brothers expected restitution for the twelve dead girls, but Johnny Doc, after a series of delays and feints still does not have the cash.

Which means things have passed into Phase Two.

The Bowen Brothers have commissioned some serious hurt.

Raychard Balen, Johnny Doc's lawyer, had talked to the Bowens' lawyer, Nathaniel Laine, who in the spirit of professional courtesy laid out the details and a timeline.

The serious hurt will arrive between Friday and Sunday night. One operative and one driver. To avoid unnecessary attention from witnesses or police, it's recommended the session occur at Johnny Doc's home. Also recommended is a physician on retainer who makes house calls. Emergency rooms are a complication better avoided.

The inevitable coda: *Don't run. It will go harder and longer on you if you do.*

The beating will serve a dual purpose. One, an object lesson for potential rivals or any others who owe the Bowen Brothers. Two, some concrete motivation for Johnny Doc to find a way to get the cash and avoid Phase Three.

Johnny Doc isn't going to run. He has something else in mind. Outside the living room window, the tide is withdrawing from the Inlet. Egrets leave, taking flight like pieces of paper lifted by the wind. Across the Inlet, the stalled stretch of West Wind Estates fades out. It's as if the world's pulse has slowed.

Johnny Doc walks into the kitchen and draws a glass of water. He makes a sandwich. He sits at the table and works his way through both.

Later that evening, the phone rings. It's Carl Adkin.

"Get out your checkbook. I got some good news for you," he says. "I found your Charlie Chan."

THE LENGTH OF DAYS – TWENTY-FOUR

The text comes through just as Pam Graves is headed for her car. The wind is running warm and steady and carries undertones of the ocean, a high clean smell, and around her, spring is beginning to crowd in, the sky above a light blue, late morning light spreading through white clouds stretched thin as a set of threadbare curtains.

The text is from Madison Hopewell and simply reads *At the Colonial*. A change of plans then. They were supposed to meet at In Your Cups, the coffee shop off Atlantic Avenue near the Mission Field Pier.

The Colonial Hotel is six stories of red brick, wrought iron railings, and hurricane-shuttered windows. It's an old Magnolia Beach landmark, a cousin to the Greek Revival city-county courthouse occupying the center of the town square. The Colonial was built by Yellow Dog Democrats in the early twentieth century and after a long period of steady decline eventually rehabbed by New South Culture War Republicans.

Madison Hopewell is in room 621. She answers the door in her bra and slip and with her hair still wet from the shower. She points toward a circular oak table holding a pot of room service coffee, a plate of warm cinnamon rolls, and a pint of Southern Comfort.

Pam pours herself a cup of coffee and looks out the bay window. She can just make out a thin blue line of ocean over the top of a grove of magnolias and live oaks on the east grounds. Madison Hopewell walks back over to the second bed in the room and the three opened suitcases covering it.

"I don't understand," Pam says, frowning.

"It's not exactly a novel concept, Pam. I believe it's called packing. Something that's usually a prelude to leaving."

"I still don't understand. Why and where?"

"Haven't you seen the news this morning?"

Pam shakes her head no.

"Galena, Illinois. A small town northwest of Chicago. A primary school. Looking at a high body count."

"What about the one here?"

Madison Hopewell shakes her head. "Once again, reality time, Honey. We're talking school shooting. Dead kids will always trump dead sex workers. For one, kids have names. Kids have interests and hobbies and pets and favorite colors. Kids have families. Those families have fingerprint identities. We're talking stories within stories within stories and lots of air time and special reports. You take dead and wounded schoolkids and put that up against twelve dead sex workers, most of them no-name, and heartrending beats prurient every time."

Pam sets down her coffee cup. She looks out the bay window. "So the ones here don't matter?"

Madison Hopewell slowly lets out her breath. "Everything matters. Everything. In the long run, that's the problem."

"That's too easy."

"No, what's easy is saying it's too easy." Madison points at Pam. "Time to grow up, Sweetheart." She crosses the room, stops at the oak table, pours a cup of coffee, then adds a generous dose of Comfort.

"I named them, you know," Pam says. "Eight of the twelve who didn't have one."

Hopewell takes a sip from the cup, then dips it in Pam's direction. "Of course you did." She shakes her head, then says, "Jesus."

Madison Hopewell looks over her shoulder and says, "Do you ever wonder why at this stage of the investigation, we've gotten no further than we have?"

Madison closes and locks the suitcase and sets it on the floor next to the bed. "What it should tell you is that no one is really interested in or in any real hurry to close this one out."

"Who's no one?" Pam says. "You're not no one. Neither am I."

Madison drops a fistful of bras and panties into the second suitcase.

"No one, Honey," she says, "is Andrew Findley and the Tourist Bureau crowd, the mayor, and the police commissioner. No one is also local businesses represented by the Chamber of Commerce." Madison crosses the room and picks up her coffee cup and then the Southern Comfort and a moment later sets both back down on the table. "Beach towns need bodies. Live bodies. Those live bodies carry cash and credit cards. Dead bodies don't carry either. Dead bodies don't book rooms in hotels or eat in restaurants. They don't play golf or go to outlet stores. Dead bodies, whatever their number, are not welcome in beach towns."

"So we just forget about them?"

"If it's Magnolia Beach, South Carolina," Madison says, "and if you're twelve trafficked women dead in a house fire, you're a bottom-line inconvenience and yesterday's news at best."

"So that's it?"

THE LENGTH OF DAYS

"Actually, no," Madison says, turning toward Pam. "There is one more thing. Watch out for the Tourist Bureau. Findley and that crew have an extra set of teeth behind their smiles."

She looks over at the bedside clock. "Best of luck, Honey," she says, "but I'm putting my ass and Moral Outrage on the noon flight to O'Hare, and I need to finish packing."

THE LENGTH OF DAYS — TWENTY-FIVE

Carl Adkin sends Kwan Lee back into the house for the suit, and then he begins to worry that Kwan might rabbit on him, so he backs the Cherokee down the driveway, intending to circle the block to cut Kwan off if necessary, but before Carl can drop it into Drive, Kwan Lee has opened the front door and starts down the lawn with the suit draped over his shoulder, crosses in front of the Cherokee, and gets in the passenger side.

Kwan Lee's wife waves goodbye from the front stoop.

"I did not bring the dress shoes," Kwan Lee says, "because you told me the others were of the same size."

Carl nods. He takes the Cherokee down East Barber Street through a neighborhood of small two-bedroom brick homes, the lawns small squares and the property lines defined by hedges of Tea Olives and Ligustrum and ranks of satellite dishes.

It's a neighborhood as bland and anonymous as a drawerful of socks, a neighborhood functioning as protective coloration for a guy like Kwan Lee who owns and runs an independent grocery store as well as a small but lucrative neighborhood casino in the back rooms of the warehouse adjoining it.

"I think I should point out," Kwan Lee says, "that I am currently of two minds concerning this weekend."

Carl slows and eases the Cherokee through a stop sign. "Long view, Kwan. Monday, you'll be back running blackjack and poker games for all your pals in northwest Magnolia Beach."

"My wife," Kwan Lee says, "she has dreams that frequently turn out to be omens. She has had three dreams in succession, one for each day of the upcoming weekend, and none of the dreams have been good."

"The only dreams I trust," Carl says, "are wet." When Kwan Lee doesn't respond, Carl says, "Hey, that was a joke. Put you at ease."

Kwan Lee keeps his gaze focused out the passenger side window. "I have a low pain threshold."

"We've been over this." Carl shakes his head. "Omens, dreams, whatever you want to call them, it's one weekend, and you're the Star."

"I can offer you more money," Kwan Lee says, "than I'm getting."

"You've had a free pass for three and a half years, Kwan," Carl says.

THE LENGTH OF DAYS 111

Everything's a matter of timing. Carl could have shut down Kwan Lee's gambling operation at any time, but he let it ride. He trusted his instincts and intuition. The world presented opportunities. The trick was knowing when to wait for and act upon them. Favors bred more favors, and favors were money in the bank, ready to be cashed out as needed.

A roster and ledger. Carl kept both in his head and could bring each up at will. People and what they owned. What they were owed. Short and long term. What you cashed in and what you let ride.

Carl did not overreach. Everything had its place. He made sure the ledger he kept in his head had the books balanced. Opportunities produced results. And results, if carefully marshalled, produced a friendly supplement to his yearly salary.

Which is why he is driving across Magnolia Beach toward Johnny Doc Nowell's place.

He's delivering the answer to Johnny Doc's problem.

Carl's careful to not underestimate Johnny Doc Nowell. Under the black-suited respectability and dead serious demeanor, Johnny Doc is a survivor, and survivors are hard to read. Survival sets its own morality, and Carl doesn't trust the dictums of its Old or New Testament. A survivor will do anything to be what it is, and what it is is always unpredictable. So Carl keeps it careful and low-key and a show of a couple IQ points below average whenever he's around Johnny Doc Nowell.

Carl takes Queensland Highway east and skirts the old downtown section of Magnolia Beach by hitting 17th Avenue north, moving through neighborhoods in stutter-step gentrification, everything in suspension since the financial fallout of 2008, and then he follows Atlantic Avenue and a blitz of tourist attractions and cut-rate restaurants until he can branch true north again onto Elizabeth Avenue, following that through North Magnolia Beach and more arrested and hit-or-miss gentrification, renovation, and rehabbing.

Kwan Lee, in the passenger seat, is running more and more on an alternating current of frown and fear.

Carl, finally, pulls into a Church's Fried Chicken and parks, but he leaves the Cherokee running. "We're almost there. No more second thoughts at this point. No more two minds. You leave your life and everything else behind for three days, and then I take you home on Monday."

Kwan Lee still keeps his gaze angled out the window, away from

Carl. "What if I have changed my mind altogether?"

Carl waits before responding. He adjusts his hold on the steering wheel. Even with the windows closed, the smell of old grease and over-fried chicken pieces works its way into the front seat.

"To answer your question, there aren't enough fire extinguishers or insurance policies to keep your grocery store, home, and warehouse intact." Carl waits and adds, "And that's no omen, friend. That's fact."

Kwan turns and looks at Carl. "What do you receive from doing this? I am wondering."

Carl doesn't answer. Instead, he turns and hits Kwan Lee in the throat, then drops the Cherokee into reverse but keeps his foot on the brake. He listens to Kwan Lee hyperventilate.

After a while, Carl says, "Ask too many questions or not enough, what you'll run into is pain. And pain is always its own answer."

Kwan Lee lowers his head. Carl pulls back onto Elizabeth Avenue and heads north. The sky is low and full of wind-sheared clouds. He starts to turn the radio on but then changes his mind.

"Think Warner Oland and Sidney Toler," Carl says.

Carl had to give Johnny Doc Nowell credit. The guy had figured his own escape hatch from the Bowen Brothers' Phase Two: a serious beatdown in lieu of reparations due.

The Bowen Brothers always kept things in-house. They inevitably sent White Bread Muscle.

Johnny Doc Nowell had counted on that Muscle, like a lot of Americans, not being able to distinguish Japanese from Korean, Korean from Chinese, Chinese from Vietnamese, and Vietnamese from Thai.

Warner Oland and Sidney Toler had played Charlie Chan in dozens of films. The fact that neither was Asian didn't matter. Each was Close Enough.

So was Kwan Lee. Put him in a black suit and white shirt and black dress shoes and drop him in Johnny Doc's house. Then wait for the Muscle to show up.

Pain is always its own answer.

Johnny Doc needed his own Oland and Toler. Carl delivered up Kwan Lee.

Carl follows Elizabeth Avenue until they reach the uppermost portion of North Magnolia Beach. They take Danvers Lane along the Inlet and follow its long slow curve past high-end homes with bloated mortgages.

Johnny Doc Nowell is waiting for them. Carl reviews things one more time with Kwan Lee. Kwan nods and gets out of the Cherokee. Carl

THE LENGTH OF DAYS 113

takes the envelope Johnny Doc passes over.

He drives south.

He suddenly finds himself thinking of his wife, of the life they've made, the kids, the reach of their vows, the whole package deal, and he's happy and centered. He's known Linda since they were kids, dated through high school, got married when he marshalled out of the Marines. At bottom, he loves his wife because she doesn't ask questions or at least none that he can't answer. She loves him because those answers match the length and width of their dreams.

Carl, driving south on Elizabeth, takes out the envelope that Johnny Doc Nowell gave him. One-handing it, he tests its weight and thickness and nods.

He's about to get on Queensland Highway and then take Old Market Boulevard home when he changes his mind and leaves Elizabeth for Atlantic Avenue. He drives through old downtown Magnolia Beach, past the boutiques and restaurants frequented by Old Money, segueing a few blocks later into a long stretch of clutter catering to tourists that Carl and most of the others on Patrol called Greenland due to the amount of money the tourists habitually spent there.

He eventually leaves Atlantic for Spencer. He knows what he's going to do. It feels right. His wife's birthday is in little over a week. He's already talked to Truman Cooke and Truman's wife, Denisha, about having a surprise party for Linda. The details for the party are in place. Her present isn't.

Carl pulls into the lot for Webber's Marine Sales and Service. He takes the envelope Johnny Doc Nowell gave him and slips it into his back pocket and gets out of the Cherokee. By the time he gets back in some twenty-five minutes later, he has put the down payment on a Bayliner Element with a 125-horsepower outboard and a seating capacity for nine. By the time he gets back on Spencer, Carl is already planning the first family outing on the Intercoastal Waterway.

Spencer to Eleventh Street is a shortcut to Old Market Boulevard and then south and home. Along the way, Carl passes the southeast entrance to Garrison Park. He looks up and hits the brakes, then pulls to the side of the street and starts laughing.

Sometimes, he thinks, the Universe is your pal.

According to Mitch, one of the homeless regulars, Carl is near the landing site for Jesus's saucer when He swings by to pick up the faithful and pure of heart.

It was also the last time and place Mitch had seen Wayne Summer,

Carl's snitch-in-the-wind.

Carl checks the sky but doesn't see any sign of Jesus winging His way earthward in His spaceship.

He does, however, find the Dead Rat That Lives In The Sky.

It had been there all along. Carl had not made the connection.

According to Mitch, he met Wayne Summer under the Dead Rat.

Carl can smell a bonus from Johnny Doc Nowell. Wayne Summer will lead Carl to Gary Lidd who worked at the house at 805 Jefferson that burned down, killing the twelve young women. Gary Lidd will lead him to the Eric-no-last-name who hung out at the house and who Carl suspects was more than likely behind the fire, or at minimum, was the one behind the murder in the front yard.

Carl will serve all of them up to Johnny Doc Nowell. Johnny Doc Nowell can serve them up to the Bowen Brothers.

To get things rolling, all Carl has to do is wait for Wayne Summer to show up under The Dead Rat That Lives In The Sky.

And it's right there, between a break in the live oaks and white pines, a billboard set high on pylons and holding the image of a large rat lying on its back with its legs pointing straight up and haloed by the slogan, DOWN FOR THE COUNT WITH MAXWELL'S PEST CONTROL.

THE LENGTH OF DAYS – TWENTY-SIX

Johnny Doc Nowell squashes the temptation to drive by the house. Getting anywhere near his home would be utter folly. He must exile himself for the weekend. He understands that, but there is an empty bubble painfully nesting under his rib cage, and it expands and contracts with each breath.

It's early evening, and he's been driving around Magnolia Beach for a couple hours. He's rented a nondescript SUV for the weekend and left the black Dodge Ram 4 x4 parked in the driveway of the house on Danvers. On Patrolman Carl Adkin's advice though, Johnny Doc has kept the keys to the Dodge. He does not want to give the Korean impersonating him any opportunity to run before the Bowen Brothers' Muscle shows up. The subsequent beating is preordained, a necessary warning and object lesson, and part of the way the Bowen Brothers do business.

Kwan Lee's stand-in beating will buy Johnny Doc a little time, and that is what he needs right now.

Patrolman Adkin has promised Johnny Doc he is close to delivering up the full identity of the Eric who had been part of everything that had gone wrong at 805 Jefferson Street.

Johnny Doc has more than a few questions for that Eric before he passes him on to the Bowens.

Johnny Doc supposes he should get something to eat. He has yet to decide where he will spend the next couple nights either. Right now though, with the horizon burning in a red and orange-banded sunset, he drives toward the airport and takes the SUV into short-term parking where he has a good view of the western stretch of runway.

He is practicing his evacuation, if necessary, from Magnolia Beach.

Arrivals and departures. Something basic. The sky threaded with the lights and submarine shapes of aircraft approaching and departing.

The horizon gone down to darkness now, Johnny Doc watches what he figures must be the 7:30 commuter flight coming into Magnolia Beach from Atlanta, and then he leaves short-term parking for Old Market Boulevard, one of the city's main arteries along with Atlantic Avenue.

He's hungry. He drives northeast. He tries not to imagine Kwan Lee bleeding out in his living room.

Old Market Boulevard is one long smear of lights. He pulls into a King of the Sea's drive-thru and orders two fish sandwiches. He tries not to think too long about the fact that the type of fish is never specified. He is hungry, and right now his hunger is direct and insistent as a newspaper headline. He parks and eats down from the dual dumpsters on the north side of King of the Sea.

Above the lights of Old Market Boulevard, the sky is clear and swollen with spring constellations. Johnny Doc knows they are supposed to be there, but he has never been able to see them. For him, they are stars without stories. Or if the stories are there, they are someone else's.

Johnny Doc leaves King of the Sea and heads toward downtown and Atlantic Avenue. He has one more stop to make before finding a place to sleep for the night.

Motels. Fish sandwiches. Constellations made of stars but holding no stories. A broken spring evening.

Johnny Doc pushes the rental up Old Market boulevard, but he's also sitting in the Colorado Bar on To Du Street in Saigon and listening to John Sloane explain how a country can lose and win a war at the same time.

It came down to Faces. And the cost of wearing, saving, or losing them.

A lesson in the way the world worked when it didn't, John Sloane had said. You start with the City on the Hill, America the good guys, God's Chosen, all that shining virtue, morality in every breath, and you ship it here, to Viet Nam, and put it to work, but then you find out it doesn't, at least not like you thought it would, and one day you look around and you find that the City on the Hill is now nothing more than a run-down 7-11 on Route 66.

The same with the heroics, Sloane had told him. You started out with John Wayne and grit in the gut and ended up with Marion Morrison in a bad toupee under a secondhand Stetson.

That's why happens, John Sloane said, when the face you think you're wearing isn't the one you are wearing, and then you compound the problem by trying to save the face that isn't there, and you end up losing both.

Johnny Doc makes Atlantic Avenue and heads south for six blocks. The moon, three-quarters and insistent, and the ocean are on his left, the constellations he can't name spreading above him like a broken umbrella. The rest is tourist sprawl, burning in its own light and

THE LENGTH OF DAYS   117

spilling like high tide over the width of the sidewalks and into the street.

The Full Moon Massage Parlor is on the 2300 block of Atlantic Avenue. Its façade is white vinyl siding, a blue tin roof, a freshly asphalted lot with crisp white parking lines, the Parlor's name and logo streetside atop a stanchion tall enough to be seen for at least two long blocks in either direction.

Johnny Doc pulls into the lot across the street and parks so that he's facing the entrance to the Full Moon head on. Its world, overseen by Bishop Conover and his wife Nina, ran on a basic Old Testament managerial style, keeping the women at the Full Moon in place by dispensing punishments and rewards arbitrarily and unpredictably. The women were never sure if they should be grateful or afraid or both.

Bishop Conover and Nina understood that Fear and Gratitude were powerful motivators. They became even more powerful when you made them synonyms.

There was a truth behind that truth that Johnny Doc had glimpsed more than once. The first time was after John Sloane repeatedly played B-10 on the Colorado Bar's jukebox at closing. The second was after the fall of Saigon at the reeducation camp courtesy of Colonel Le Van Thu. The third time was tied to his original negotiations with the Bowen Brothers about the price for keeping the women at the safe house on 805 Jefferson.

The Bowen Brothers had interrupted him mid-sentence. Not women, they'd said. We're talking merchandise. Bar codes with a pulse.

Johnny Doc had started to object but stopped. He understood. He understood, however, in a way that the Bowen Brothers never could. Colonel Le Van Thu had seen to that.

Over the next hour, Johnny Doc Nowell sits behind the wheel of the SUV and watches a line of men enter and leave the Full Moon. They are men who have run out of faces. They've lost them to loneliness, blind need, or desperation. They are men who are now as generic as motels, fish sandwiches, constellations without stories, and bar codes with a pulse.

Right now, the view on the other side of the SUV's windshield holds the truth behind the truth, the one that resides at the core of the universe: that there is always something inviolate, irreconcilable, and unjustifiable, a lump of truth that is indigestible, some black hole where all ethical distinctions collapse upon themselves, revealing something finally appalling and indefensible at its own core, the equivalent of what happens when God blinks and in that long moment morality and anything resembling judgment or justice absolutely disappears and what you're left with in that long moment is simply the zero gravity of your own heartbeat and the Full Moon Massage Parlor and the women working there and the men who pass through its doors.

THE LENGTH OF DAYS — TWENTY-SEVEN

Samuel Fulton finally has to enlist the aid of Arturo Morales to extract Weldon Trulane III from room D-8 in D-Wing of Bayview before Security arrives.

Samuel and Arturo each take an arm, and half-hustle, half-drag Weldon to the employee entrance where Arturo one-hands the code keys and ushers Samuel and Weldon out the door before it's half open. Samuel has a wishbone grip on Weldon's upper arm. He pilots Weldon down the sidewalk past the employee parking lot and back of D-Wing and follows the long slow curve of sidewalk toward a trio of benches facing an acre and a half lake, Weldon providing an accompanying soundtrack of invectives, curses, obscenities, threats, and entreaties with each step.

Today, Weldon Trulane III is an unruly combo of disheveled and disreputable, his out-of-season seersucker jacket wrinkled to the point where each blue stripe is irreconcilably bent in competing directions. His khakis hang like bad drapes. His shoes plead the Fifth when it comes to polish. His morning shave is a faulty memory, and his haircut follows its own calendar.

Weldon keeps trying to pry his arm from Samuel's grip, but Samuel refuses to let go. With his free hand, he points further down the sidewalk where crews are digging up and prepping future flowerbeds. Samuel then swings his free arm toward the eastern end of the lake and the marina where this afternoon, crews are doing their own version of dry-dock. They've taken the rowboats, pedal boats, canoes, and kayaks out of storage and laid them out in rows and begun cleaning them.

Samuel points at the crews. "Just watch, okay, Weldon? They're working. Watch them. The flowerbeds and boats and workers. Just watch. They're trying to show you something. They're doing what they're supposed to. It's not complicated."

Weldon's breathing levels. He looks over at Samuel. "You know, you can be a real asshole at times."

"I'm not the one who went off on the nurse," Samuel says. "You're lucky I was heading back to the townhouse. That and the fact that Arturo was working this afternoon."

"That bitch, Marsha, she's Florence Nightingale by way of Eva Braun."

120 LYNN KOSTOFF

Samuel lets go of Weldon's arm. "Her name's Martha, not Marsha. Martha Dashe. She's helped with Glenda. She's all right."

"There's too much *all* to her *right*."

"You didn't need to take it as far as you did."

Weldon waits a moment before responding. The crews digging flowerbeds take a break. The men lean on shovels and smoke furtive cigarettes and check cellphones.

"I was trying to talk to my dying friend. She comes in the room. I told her I needed some more time. She wouldn't listen and starts quoting doctor's orders and in-house policy."

Samuel raises his right arm, then lets it fall. "Her job, Weldon, that's all she was doing."

"HT is my best friend. I haven't had a lot of them, okay? I had some things I needed to tell him, some things I needed to ask him too, but that nurse kept interrupting."

"Why Security?"

Weldon makes a show of shrugging. "One or two of my observations and comments might have been misconstrued as threats of bodily harm."

A short glance over Weldon's left shoulder is the point where an arm of the sidewalk breaks toward the Bayview Manor and its townhouses, and beyond that, in a southeast patch of sky, three planes circle the regional airport like impatient birds.

"Oh shit," Weldon says. "It never stops." He shakes his head. "You know, Samuel, there are days that call for nothing less than SWAT teams." Weldon points to the east and the approach of two figures, the one trailing easily twice the size of the one leading. "We're about to meet Dr. Empathy and the Long Arm of Policy. That nurse sicced them on me."

The doctor turns out to be a young woman in a white lab coat and Mr. Policy an overweight and oversized security guard wearing Bayview's navy-blue uniform. The young woman introduces herself as Dr. Thomas. She's wearing minimal make up and the expression of a pet lover who's just found a dog in dire need of rescue. The security guard stands over her shoulder like an immense shadow. There's a small plastic rectangle pinned over his left pocket reading Gerald. His fists are the size of grapefruits.

"He necessary?" Weldon asks, nodding toward Gerald.

"I didn't—" Dr. Thomas starts.

"I asked to come along," Gerald says and smiles. "I was hoping you'd

THE LENGTH OF DAYS 121

try something again."

"You sound like something from a B-movie," Weldon says.

Dr. Thomas breaks in, her voice calm and even. Her bedside manner is reasonable, respectful, concerned, empathetic, deferential, and accommodating.

Weldon Trulane, of course, takes exception to each shading.

"When's the last time you had your blood pressure checked?" Dr. Thomas asks Weldon. "Your color's not good."

Gerald, the security guard, leans in and says, "My book, there are certain individuals who need to be put down. No room for them on the earth. There's a lot to say for the common good and keeping it that way."

Dr. Thomas holds up her hand. "That's enough. Mr. Trulane's friend is dying. People respond to the reality of death in different ways. We need to respect that."

"My friend HT is not dying," Weldon says.

"It's part of Life. A natural process," Dr. Thomas says.

"Stop it," Weldon says, "right there."

"As difficult as it is to accept at times, things end. They conclude. But acceptance leads to closure, and closure heals."

"I call bullshit," Weldon says. "HT's not dying. He's being snuffed out. That's the difference. There's nothing to accept."

The security guard taps Dr. Thomas on the shoulder. "I warned you the little fucker was crazy."

"I really think we should check out that blood pressure," Dr. Thomas says, leaning closer.

"Snuffed out is snuffed out," Weldon says, shaking his head. "We're not talking semantics here. We're talking the Nature of Things."

Oh no, Samuel thinks. Here we go.

Weldon slips into his rendition of what was necessary in the face of the Universe's equal opportunity push for each individual's eventual extinction. What was needed, he maintains, is Professor Longhair and "Tipitina" and medium-rare rib eyes and boiled shrimp and fresh peaches and Samuel Beckett and Tennessee Williams and Billy Wilder and Orson Welles and the butterflying of July 4th fireworks and Louisiana Frank's Hot Sauce and hymns like "Be Thou My Vision" and chicory coffee and powdery beignets and the smell of flesh pre-and-post orgasm and the Crayola colors of blooming hibiscus and the exact moment of take-off when a plane's tires leave the runway and the basic truth of dark chocolate on your tongue and the full menagerie of summer cloud formations and the sweet last-ditch promise of a three a.m. breakfast on the coattails of last call and finally the long ache in the face of beauty and everything, absolutely everything, that satisfied and sustained that ache.

"I told you he was batshit crazy," Gerald says when Weldon finishes. Dr. Thomas holds up her hand again. "I'm concerned, Mr. Trulane."

Samuel, tired and hungry, is ready to head back to the townhouse. He's about to add to the mix, pointing out that Weldon's problem is that he never talks or listens. Instead he searches out captive audiences and gives speeches.

He stops short of delivering that observation though when he looks over and sees that Weldon Trulane III is crying uncontrollably.

THE LENGTH OF DAYS — TWENTY-EIGHT

Carl Adkin is off-shift and out of uniform and sitting in the family car, a 2006 Ford Escape, its paint job lightened by at least two shades from the South Carolina sun. He's parked near the southern border of Garrison Park a block away from the Maxwell Pest Control billboard featuring a large dead rat on its back and the company name and phone number underneath in blocky red letters.

There's a large takeout coffee, cooled now beyond drinking, resting on the dash. Carl has his cellphone out and is thinking about calling his wife again to see if her period has started. Linda is only a few days late, but her periods are usually regular and on time. Carl is not sure how he feels about another kid possibly on the horizon. He seems to change his mind about it every fifteen minutes.

Police work often felt like a Rube Goldberg Machine. You had a clear end in sight, but how you got there, if you got there, took some strange and unpredictable paths. Technically, though, Carl had to admit what he was now doing didn't exactly qualify as police work. The line, however, between police work and off-the-books work could all too easily blur or disappear altogether at times.

It was like this: there were twelve dead girls and two missing. The Eric guy appeared to be responsible. No one had a last name on him. As far as Carl can tell, Magnolia Beach homicide had no real leads pointing to the Eric guy. They didn't seem to know he existed or if they did, were keeping it under wraps. Homicide's investigation seemed tailored for local, regional, and national sound-bites. The investigation was a lot of movement but with no real direction. Carl's off-the-book work for Johnny Doc Nowell followed the opposite dynamics. He knew what he needed to do, but getting there had turned out to carry its own complications.

Carl needed to find the Eric guy, but everything went Rube Goldberg after that. To find Eric, he needed to find his snitch Wayne Summer, but to find Wayne Summer, Carl needed the tips from a homeless man named Mitch who believed Jesus was landing his flying saucer in Garrison Park in order to ferry the truly faithful to their heavenly home and reward, and Carl once he found Wayne Summer needed Wayne to point him to his friend and dopehead pal Gary Lidd who it seemed to have worked out some kind of arrangement with the Eric guy at the house and the women at 805 Jefferson.

In the meantime, the Bowen Brothers, Don and Danny, expected restitution for the dead women who had been in transit at the safe house. Carl was hoping that Johnny Doc Nowell stayed alive long enough to pay for the off-the-books work he had commissioned.

Johnny Doc had bought himself a little time with Kwan Lee standing in for him. That had worked out even better than expected. The Bowen Brothers' Muscle had taken the impersonation at face value. Kwan Lee had ended up with a couple broken ribs, a bruised kidney, mild concussion, and some future dental work.

Carl powers down the window on the Escape. He empties the cooled cup of coffee. His cellphone begins buzzing. He lets it run to Voicemail. He waits a full minute before checking it.

It's okay, his wife says. *I'm bleeding.*

Carl can't read her tone. He is relieved and angry at the news.

He watches a line of sparrows spin across his windshield and into the park.

And then, less than fifteen minutes later, he spots Wayne Summer skulking outside the park entrance. It's as if the birds have flushed him out.

Carl starts the Escape. He follows Wayne down the street. When Wayne is abreast a Toyota, Carl hits the gas and angles, pinning Wayne between the Escape and Corolla. He powers down the driver's side window the rest of the way.

"You've been AWOL, Wayne."

Wayne starts wiping at his nose. "Not intentionally, Officer Adkin. Just busy."

"What are you on?" Carl asks.

Wayne looks down and then away. "Busy. A lot. It's been that."

Carl reaches out the window and taps Wayne's wrist. "That's not what I asked you, Wayne."

"It wasn't?"

"I'm looking for a friend of yours," Carl says. "Let's start there. I need you to focus, Wayne. It's important." Carl waits a moment. "Gary Lidd."

Wayne starts trying to edge away from the Toyota, but Carl opens the door of the Escape, cutting him off.

"Gary Lidd's my friend," Wayne says.

"That's already been fully established," Carl says. "What hasn't is what you intend to do to help me find him."

THE LENGTH OF DAYS

Wayne tilts his head. "And if I do?"

Carl levels his smile and locks in his gaze. "We're beyond bargaining, Wayne. You need to understand that. I need to find Gary Lidd. Yes or no, can you help? Your answer will determine whether I let you keep that dope you're carrying or bust you."

"Okay, okay, okay." Wayne pulls out a cellphone. "What am I supposed to say?"

"Anything that will get him to meet you at Pinewood Bowling in the next hour."

Wayne squints, furrowing his brow, then punches in a number and turns away, swiveling at the hips and talks in low tones, then less than a minute later, turns back to Carl and tells him that things are okay and in place.

"Hop in then," Carl says.

Wayne looks right, then left. "I was thinking we were done here."

"In your case, thinking will always get you in trouble," Carl says. "Hop in."

Once Wayne's inside, Carl cuffs him and tells him he'll take them off when they get to the Pinewood. Carl then drops the Escape into Drive. The Pinewood's on the other side of town, a good half hour drive, given afternoon traffic.

Wayne's a compendium of slow-motion twitches and scratching. His skin has taken on the texture and color of hardboiled eggs. He's wearing a small tarnished silver skull earring and a camo jacket with a half dozen pockets, a faded green tee-shirt, and a pair of jeans that look two sizes too large and which are held up by a yellow and black banded bungee cord in lieu of a belt.

"You got Gary all wrong," Wayne says. "In fact, me too."

Carl nods. "No doubt. You two are charter members of the Universally Misunderstood Club, right?"

Wayne looks out the passenger window. "The police turn everything into a joke that isn't one."

"You see me wearing a uniform, Wayne?"

He turns back to Carl. "I was wondering about that." Then the delayed-action light switch and the bulb finally coming on, and Wayne says, "Oh shit."

Carl takes a right on Hanover Street that will lead to Old Market Boulevard. He's thinking about the child that had almost entered his days and what he'll say to his wife Linda when he gets home later today. *I'm sorry* or *I love you* feels paltry and inadequate right now.

There are times when he'd like to be able to live outside words. When his days could be governed by something like muscle memory.

"It was the hamburgers and the smoke detector," Wayne says. "That's where everything started."

Carl glances down at the dash clock. Wayne continues explaining what happened at 805 Jefferson that led to the fire and twelve dead bodies.

According to Wayne, Gary Lidd made good hamburgers. Medium-well, just shy of pink inside, they were his specialty. Fourteen hungry women eat a lot of hamburgers.

Earlier in the day, pre-hamburgers, Gary was putting up a new smoke detector. Just after he put the nail in the wall, he set down the hammer to take a phone call. Then he went to look for batteries, but before he located them, he figured he'd better start supper for the women and started frying up the first round of burgers. He had the skillet popping when suddenly a girl ran down the hallway past the kitchen. The guy named Eric chased her. Gary kept frying burgers until he heard screaming from the front lawn. When he ran outside, he saw the Eric guy hitting one of the girls. Gary waved, trying to get him to stop. Then two more girls ran out of the house. Gary couldn't get Eric to quit hitting the first woman. There was a storm and a green car at the curb. The driver hit the horn, and Eric dragged the woman toward the car. Back in the house, Gary had forgotten to turn off the stove, and the hamburgers started a grease fire. Gary started to call the fire department, but Eric stopped him. Eric had also dragged the woman he killed back into the house. The fire kept getting bigger. Eric told Gary they needed to leave. He didn't tell Gary he'd taken the hammer and box of nails and nailed the door shut on the other girls in the walk-in pantry. Then there was a lot of smoke and heat and screaming. Eric ran. So did Gary.

Carl doesn't say anything. He turns right on East 4th Street. They pass the Andover Middle School, then three blocks that segue into a steady mix of stores and strip malls holding eclectic collections of small businesses, everything from tanning salons to florist shops to vacuum sales and repairs.

"You don't believe me, do you?" Wayne says when they stop for a light. "I just told you what happened, man."

"I believe you believe what Gary told you," Carl says. "But you weren't at the house when everything went sideways. There's that and the fact that you put shit in your veins, Wayne, and those veins carry that shit

THE LENGTH OF DAYS

to your brain. Bottom line, you're tainted. Everything that lives in your head is tainted."

"Tainted doesn't mean it isn't true." Wayne looks down at his cuffed hands and then out the window at the sign for Pinewood Bowling.

The Pinewood is one of Johnny Doc Nowell's properties that the bank has foreclosed on but not been able to unload. Johnny Doc explained that it's still possible to gain access through the back because the bank has been careless about changing locks. Carl takes the Escape through the empty front lot and parks it out of sight at the rear of the building.

He uses the keys Johnny Doc had given him to let Wayne and him in. Then he opens the front doors from within. They're still chained on the outside, but there's space enough for a body to squeeze through.

Carl turns back to Wayne. "You sure Gary's coming?"

Wayne starts nodding. "Yes. He's my friend. He trusts me. He promised he'd show."

THE LENGTH OF DAYS — TWENTY-NINE

The Crosshairs Firing Range is the eastern anchor of a strip mall on Newberry Street in northwest Magnolia Beach. The slot, formerly Baylor's Barbershop, next to it is empty, and that's followed by Healthy You, Frank's Subs, and Hanover Realty.

Samuel Fulton has been spending three days a week practicing at the Crosshairs with the Bersa 380. He's surprised to find he's adept with the pistol. More than adept. According to the manager, Davis Tremont, Samuel is a natural. He knows how and where to place his shots. Samuel attributes each to his years working at Ryland Iron and Steel as a welder, the combination of muscle memory and a dead-on eye. Aiming and pulling a trigger were almost too easy. He shredded the targets crossing his field of vision over and over again.

At first, the half-torso silhouettes at the Crosshairs were conveniently abstract, and Samuel concentrated on grouping his shots—head or heart—until they were a tight cluster. It took a while before he started to put a face on the silhouette.

But he had. Eventually it became natural to imagine the overripe features of the young man who sat across from him in the coffee shop at the base of the Mission Field Pier. The young man with the lively dead eyes who'd shown him a cellphone photo of Glenda with the top half of her nightgown pulled to her waist. The young man who'd snapped a young woman's neck.

Samuel did not have a name for him, but Samuel would never again forget his features, and Samuel kept working on where to aim and place the shots.

This afternoon, though, at the Crosshairs something else has happened, something Samuel is not prepared for.

Samuel has managed to ambush himself.

The target with the anonymous silhouette had become the young man with the All-American features, but then returns to the black silhouette, and when he finds himself superimposing the features of men he suspects may have slept with his wife, Samuel keeps firing and reloading and firing again.

Samuel has never seen an iceberg firsthand, but it has become all too easy to imagine accidentally sailing into one, the love letter its tip and

THE LENGTH OF DAYS   **129**

the immensity of the dark mass hidden below the surface portending all the confusion and despair that the letter produces whenever Samuel lets himself think about the accumulated mass of illicit details beneath the days of his marriage.

But by the end of his session at Crosshairs, there is nothing more than shredded paper from the targets, nothing more and nothing changed.

Samuel crosses the parking lot, unlocks the Taurus, and eases into the front seat. He waits a moment before slipping the key into the ignition. Right now, he wants to forget real or metaphorical icebergs.

Samuel drives back to the townhouse at the Bayview Complex. With the aid of a couple detours and cut-through shortcuts, he's able to beat the headaches of rush hour traffic.

He's surprised to find the townhouse empty. No sign of Weldon Trulane III. No note either. On the floor near the couch, he picks up two sections from a discarded *Magnolia Beach Monitor*. He takes them to the dining room table, opens each section, and spreads their pages across the top. Samuel sets the Bersa 380 down and then unpacks his cleaning kit, laying out the muzzle guard, oil, brushes, solvent, aluminum cleaning rod, and cotton patches.

A long growl from his stomach reminds Samuel he had missed lunch. He stops to build a ham sandwich, then garnishes it with a couple dill pickles, and adds a handful of chips. On impulse he decides to follow up with a cold beer.

He carries everything into the living room and turns on the television and settles back on the couch. While he eats, Samuel watches a news segment called *This Week At The Beach* highlighting local events, and then a special on bracketology for March Madness, all of which is heavily interspersed with commercials for new and used cars, fast food restaurants, heating and cooling repairs, banking and investment services, over-the-counter and prescription drugs, and lawyers specializing in personal injury suits.

His stomach full and the beer almost done, Samuel feels the accumulated effects of a long stretch of nights broken by persistent insomnia and some deeply entrenched bad dreams. He starts to drift into a nap, barely registering a commercial with two overweight men named Don and Danny who are pitching some cleaning service named Floor to Ceiling opening soon in Magnolia Beach. The last thing Samuel remembers hearing before dropping off is "No Job Too Large or Too Small or Too Dirty for us and Floor to Ceiling."

Asleep, Samuel catches a small reprieve. His dreams are summer-run, their details first cousins to actual memories, and those memories sweet and with a half-century reach which leaves them a little blurred at the edges but still real enough to hold some of their original juice.

Glenda and Samuel on the porch of their house in Ryland, Ohio. The heart of a Midwestern summer night. The drunken weave of bats. The distant sound of a train. Closer, a neighbor playing a Top-40 radio station. The air July-heavy. A bone-white half-moon. Glenda with a glass of wine, Samuel with a cold beer. Glenda in a thin summer dress, her long legs bare. Samuel in a pair of jeans and a white Saturday end of work T-shirt. The night ripening around them and Glenda lightly touching the back of Samuel's hand and Samuel following her into the house and up the stairs to their bedroom where they undress and map the longitude and latitude of their desire.

At what sounds like a toilet flushing, Samuel wakes up. He's disoriented at first. He looks around and checks his watch. His nap has ballooned into an hour and a half. His neck is stiff. The television is running a trailer for a movie about creatures giving off electrical charges.

Samuel climbs to the second floor. He figures a long shower will set him up. He grabs a towel from the linen closet and walks down the hall to his bedroom.

Where he finds Weldon Trulane III standing at his maple dresser with the top drawer open.

Samuel clears his throat.

Weldon starts to close the drawer, stops, and turns. "Mighty sorry, Samuel. Didn't mean to wake or bother you. You looked peaceful there, on the couch."

"What are you doing in my bedroom?"

Weldon tosses out a quick smile. "I was thinking about borrowing the car. I needed the keys."

"They're not up here. You know that. They're hanging in the kitchen where they always are."

"Okay, okay," Weldon says.

"Okay what?"

"Don't get all Perry Mason on me," Weldon says. "I was looking for your wallet. I needed to borrow a little walking-around cash."

"You could have just asked," Samuel says.

"Well, you know," Weldon says with a half-shrug. "Among friends."

"I thought that's what we were."

THE LENGTH OF DAYS

"Whoa there, Samuel."

Samuel remains in the doorway. He decides to keep pushing. "Okay then. What's in your hand?"

Weldon cups his right ear. "Sorry. Didn't catch that."

"There's nothing wrong with your hearing, Weldon." Samuel's jaw feels heavy and tight. "I'm still waiting."

"For what?"

"For you to tell the truth," Samuel says. "To not make me shame it out of you. And maybe a chance to get my anger under control because right now it barely is."

"Aw shit. It was just a couple paragraphs, that's all," Weldon says. "You told me about it, so I was curious, okay? I wanted to take a look for myself."

Samuel starts into the room, stops, and backs to the doorway. "Not the point."

"Oh, I almost forgot," Weldon says. "With you, there's always got to be a point."

"Well, what about this one?" Samuel says. "What about you packing your stuff and getting the hell out of my house?"

Weldon looks down, but Samuel just catches the abrupt and confused hybrid of anger, panic, and fear crossing Weldon's features.

"It's just a goddamn letter," Weldon says after a moment.

Samuel doesn't retract what he said and steps aside to let Weldon pass. He waits for the inevitable *Fuck You* and then the slam of the front door before he crosses the room to the chest of drawers and picks up the love letter someone had written to his wife.

It's not just a goddamn letter, Samuel thinks. It's a rent in the known fabric of his universe, the black hole swallowing everything he held close and believed true.

He slips the letter back into the envelope and replaces both in the top drawer. He checks a second envelope, one that's unmarked and holds his emergency cash fund: three hundred in small bills. Now, courtesy of Weldon Trulane III, reduced to two tens, three fives, and a fistful of ones and an IOU that might as well have been written in disappearing ink.

Samuel sits on the edge of the bed. He listens to the silence descend. Then he gets up and takes a shower.

Later, as Samuel walks into the kitchen, he discovers what he should have realized earlier: the Bersa 380 and the keys to the Taurus are gone.

THE LENGTH OF DAYS – THIRTY

Carl Adkin stands behind the empty concession stand at Pinewood Bowling and watches Wayne Summer walk slow circles between lanes four and six. The empty shelves of the stand are all glass, and Carl's reflection is dim and watery, like something spilled and only partially dried.

On every other circuit, Wayne Summer lifts his hands and shakes the cuffs, rattling them and pleading, "Hey Officer Carl, come on, you told me you'd take them off when we got here."

"The eyes," Carl says. "I need to get used to what light we got here."

"The thing is, I'm asking because I need to use the bathroom." Wayne keeps making circuits, moving like an old man.

"How bad, exactly," Carl says.

"I don't think I should have ate those hot dogs for breakfast," Wayne says. "They're really fucking with my stomach."

"I'll only ask one more time," Carl says. "How bad, exactly?"

Wayne stops mid-circuit. He taps the front pocket of his camo jacket. "I need to get things right. Gary Lidd's my friend. Setting him up like this is doing things with my mind." He lifts his hand again, presenting the cuffs. "My head's not in a good place."

"It's where it usually is, Wayne," Carl says. "Up your ass." He sighs and moves to the front of the concession stand and takes out his keys. Wayne holds out his hands. Carl uncuffs him. Wayne starts toward the bathroom.

"Hold it," Carl says. "Your cellphone, Wayne. Hand it over. Then you can go about getting your head where's it's supposed to be."

Wayne hands over the phone and starts shuffling across the rest of the lanes and eventually disappears into the men's room.

The light in the Pinewood is like the one in a theatre just before the movie starts. Carl watches Wayne's cell come to life. A text from Gary Lidd. *Almost there.*

Carl texts back. *Front door's unlocked.* He doesn't want Gary Lidd to see the Escape parked in the rear of the Pinewood and get spooked. He's counting on the element of surprise and the opportunity to extract some answers from Gary.

Carl double-checks the door and steps to the right where he'll be out

THE LENGTH OF DAYS
133

of the light when it's opened. He checks the safety on the Walther P22, a throwdown he'd pocketed from a small-time catch and release drug bust a year ago.

Carl's calm. He's focused. He's thinking Slot, the inevitable way people and things fit when you understood your place.

He needs Gary Lidd to cough up the full name of the Eric who'd been at 805 Jefferson when all the young women died. He'll deliver the name to Johnny Doc Nowell, collect his finder's fee, and step aside. Johnny Doc can take it from there. Carl's part in the whole deal will be over except for cashing a check.

That's the whole point of a Slot. Carl understood the depth and width of its fit.

Carl tilts his head, listening to a car approach the Pinewood. The engine needs a tune-up. The car coughs to a stop. Carl listens carefully, making sure there is only one door that opens and closes.

A moment later, Gary Lidd enters the Pinewood. With the front doors partially open, and in the slice of available light, Gary Lidd is the Gary Lidd that Carl has always known: a skinny guy with bad posture and rockabilly sideburns and the flattened oval-shaped face of an owl and a chin dotted in an archipelago of blackheads.

Gary moves deeper into the Pinewood and starts calling out for Wayne. Carl closes the distance between them in three quick steps and has the Walther P22 pressed against the back of Gary Lidd's head before Gary can turn it in Carl's direction.

"A lot of people have been looking for you, Gary." Carl taps his neck with the Walther. "And those people have a lot of questions about 805 Jefferson. I, on the other hand, only have one."

"I didn't do anything wrong." Gary glances back over his shoulder. "I just helped out around the house. Little things, you know, like cooking."

"Wayne has already filled me in about your legendary culinary skills with ground beef." Carl lifts the Walther and taps the right side of Gary's neck twice. "I'd like to hear about your friend Eric instead."

"He's not my friend. The guy's a Freak. Doesn't matter if he's good-looking or has money." Gary starts shaking his head. "A Freak's a Freak."

"Why'd you let him in the house then?"

Gary glances over his shoulder again. "You listening? I told you he's a Freak with money. You have any idea how much Johnny Doc pays for watching the girls and keeping things going? I mean, this Eric shows up at the house. I look the other way until he's done. I get paid.

Sometimes, on the side, a little dope too. What he called gratuities." Gary's voice breaks. "I mean, come on, can you blame me? How about a break here? I needed the money. I got a kid on the way."

"You might get to meet him yet," Carl says. "All I need is a full name for this Eric you say is not your friend."

"I'm not sure that's such a good idea." Gary lifts his arms in surrender and slowly turns to face Carl. "They guy is not just a Freak in the bedroom. I saw what he did to that girl and her neck." He waits a moment before adding, "The thing I'm saying is that I haven't been hiding from you. It's him I was. The guy is bad news and serious."

Wayne Summer opens the bathroom door and zombie-walks toward the first lane. Carl waves Gary in that direction too. They stop at the head of the lane near a cardboard box filled with mismatched bowling shoes and discarded pins.

"Show time," Carl says and keeps the barrel of the Walther pointed at the middle of Gary's forehead.

"Okay, okay," he says. "You asked for it. Remember that."

"I'm still waiting."

Gary looks over at Wayne who's slowly weaving, trying to keep his balance. "Eric Findley," he says. "That's the guy's name. Eric Findley."

Carl nods, smiles, and says, "There we go. That wasn't so bad." Carl starts to lower the Walther and realizes the mistake a heartbeat or two too late when Gary Lidd takes one step toward him and knees him in the groin.

The Walther jumps off his fingertips and slides toward the concession stand. Gary picks up a bowling pin from the box. Carl tries to roll over, but Gary brings the pin down on his right shoulder. Carl fights his way through an electric blizzard of pain. He momentarily loses sight of Gary and kicks out and manages through blind luck to hook Gary's ankle and pull him off his feet.

Then it's an inarticulate struggle, a clumsy collection of flailing arms, fists, knees, and feet, Gary calling out to Wayne for help the whole time.

Carl, momentarily pinning Gary, sees Wayne approaching in his peripheral vision and Wayne fumbling with one of the pockets on the camo jacket.

Wayne loses his balance while trying to pull something from a pocket. He falls on Carl and Gary, adding more flailing to the mix.

Then Carl sees what Wayne is fisting.

A syringe.

THE LENGTH OF DAYS

Carl kicks Wayne twice, then forearms Gary, rolls off, and starts for the Walther lying at the base of the concession stand.

Wayne yells out, "Too late, fucker. I got you. Just delivered an oldie but goodie. A speedball express. Welcome to Heart Attack City."

Carl grabs the Walther. Gary's on his feet and coming fast at him with the bowling pin again.

Carl shoots him in the chest and head.

"Oh shit," Wayne says.

Carl leans against the concession stand. He's choking. His breath feels miles away.

"Oh shit," Wayne says again. "I missed. I thought it was yours." He points to his left leg. The syringe is buried in his thigh.

Carl continues to lean against the concession stand. He listens to Wayne rasping his way through an overdose, Wayne invoking his mother and what Carl assumed was a childhood pet, a dog named Maxi.

It takes Wayne another five and a half minutes to die.

Carl tucks the Walther behind his back in the waistband of his jeans. He's thinking fingerprints, where he left them and how many.

Once he erases his presence, it should be a straightforward move to pass off the scene as a drug deal gone bad. It's practically paint-by-the-numbers. All he needs to be is careful and methodical in the setup.

Carl finds an old tee-shirt in the box with the discarded shoes and pins and then steps over to Wayne's body and uses the sleeve of the T-shirt to pull out the syringe. He replaces it in the pocket of the camo jacket and starts to work out the correct angles for the placement of the two shots. He moves Wayne's arm sixty degrees to the northeast.

He's about to pull out the Walther and put it in Wayne's hand when someone steps through the front door and says, "I told you kids to stay out of here. This is private property."

Carl recognizes the voice. He's known it for most of his life.

"Easy," Carl says. "It's me, Truman." He slips the Walther in the back of his jeans.

Truman Cooke, Carl's fellow officer, best friend, neighbor, godfather to Carl's three kids, and closest thing Carl has to a brother, steps over. He looks down at where Gary Lidd has bled out, then over at Wayne whose skin is already starting to take on a pale blue tint. Finally, Truman looks at Carl.

Seemingly out of nowhere, Carl flashes on Salt and Pepper, the derogatory nickname Truman and he had been tagged with as kids.

The nickname had followed them through high school where it changed tone and became part of the cheering when they stepped onto the football field and changed again into a private joke between them when they joined the force.

Salt and Pepper. You couldn't have one without the other.

Truman's standing six feet away from Carl. His hand has moved and now rests on the holstered butt of his Glock 9. He keeps his gaze steady. He's giving Carl a chance to explain though it's becoming more and more apparent by the second that Carl can't produce anything approaching an explanation that will satisfy Truman. Carl's out of uniform and off-duty and there's no little blood, literally and figuratively, on his hands.

Officer Truman Cooke who doesn't split hairs or take shortcuts or cut corners or look the other way or do anything that might be construed as compromising himself. Truman's strictly by the book. He's proud to have set up shop in every cliché and stereotype for a good man and good cop. Truman would never separate the two.

"I'm waiting, Carl."

Carl can't meet Truman's gaze. He also can't dismantle a thought that's slowly taking shape and gaining weight.

"At least give me a who, Carl. You told me you were clean." Truman lets out his breath. "Every time I asked. That's what you said. Clean."

Forever, Carl thinks. I will be, damned forever. He can't go further than that, but he's afraid of the things that are gathering in his head.

"It was Johnny Doc Nowell," Truman says. "That's the who, isn't it?"

Carl nods.

Truman unsnaps his holster. "You know where this is going." He doesn't pose it as a question.

Carl throws out an eleventh-hour appeal. "Just this once, Truman. I know I fucked up bad. But it wasn't for me. It was for Linda and the kids. The money was good and right there." Carl closes his eyes for a moment. "All you have to do is back off, Truman. Turn around and leave as if you were never here."

Truman hesitates for one agonizingly long moment before he finally pulls out the cuffs and tells Carl to turn around. He begins to read Carl his rights.

Forever, Carl thinks. I will damn myself forever.

Carl starts to turn around. Truman is ready with the cuffs.

"I'm sorry, Carl," Truman says.

Carl, mid-turn, pulls the Walther P22 and shoots Truman. He was

THE LENGTH OF DAYS

going for a quick head-shot, but his aim is off, and he ends up shooting Truman in the neck.

There's a bright red arterial fountain each time Truman moves.

Truman opens his mouth. He's trying to find his words when Carl leans over and sets the Walther against Truman's lower teeth and pulls the trigger.

Carl steps back and closes his eyes and counts slowly to one hundred. He picks up the T-shirt he'd found earlier and starts wiping down the scene.

Forever, Carl thinks. He remembers a message board he'd once seen outside a church while on patrol. *Forever is God's Clock.*

He puts the Walther P22 in Wayne Summer's hand.

He takes out Truman's Glock 9 and puts it in Truman's right hand.

He double-checks the shooting angles.

Let the others sort out and come up with a reasonable scenario about drug deals gone wrong and three dead bodies at Pinewood Bowling.

Most likely, the way the investigation will play, Truman Cooke will come out a hero.

Carl, at least, can give his best friend that.

THE LENGTH OF DAYS – THIRTY-ONE

A pale orange sunset bisects the rearview mirror each time Pam Graves glances up at it. She's parked a half block down from the Second Wave Bookstore. She's been sitting there ten minutes and hasn't turned the Hyundai off yet.

Her cellphone goes off. "You coming in?" her mother asks, "or are you going to sit there all night?"

Pam Graves closes her eyes for a moment, then she drops the car into Drive but doesn't touch the gas. She can see her mother watching her from the front window of the store.

She turns off the car and gets out and cuts across the street on a diagonal and continues up the block. Foot traffic is minimal tonight.

The Second Wave is housed in a former neighborhood grocery, part of a four block gentrification project in North Magnolia Beach.

Painted on the front door underneath the store's name and street number is the Second Wave's slogan: *There's no testosterone on these shelves!*

Along the walls of the Second Wave are a series of poster-sized framed photos of Betty Friedan, Simone de Beauvoir, Gloria Steinem, Kate Millet, Germaine Greer, Bell Hooks, Alice Walker, and Adrienne Rich. When Pam was an early middle-schooler and visiting the store, her mother would test her on the name of each woman. Pam, self-conscious and eager to please, froze up every time until she came up with *Best save good karma. Go back and arrive.* Pam, whispering to herself, attached the first letter of each word to the sequence of photos and managed to gain her mother's approval, but the approval was short-lived after her mother picked up on the mnemonic device and began mixing up the order of the photos. Pam went back to tongue-tied.

"What were you doing out there?" her mother asks.

"Deciding."

"I could use a glass of wine," her mother says. She walks over to the door and flips the "Sorry, We're Closed" sign streetward. She then hooks her arm with Pam's and leads her to the rear of the store where there is a small area that passes for a reading room or lounge. There are a hot-plate, coffee pot, and a small dorm-sized refrigerator along one wall, a faded floor rug, a couple chairs, a small couch, and coffee table.

THE LENGTH OF DAYS

She pours each of them a glass of white wine. "It's good to see you," she says. "You don't come around much anymore."

Her mother's wearing her customary look: a white oxford shirt, tight jeans, and espadrilles, her silver-white hair in a thick ropey braid falling past the middle of her back. No make up.

Her head-turning longevity is intimidating because Pam's mother has always taken it for granted or doesn't seem to notice it at all. Pam's conscious of the contrast, her five-feet-four to her mother's five-eleven, the extra eight to ten pounds she's carrying, the faint but still anachronistic spray of freckles. Pam's always been saddled with "cute" and on occasion "pretty."

"I've been calling all day," her mother says. "Leaving messages too."

"I'm here."

Her mother points at a hardback lying on the room's coffee table. It's entitled *Mirrors, Windows, and Doors* by someone named Josephine Tremont. Her mother had given Pam an early review copy and asks if Pam has read it yet.

"I've dipped into it."

"Nice try. I bet you didn't get beyond the table of contents if that."

"I haven't had the chance to start it, okay? I've been busy."

Her mother tops off each glass and hands one over to Pam. "Your hair, it looks good. Is that a new cut?"

It's Pam's turn. "Nice try, Mom."

Her mother drains half her glass, then reaches over and refills it. "Okay then."

With her mother, it's always been an *Okay then.*

"What?" Pam asks.

"A favor."

Pam waits out a full answer.

"I lost track of the time," her mother says, "so the favor."

"I don't know."

"Barton's Bar and Grill," her mother says. "Your father. A favor. A couple details."

"A couple details?" Pam says. "You mean lies."

"Let's call it a little corroboration. Nothing more than that."

"What is it this time?"

Her mother once again drains half her glass and refills it. She holds the bottle up to Pam, but Pam waves it off.

"I lost track of the time," her mother says. "I was in Charleston for the day with a friend and got back late. I was supposed to meet your

140   **LYNN KOSTOFF**

father at Barton's Bar and Grill for drinks and a meal." She waits a moment before adding, "It was one of your father's 'special anniversaries,' you know, the ones only he keeps track of. In this case, it was at Barton's that he supposedly first said he loved me."

"And you want me to help explain away your absence."

"Unruffle a few feathers, yes." Her mother smiles. "When it comes to our lives together, your father never forgets. He's just never been very good at noticing things."

Therefore, Pam thinks, a couple details. A little corroboration. When it comes to his wife, Dave Graves always took all her lies, excuses, and evasions at face value. And Pam, the perpetual family peacemaker, had inevitably helped to maintain the status quo.

Catherine Connolly-Graves and Dave Graves: the couple that had always seemed anything but. People commented on that behind her parents' backs. Those that didn't more than likely thought it. The surprise, the shock, the incredulity of seeing them together, her mother statuesque and running on full-bloom beauty, her father four inches shorter with a countenance whose features seemed like an afterthought. The same deep differences holding true with their personalities too. Pam, like everyone else, wondering what had brought and kept them together.

She's still not sure she can answer that now.

"Charleston and a friend," Pam says. "He have a name?"

"Yes," her mother says, "but it's beside the point."

"Don't you ever get tired of it all?" Pam asks. "All the long-term cheating? The lies?"

Her mother pours more wine. "I asked for a favor, Pam, not your judgment."

"I know, just a couple details, right?" Pam leans back in her chair. "Maybe I should tell him. Dad, I mean."

Her mother sits up a little straighter. "Really? Now, after all this time? You're going to do that to him?"

Pam nods. "Maybe I should."

A text pops up on her mother's cellphone. It's followed by another. The phone is on the table next to the wine. Her mother glances at the phone message and then points at the bottle. "You'd better hurry and catch up. This one's on the way out."

Pam waves off the offer. "I'm good."

Her mother shrugs and tops off her glass. "FYI, Daughter, your father knows. He has for a long time."

THE LENGTH OF DAYS

Pam frowns. "Why all the lies then?"

"Because," her mother says, "there's knowing and then there's *knowing*. The world's built on arrangements, and those arrangements are built on questions you don't ask and answers you don't question." Her mother tips the wineglass in Pam's direction. "That's the closest thing to happiness for us mortals, Honey."

Pam looks away, toward the front of the store. The streetlights have turned the front window of the Second Wave opaque.

Another text pops up on her mother's phone. A moment later, the phone starts ringing. Her mother ignores both.

"A couple details," she prompts. "Bottom line, we both love him. It's why each of us goes so far to protect him." Her mother waits until Pam makes eye contact. "You'll lie to him to protect him, and he knows, no matter what, that I'll save him from the full truth and never leave him. That's Dave Graves, husband and father."

Not for the first time, Pam has the sensation that her mother can read her mind, and Pam starts wondering if things will ever change between her mother and her. The title of the book next to Pam's wineglass—*Mirrors, Windows, and Doors*—now feels vaguely accusatory, as if Pam had run her life avoiding each and every one of them and what they held or led to.

"I don't know how you can live with yourself." Pam's words, unexpected, surprising even herself, and in that moment, she can't say for sure if she's talking about her mother or herself.

"Don't ask that unless you're ready to hear the answer," her mother says, keeping her voice even. "And I can tell by looking at you, you're not." She stops and looks out the front window of the Second Wave, then back at Pam. "You may think you're ready, but you're not. Not by a short or a long or any kind of a shot."

THE LENGTH OF DAYS – THIRTY-TWO

Donell—P for Purple—Hayes is the de facto mayor of twelve square blocks in South Magnolia Beach, a mini-province that enjoys a separate peace from the standard-issue poverty, squalor, and violence of the blocks surrounding it. It's a hard-won peace and one maintained by Donell's early reputation and his present connections to the powers-that-be in greater Magnolia Beach.

Donell P. Hayes was known for saying that his left hand always knew exactly what the right was doing. He was also known for following that up with a wide smile meant to simultaneously put its recipient at ease and on guard.

Earlier in the evening, at the 4 Star Laundromat, Too-Wide, who'd brokered the intro to Hayes, had warned Arturo Morales about him. "Don't be trying to put anything over on Donell," he said. "Donell, his mind always working at the same time on three different level, and he gonna beat you on every one of them." He'd waited a moment, then added, "Donell, he plugged in, that's all I'm saying, and if you got even one ear, you heard what I meant."

Arturo parks on Amelia Street and checks his watch. Even with Saturday night traffic, he's on time for the meeting. He walks down the block to Hayes' office, a small squat building carrying the weight of borrowed authority. It had once been a post office substation, one that was eventually closed down by the Feds in a series of consolidation moves close to a decade ago.

Arturo gives his name to the man fronting the entrance, and after being checked for weapons, he's ushered inside where he takes a seat in a small waiting area with an old leather sofa and four matching chairs. The receptionist's desk is empty. Arturo is the only one in the room.

Then, a door softly opening and closing, followed by light footsteps, and Donell P. Hayes enters the room. He's wearing a nicely tailored light gray suit over a pale green shirt and a deep purple tie held in place with a diamond stickpin. His hair is cut close to his skull and beginning to gray on the sides, and he's sporting a goatee whose lines are as carefully defined as calligraphy.

Arturo swallows his self-consciousness and reminds himself why he's

THE LENGTH OF DAYS

here, but he can't quite get on the other side of the same sort of feeling that Luis Sorbano, Felina's husband, evokes in him, a sense of a divide that no wardrobe, money, or luck will ever be able to bridge.

For a long moment, Arturo Morales is afraid he'll never be more than Arturo Morales, a short dark-haired man in a pair of battered cross-trainers, black jeans, and light blue shirt with snap buttons.

Donell Hayes checks his watch, then looks at Arturo. "Let's take a walk."

They cross Amelia Street and start down Desmond. The evening's on locked-down Spring, and many of the neighborhood businesses have their doors open. Too-Wide had explained to Arturo that Donell had a controlling or significant interest in each of them.

They pass The Razor's Edge Barbershop, In Your Pocket Payday Loans, and Melanie G's Fashions. The sidewalks are crowded.

"Did you bring the money?" Donell asks.

Arturo nods and starts to reach for his back pocket, but Hayes stops his hand and says, "I just wanted it understood that this walk is all your money buys." Donell stops and turns to Arturo. "When I get to know you, I'll decide how much information you get or if I'll pass on any at all."

Donell Hayes starts walking again. He asks if Arturo has ever killed a man, woman, or child. Arturo answers no to each.

Hayes asks if Arturo has ever seen anyone die then. Arturo tells him he works at the Bayview Assisted Living Center and lets Hayes draw the rest of the conclusion.

They pass Papa Lou's Groceries, LaRhonda's Beauty Emporium, and Uncle Chad's Chicken Place.

"You need to have dirty hands before you can clean them," Hayes says. "I believe that's better and more to the point than the other way around. Too many people do it backward and then can't find the soap."

Arturo holds his hands out for inspection. "I'm not exactly a candidate for sainthood, Mr. Hayes." Too-Wide had filled Arturo in about Donell's past. If asked if he'd ever killed a man, woman, or child, Donell would say yes and leave it at that. The same held true if you asked him about selling guns, dope, or girls. The soap in Donell Hayes' life took the form of his marrying a beautiful woman some twelve years his junior who was the daughter of one of the inner circle of Magnolia Beach's Tourist Bureau and that woman delivering two bright and beautiful daughters of her own.

Donell Hayes had made sure he never ran out of soap. He also made sure people never forgot why he needed it in the first place.

They pass the Cloudy Day BBQ and Baba Jenny's Bakery and JAK's Used CDs and DVDs. Donell smiles and nods and occasionally stops to speak to someone in the crowd. It's Saturday night, and everyone is living in its pulse and moving things along.

"I'm curious about something," Hayes says. "You've been seen more than a few times around Houston Street parked across from the lot where the United Trucking warehouse burned down. Just sitting in your car. Looking at ashes. Why?"

They pass a bar called The Lounge, then Sister Mama's Psychic Center, and a half block later, a second bar named The Other Lounge. Arturo is aware of Donell Hayes' eyes on him the entire time.

"Silence is its own answer, Friend," Hayes says. "That and the change in your step and posture. I'd say there's some anger and hunger deep in you. Maybe deeper than you yourself know."

"I didn't come here to talk about me," Arturo says finally.

Donell stops to shake the hand of a man in a dark blue suit and open collar and then to kiss the cheek of the woman with him.

"Tell me, then, why I should help you," Hayes says when they start walking again.

"It's important that I find somebody."

"You know I don't need your money." Hayes stops and checks his reflection in the front window of Edwin's Pharmacy and readjusts the knot in his namesake purple tie.

"Why'd you agree to see me then?"

Hayes shrugs. "I heard some things. Was curious to see if they were true."

They stop at the Helping Hand Food Bank where Hayes tells the manager that the next delivery will be Monday before noon.

"What do you want to know?" Arturo asks finally. He's already decided he won't tell Hayes about the lot on Houston. That's mine, he thinks, not sure if it's anger or hunger or something else entirely that drives the decision.

"I would like your thoughts on Vaginas," Donell Hayes says. "Rare. Sweet. Necessary. How would you rank them?"

"You're serious," Arturo says. "That's what you want to know?"

Hayes nods. "Rare. Sweet. Necessary. How does that sound?"

Arturo frowns. "Backwards. That's how it sounds to me. It should be Necessary, Sweet, and Rare."

Donell Hayes nods and laughs. "What I'd expect from you. Spoken

THE LENGTH OF DAYS   **145**

like a True Romantic."

"I don't understand any of this."

"You've been showing a photo of a girl all over town. Why are you looking for her?"

"She's the niece of a friend of mine," Arturo says. "One of those trafficked girls that didn't burn up in that house fire."

"So you're not looking for this girl to put her out there yourself?"

Arturo shakes his head no.

"And I'm betting this 'friend' is more than that to you."

Arturo reluctantly shakes his head yes.

"And I'm betting there's something else there too," Donell says. "I'm betting it has something to do with your hands and how much dirt's on them."

Arturo looks down at the sidewalk, then up again.

They pass Closet Consignments before he can find the words. "My friend's husband offered me money to find her. Enough that it was hard to turn down."

"A Romantic still has to eat," Donell says. "No shame in being hungry. And there's a lot of ways to feed that. Some worse than others. Some better."

Donell Hayes takes out his wallet, opens it, and shows Arturo a photo of his wife and two daughters.

"You wanted a name. It's Eric Findley," Hayes says, slipping the wallet back into his pocket. "This wouldn't be the first time Eric stepped over the line. His daddy is a big dog in Magnolia Beach tourism. Eric's had a Free Pass ever since his momma squeezed him out. Daddy's been there to make sure of that."

Eric Findley. Arturo repeats the name over and over to himself. Right now, it carries the same weight and promise as a check in the mail.

At the end of the block, they come to the entrance of a small playground. Next to its gate, there's a plaque announcing it's named for Donell Hayes Sr. Across the street is the tan-bricked and slender-steepled A.M.E. Church, and above the steeple is a sky whose stars have been eclipsed by the city's ambient light.

"There's something else you need to know," Donell Hayes says.

THE LENGTH OF DAYS — THIRTY-THREE

Dusk on Chestnut Lane in the Delmar Woods subdivision that Carl Adkin calls home and above it, the bats are doing elliptical cartwheels. Carl Adkin tracks their movement and cracks open another beer. He helped put Truman Cooke, his best friend and fellow patrolman, in the ground five and a half hours earlier.

When the family and he got back from the funeral, the Bayliner Element and its trailer were setting in the driveway. Webber Marine had screwed up and delivered the boat early. His wife Linda's birthday is still three days away.

Linda thanked him and kissed him on the cheek. She even tried to dredge up a small smile at the name painted across the Bayliner's bow—*Material Girl*—but her eyes were still red and almost swollen shut after she'd cried herself out at the funeral.

Carl's sitting behind the wheel of the Bayliner. He's wearing one of the two complimentary captain's caps that Webber Marine had left on the front seats. The cap's white with a shiny black bill trimmed in gold braiding. Linda's is the same except for pink braiding.

From his vantage point, he can see into the house and dining room where his wife and three kids are eating supper. Carl knows he should be inside with his family, but there's no room, right now, for anyone or anything except his dead friend. Carl's working his way through a new twelve-pack. He figures he's a beer or two from admitting to himself that Truman Cooke is dead and probably three or more before he can approach the truth that he himself had killed Truman.

In the meantime, he adjusts the fit of the captain's cap and watches the bats whirl and tumble through the twilight on a search and destroy for bugs.

He considers taking out his cell and calling Johnny Doc Nowell and putting the squeeze on him for the money he's owed. Carl had already talked to him twice, but he wants to remain in the forefront of Johnny Doc's thoughts. He, after all, had delivered the full name of the guy who had killed the women on Jefferson. Johnny Doc had promised the money soon and had even thrown in a bonus for Carl's patience. That should have been enough, but Carl had not liked the hesitation, however slight, when he'd talked to Johnny Doc the last time and what that

THE LENGTH OF DAYS **147**

hesitation might point to.

Carl breaks open another beer. He's decided to wait for a face to face with Johnny Doc Nowell when he can lean, and lean heavily, on him not only for what he's owed and the bonus but for a bonus on top of the bonus. Carl had done some checking into the Findley name and discovered how much cash and holdings underwrote it.

He palms the second of the three valiums he'd lifted from Linda's prescription that morning and chases it with a hit from the beer.

A little relief, that's all he can hope for. All day he's wanted to position himself just south of sober to keep himself cushioned against whatever his conscience threw his way.

The funeral had been excruciating. The Department had gone full platter—dress blues, music, and testimonials, and the church and gravesite had overflowed with Truman's and Denisha's families, friends, and neighbors. It was as if the crowd had invented grief. A good man had departed this life, and there was no place to hide from the raw yawning aftermath of that departure.

After the service, Carl stood in line with the others, and when his turn came, he hugged Denisha and the kids, and he said the words people at funerals expected to hear, and at the reception hall, he ate fried chicken and potato salad and baked beans and said more words people expected to hear, and eventually he ended up in a cluster of cops surrounding John McKelvey's Chevy Silverado and the coolers of iced-down beer, and Carl listened to them tell Truman Cooke stories, Carl tossing in a few of his own, and by the time the coolers were empty, Truman Cooke had pretty much been canonized into cop sainthood, and the talk then shifted to the crime scene and the fact that Truman had been holding the Glock in the wrong hand and the belief all around that two losers like Gary Lidd and Wayne Summer could never have gotten the drop on Truman except with an inordinate amount of blind luck, and probably not even then, the tailgate session ending with oaths to get to the truth and avenge Truman, preferably without the niceties of a trial.

Carl opens another beer and briefly rests the can against his forehead. He's still in his dress blues though the fit's decidedly tighter since the last time, probably a year ago, he wore them. He leans on the wheel of the Bayliner and watches Linda and the kids clear the table of supper dishes.

He looks around for the bats, but they've disappeared. The evening sky is fat with stars.

And Truman Cooke is standing at the end of the driveway.

For a moment, Carl is afraid he's going to come up and sit next to him in the Bayliner.

But Truman remains where he is.

Carl takes a long swallow of beer and then asks Truman what he's doing out of his grave.

Truman can't answer though because he's been shot in the neck, and each attempt at speech results in a hot spray of blood and deep gargling sounds.

"I'm sorry, Truman," Carl says. "You know I am. I wish it had been anyone else."

Except it hadn't been.

Carl looks up at the wide spill of stars. He's hoping Truman will be gone when he looks back down.

Truman Cooke is still there, however. He's given up trying to talk. Instead he's holding his hands out in front of him, and he is trying to bring them together.

He can't do it. It's like a sideways pantomime of clapping or a slow-motion palsy. His hands never quite meet. They approach, dip, and fall away.

Carl doesn't get it.

Truman won't quit.

Carl cracks another beer.

He's afraid Truman is going to be there all night bleeding out and doing the hand stuff.

He's halfway through the beer when he finally gets it.

"The Cypress Bar and Grill," Carl says. "Last summer."

Truman gives him a bloody smile. The hands continue moving.

Last June, Truman and Carl had spent the day fishing the Two Bridge River and late in the afternoon ran into McKelvey and Williams at the Cypress. A couple rounds in, Carl started in on his monster catfish story, limning his fight with the Moby-Dick-sized cat he'd pulled from the depths and almost landed.

Carl had been deep into the details, and McKelvey and Williams were smiling and laughing and nodding, not in appreciation of Carl's fishing prowess, but rather in reaction to Truman Cooke and his hand gestures, Truman standing behind Carl and constantly adjusting and readjusting the size of the catfish and Carl's lies.

All those hand gestures. Truman as usual insisting on the truth. Measuring it. Spelling it out for McKelvey and Williams and everyone else.

THE LENGTH OF DAYS — THIRTY-FOUR

Arturo Morales's first errand this afternoon is easier than the second. *Errand*, though, he's not sure if that's the word for either one, but he supposes it's close enough. There are days when words don't quite fit things, and you learn to live with approximations.

The sky outside and above Arturo's Chevy Impala, however, has no room for approximations. It is an adamant March blue and empty of clouds. Spring has elbowed its way into the day, and Arturo drives with the window down.

Samuel Fulton, sitting in the Impala's passenger seat, says, "I appreciate this, Arturo. The lift and everything else."

Arturo tells him no problem. Arturo had been ghosting the area around the Horizon Inn, hoping to catch sight of Eric Findley again and through him to finally locate Connie Fuentes, when he discovered Samuel Fulton's green Taurus setting in the northeast corner of the Horizon's rear parking lot.

Checking in with the bartender, Arturo discovered that Weldon Trulane III had put the car up as collateral to cover his bar tab. The bartender was holding the keys to the Taurus until Weldon or someone acting as his proxy paid up.

"Did he have any idea where Weldon is?" Samuel asks.

Arturo shakes his head no. "I'm sorry you and Mr. Weldon had a falling-out."

"It was bound to happen sooner or later. He is what we used to call a Bad Penny. I should have paid more attention." Samuel starts to roll up his window, stops halfway, and then seems unsure if he should continue or not. "I don't suppose the bartender managed to get ahold of the pistol Weldon took along with the car?"

Arturo again shakes his head no. His attention is snagged by how much at this moment Samuel Fulton reminds him of his father. Not physically, except perhaps for the same fencepost posture. More along the lines of how his values seemed to inform each breath. Two men run on duty, love, hard work, and a measured silence. Two men who smiled but had no sense of humor. Two men deadlocked with the world and their lives.

When Arturo leaves the downtown district and hits south Atlantic

Avenue, he runs into Spring Break, the street bursting with teenagers and twenty-somethings, all of whom are loud and only marginally sober, the mass of swimsuited bodies slowing and at times outright stalling traffic.

Samuel Fulton studies the action around them as if the swarm of bodies are scattered puzzle pieces he'll never be able to finally put together. All Arturo sees is a slew of young women unnecessarily complicating his search for Connie Fuentes. More hay on the stack holding the needle.

Arturo slowly noses the Impala through the crowds, piloting through a high tide of flesh and fun.

Seemingly out of the blue, Samuel Fulton asks him how old he is.

Samuel takes in the number and after a long moment says, "You may not believe this, but I can remember thirty-one. Every second of it. My life, Glenda, every second." He slowly shakes his head. "That there's a difference between remembering and understanding, though. That's something I'm just starting to see."

"Never found the right one," Arturo says three blocks later when Samuel asks him if he's married or ever been married. The lie is a lot less painful than the truth right then. Arturo does not want to revisit the wellspring of his feelings for Felina Fuentes and then his losing her to Luis Sorbano. Not today, on a full-bore spring afternoon when the weight of memory and the pull of blue skies and freshly-minted hormones are equally oppressive.

"The right one," Samuel says, carefully measuring and spacing each word, and Arturo waits for him to continue. When he doesn't, they drive the rest of the way in silence.

At the Horizon Inn, Samuel waves off Arturo's offer to help recover the Taurus and goes on to thank Arturo for the lift, and in a move that once again reminds Arturo of his father, Samuel insists on paying for the gas getting there, slipping a five and a couple singles into Arturo's front shirt pocket.

Which then leaves Arturo facing the second errand of the day.

Home Free, that's what Arturo had thought when Donell P. Hayes had given him Eric Findley's name. In his mind, Arturo was already more than halfway to finding and then rescuing Connie Fuentes and collecting on her return, things decidedly pointing in the direction of sweet until Donell had thrown in a coda of *There's something else you need to know.*

Twelve young women were dead. Connie and one other had escaped.

THE LENGTH OF DAYS   151

Arturo had assumed both were on the loose until Donell informed him that the grapevine was running the news that one of the two girls was dead. Donell had given Arturo the name of someone rumored to have disposed of a body a little over a week ago.

Talking to Clayton Beal is the second errand of Arturo's day.

West of the airport, Arturo starts taking secondary and back roads. Most of the roads are named after nearby local families or given blunt matter-of-fact designations based on landmarks. Greene Lane. Hawkins Way. Twin Oak Drive. Short Bridge Road.

The GPS on his phone is little help. Reception is weak and sporadic. It's a matter of pure luck that Arturo finally pulls into the washed-out driveway at 125 Crow's Nest Circle.

The mobile home had seen its better days at least a decade and a half ago. What's left is a couple steps from debris. The cement blocks serving as a foundation have settled unevenly so that the home lists like someone leaning in to hear better. The windows are covered in taped cardboard. There's a large satellite dish in the middle of the front yard, and near the front steps an aluminum garbage can overflowing with empty Old Milwaukee cans. Next to the doorframe are a couple holes that look like they'd fit a .38 caliber.

Arturo knocks and keeps knocking until the door is opened by a girl in her teens wearing a baggy Hilton Head sweatshirt, leather miniskirt, and cowboy boots. Below a thatched haircut holding competing shades of turquoise, magenta, and shoe-polish black, her complexion is pale and vaguely vampiric. Her left arm is sleeved from wrist to elbow with tattooed bands of tiny fish chasing each other head to tail.

The smile she gives Arturo is open and genuinely friendly, as if she'd been waiting all day for him to show up.

"You could if he was here," she says after Arturo asks if he can speak to Clayton Beal, "but he's in jail again. Parole Violation. He won't be out for another ten days."

"I really need to talk to him."

The girl tilts her head and looks over Arturo's shoulder at the Impala. "Maybe I can help you. Clay and me, we do everything together."

"I don't think so, but thanks."

She drops an expression that's a cross between a frown and pout. "Is this about guns? Dope? I can help out."

"That's okay," Arturo turns to leave. She grabs his shirt sleeve.

"Try me," she says. "I'll make you a deal." She points at the Impala and says she's stuck out here and running low on patience, pocket

152 LYNN KOSTOFF

money, beer, and cigarettes.

"No car?" Arturo asks, looking around.

"Clay loaned his to his cousin Justin when he got popped for the parole violation." The girl stops and slides her hand under the rolled bottom of the Hilton Head sweatshirt and pulls out a crumpled pack of cigarettes. She counts the number left, takes one out, and lights it with a yellow disposable lighter she's tucked in the waistband of the miniskirt.

"Justin's supposed to check in, see how things are going or if I need anything," she says, "but Justin is kind of an asshole." She looks straight at Arturo and smiles again. "I'll help you out with your problem if you help me out with mine," she says. "If it's not guns or dope, what? Sex?" She tries a different smile on Arturo.

Arturo makes a spur of the moment decision. "I heard if the price is right that Clayton can take care of all kinds of things. I heard he was a handyman." Arturo decides to leave it at that.

The girl starts shaking her head. "What's your problem? You shy or stupid? Why don't you just say what you want? I already told you, Clay and me, we do everything together. No secrets."

Arturo slowly lets out his breath. "Okay. I heard that Clayton got rid of a body for someone."

"That's it?" she says. "Well, he did."

"How long ago?"

The girl squints and starts counting off fingers. "Around a week ago. Maybe a little longer. He got paid good money for doing it too."

"Did you see the body?"

The girl nods. Arturo shows her the photo of Connie Fuentes. She gives an exaggerated shrug. "Could be. The body was in two taped-together plastic lawn bags. The only reason I know it was a girl is there was a hole at the bottom of one of them, and a part of a foot stuck out and it had toenails painted Cherry Bomb red." The girl points at her cowboy boots. "That's my shade too."

Arturo hopes against hope about the answer to his next question. He's afraid of the direction things are tending. "Did Clayton have a look at the body? You think he'd recognize her from the photo?"

The girl shakes her head no. "We met up with this guy and transferred the body from his trunk to ours. It was already wrapped in those bags."

"This guy have a name?"

"I didn't get it, but Clay probably knows." She drops the cigarette and toes it out. "The guy had the one-two punch going. He was good-looking

THE LENGTH OF DAYS

and rich. Clay said after to me that he paid top dollar. Me, I thought he was super-cute."

She takes out her cigarettes and counts them again. "Speaking of names," she says, looking up, "you never told me yours. Mine's Pru. Pru Daniels."

Arturo gives her his first but not last name.

She gives him the open smile and nods. "Cool. That's kind of like a Zorro name."

Arturo asks the question he's been avoiding. He asks Pru is she knows where the body is buried.

"Sure," she says. "I told you, Clay and me, we do everything together."

Pru then lays out the terms of the deal. She'll take Arturo to the burial site in exchange for three twenties walking-around-money and a lift into town afterward. Along the way, she needs Arturo to buy reinforcements, a carton of Newports and a twelve-pack of Old Milwaukee. She'll throw in the shovel from the back yard of the mobile home for free.

Arturo hesitates, but finally agrees. She joins him five minutes later carrying a backpack covered in unicorns and rainbows which she drops on the floor of the Impala and then points northeast. "First stop, cigs and beer, the Corner Market. It's two miles that way."

Arturo follows her directions, but he's turning his decision over and over again in his mind. He's not sure he can follow through. The shovel lying across the back seat is a line he's not sure he wants to cross.

"Man," Pru says, "you mind I play the radio? You're not exactly a conversationalist." She starts playing with the dials and a few moments later, squeals that she's found her favorite song.

"It's by a group called Mopeds on Saturn," she tells Arturo, "and the song is called 'Quit Parking in my Head'."

Then as Arturo's afraid she'll do, she joins in, her voice thin and girlish and just enough off-key to grate. "Quit leaving trails of bread/Quit crying in my bed/Quit laughing at the dead/Quit settling for instead/Quit counting the books I read/Quit repeating what's been said/Then maybe, yes maybe, you'll quit parking in my head."

Arturo's out of the Impala and in the Corner Market for the beer and cigarettes before Pru can get to the second verse.

It takes another half-hour to get to the burial site. Arturo drives through a mix of swamp and Low Country forest filled with stands of loblolly pine, magnolias, red cedar, live and water oaks, sweetgum and tulip trees, red maple, hemlock, dogwood, cypress, tupelo, black gum, and fan and sabal palmettos. Along the way, he leaves asphalt for gravel and gravel for dirt. Above them, the skyline is threaded with hawks and buzzards.

Pru directs him to a thirty-acre hole in the landscape, a stretch of clear-cut pine harvested by the timber companies and dotted with stumps and tangled groundcover running into more marshland at its south border. It's a landscape that looks as if it's been half-chewed and spit out.

Arturo pulls over and parks. Pru grabs her reinforcements and hops onto the hood of the Impala, sitting lotus-style and immediately cracking a Milwaukee and firing a Newport. She looks over Arturo's shoulder and says, "The big magnolia? Seven stumps to the left. That's where she's buried."

Arturo nods and starts walking toward the tree, but he's gone only a few steps before Pru calls him back and hands him a Newport and the lighter. It takes him a moment to understand why. It's been a week or more since the body's been in the ground. Wet, swampy ground under a warm spring sun. He tucks the cigarette behind his ear and drops the lighter in his pocket and starts down the field.

The magnolia is at the edge of the swamp. Arturo counts seven stumps. He jabs the blade of the shovel into the ground, but he can't lift his foot and take it further.

He's roofed houses. He's planted flowerbeds and mown lawns. He's painted rooms. He's washed dishes and bused tables. He's picked tomatoes and strawberries. He's changed oil and tires. He's stocked shelves. He's vacuumed, mopped, and buffed floors. He's loaded and unloaded trucks. He's laid flooring. He's moved furniture.

But he's never ever dug up a teenaged girl buried at the edge of a swamp.

And he's not sure he can do it now.

He does not want to have to deliver the news to Felina that her niece Connie has more than likely been raped on numerous occasions and now is dead. No one forgives someone delivering news like that.

There are moments, though, that are outside forgiveness. There's no room for anything but the least common denominator of breath. Everything else falls away. You're there. You're alive. You act. No excuses.

Arturo begins digging.

It doesn't take long. The ground is spongy, a step away from mud, and Clayton Beal didn't bother to bury the body any deeper than a few feet, barely outside the range of most scavenging animals.

THE LENGTH OF DAYS 155

Three more turns of the shovel. The smell comes in waves. It fills every syllable of appalling.

The plastic bags tear. Arturo peels them back. He looks down at what is left of the corpse. He looks again, studying what's left.

It's not Connie.

The body is larger, longer-jawed and wider-hipped and heavier than Connie's frame.

It's somebody else's daughter and niece.

The makeshift grave starts filling with water.

Arturo replaces the dirt he's shoveled.

He walks back to the Impala. He hands the cigarette he forgot to light and the lighter back to Pru. She gets back in the car.

The sky is shutting itself down and running to dusk.

There are moments that are outside forgiveness.

Arturo drives them back to Magnolia Beach.

Later that night, he puts in a call to the police and leaves an anonymous tip about the location of the body.

THE LENGTH OF DAYS — THIRTY-FIVE

Everything's going to be okay. It's America. Johnny Doc Nowell has lived there long enough to be seduced by the stubborn optimism encoded like an extra chromosome in the DNA of the country's character.

A reversal of fortune. Anything's possible in America.

Carl Adkin had brought him a name.

Now there's some real talk about more government bailouts, and Johnny Doc is starting to believe that he can get out from under 2008's disastrous financial moves and their consequences. It would be nice, he thinks, to be able to reinhabit hope. Maybe get some fresh backing for resurrecting West Wind Estates and recouping the lion's share of what he lost. He likes the sound of Recovery. It carries the weight of grace, and right now Andrew Findley is its agent.

Eric Findley. Once Carl Adkin got the name, Johnny Doc felt his fortune begin to shift. Andrew Findley, Eric's father, owned and ran a dozen or more high-end hotels and condo complexes in Magnolia Beach. He was the president of the Tourist Bureau and former president of the Chamber of Commerce. At one time, Andrew Findley had also jammed Johnny Doc's bid to join both, the official reason being community standards and Johnny Doc's ownership of the Full Moon Massage Parlor, the unofficial and real reason being Andrew Findley had a younger brother killed in Viet Nam during the Tet Offensive.

Courtesy of his lawyer Raychard Balen, Johnny Doc is about to get out from under the Bowen Brothers and their demands for restitution for the twelve dead girls.

Johnny Doc sits, face to the noon sun, on a bench in the commons area of downtown Magnolia Beach. He's waiting for the noon recess of the courthouse crowd. Around him are freshly planted flowerbeds, kids throwing frisbees, people walking dogs, and others headed for restaurants or niche boutiques.

At twelve, the courthouse doors open. Johnny Doc has no trouble spotting Raychard Balen. Raychard has a way of standing out in a crowd. Johnny Doc watches him pause on the steps, look around, and start his way. Raychard Balen is a short man, small-framed with an outsized waistline barely tented by a plaid sports jacket. He's wearing the usual spilled-ink comb-over and a thin mustache resembling two

THE LENGTH OF DAYS 157

legs of an isosceles triangle.

He stops in front of the bench and checks his watch. "Already a long day. Too many people don't understand the relationship between lawyers and the law. The law's a matter of deciding which rocks to turn over. Concerning what's underneath, it's my job to flinch so that the clients don't have to."

They head for Balen's Lincoln Towne car parked along the curb. "The phone calls were not a good idea. Next time check with me first." Balen leans over and unlocks the car. "No need to give Nathaniel Laine a heads-up until it becomes necessary."

"I thought it was," Johnny Doc says. "I told Mr. Laine to pass on to the Bowen Brothers that we were looking at closing things. I thought some reassurance was in order."

Raychard Balen stops midway to keying the ignition and looks over at Johnny Doc. "Those phone calls, that reassurance, they're the equivalent of flushing before you've finished wiping. Not the kind of move you should be making at this point."

Balen backs the Lincoln out, rights, and heads toward Atlantic Avenue. "Carl Adkin, you still have him on a leash? That shootout at Pinewood Bowling is drawing some unwelcome attention. There's talk of irregularities at the crime scene. Questions like why the black cop died with the gun in his right hand when he's left-handed."

"I promised Adkin a bonus," Johnny Doc says. "He's okay." Johnny Doc does not add *For Now*. There had been two out-of-control late-night phone calls from Adkin, each rambling and barely coherent, but finally circling around and back to the question of money.

"Okay," Balen says, "but my view, nothing will get you in trouble faster than a promise."

Balen takes the Lincoln up Atlantic Avenue to Elizabeth and then into North Magnolia Beach, a section of the city that for the last quarter century has been locked in an uneasy limbo. Some of the buildings still held vestiges of Low Country glamour and ease. Others have gone all least common denominator. Each block with History alive and unraveling at the same time.

The Hook and Line Club is a Magnolia Beach institution. Small and boxy, it perches on the edge of the ocean and has survived every hurricane and tropical depression the Atlantic has brought to it. The Hook and Line runs on a battered charm. None of the tables match. The floorboards are warped in places with a funhouse tilt. The ceiling fans take their time making each rotation. The walls are hung in an eclectic mix of shrimping nets, canvas life preservers, facsimiles of compass roses, laminated newspaper clippings and tidal charts, and black and white photos of the club and its customers over the decades.

Andrew Findley has commandeered a table near the ocean-side windows of the club. He's in his late sixties, deeply tanned and lean-boned, and dressed in the out of office uniform of successful Low Country businessmen: a white oxford shirt with the sleeves turned over mid-forearm, tan khakis, and broken-in deck shoes and no socks.

The waitress steps up and takes their orders. Sweet tea and the day's special—shrimp and grits—all around. As soon as the waitress leaves, Andrew Findley clears his throat and says, "I need to make this clear upfront. I agreed to this meeting against my better judgment."

"I can't speak for Mr. Nowell," Raychard Balen says, "but you just hurt my feelings, Andrew."

"Please, Raychard," Findley says, "that sounds like the lead-in for the standard spiel about your family history you never seem to tire of delivering." He holds up his hand. "I've heard it more than once. The whorehouse. Your mom. What she collected on patrons and passed on to you after she died."

"It appears my reputation precedes me," Balen says. "The same could be said for your old man. I checked Mom's files. Your old man was a regular pussy-hound."

Andrew Findley takes out his wallet. He lays a hundred on the table. "Lunch is on me, gentlemen. I've heard enough." He starts to get up from his chair.

"I don't think so," Balen says. "You need to sit down, Andrew."

"Give me one reason why."

"Your son Eric," Johnny Doc says evenly.

Findley sits back down. The waitress brings their order and leaves. "I assumed this meeting was about the Tourist Bureau, Balen there pulling strings to get you in, and I was looking forward to again telling you no, Mr. Nowell."

Johnny Doc tells him that the meeting is not about his garnering a spot with Magnolia Beach's power brokers on the Tourist Bureau. And not about using Findley's influence to get the legs under the West Wind Estates project again.

"It's about your son and dead girls, Mr. Findley," Johnny Doc says. "Twelve of them."

"I'm telling you right now that your extortion demands are going to get you nowhere."

THE LENGTH OF DAYS

"Technically, Andy," Balen says, pausing with a spoonful of grits and one lone shrimp, "we're talking about blackmail, a subset of extortion, not extortion per se."

Raychard Balen points the spoon at Findley. "Your boy Eric snapped one's neck and left the rest in a burning house and walked. The girls did not belong to Mr. Nowell. He's expected to pay restitution and damages."

Andrew Findley takes a sip of his iced tea and then starts in on the shrimp and grits.

Raychard Balen takes out a pen and writes a figure on a napkin and sends it across the table. "And don't tell me you can't afford it, Andrew."

Findley picks up the napkin, glances at what's written, and sets it down. "Of course I can afford it," he says. "Unlike your friend here, I know how to protect my money. Any fool could see where the West Winds Estate was headed, 2008 or not."

Findley finishes his shrimp and grits and pushes the bowl away. He calls over the waitress and orders a cold beer. Nobody says anything until she brings it.

Findley looks at the figure once more, then wads the napkin. "So that's what a life is worth today."

"Your progeny," Raychard Balen says. "None of the girls were close to twenty."

Findley takes a sip of his beer. He looks around the room and then back at Balen and Johnny Doc. "Enough," he says quietly. "There are limits, finally, and I guess those limits and at some point facing them are the closest to what counts as morality. At least for me."

He sets down his beer. "So No Sale, gentlemen."

Raychard Balen jumps in and points out the obvious, itemizing the occasions over the years that Findley had bailed Eric out of the trouble and damage he caused for himself and others. "I have to say," Balen adds, "I have a high tolerance for various and sundry acts of perversity, but your son Eric comes close to giving me a permanent set of the Creeps."

"Your name," Johnny Doc says. "Your reputation. Think of what will happen to both if this gets out."

"I'm sixty-eight, almost sixty-nine," Findley says. "I have enough money to be more than comfortable for the rest of my life. I've done what I set out to do. I don't need to prove anything to myself or others anymore. I'm not interested in bailing Eric out again." Findley drops his hand on the table and taps it twice. "In fact, at this point, I'm truly sorry I had any part in bringing Eric into the world."

This isn't happening, Johnny Doc thinks. It can't. This is America, and Father Knows Best, and boys will be boys, and endings, if you have to acknowledge them at all, are always happy.

"Maybe we're talking to the wrong person," Raychard Balen says. "Maybe we should be talking to your lovely wife Kyra and see how well her maternal instincts match up with little Eric's activities."

"Nice try," Findley says, nodding. "That might have worked at one time. No, backspace that. It would have worked. I was willing to do anything to protect Kyra from having to face what her son was and the things he routinely did."

"Why change the channel now?" Balen asks. "All those girls, this is big-time ugly. Think about what it will do to Kyra."

Johnny Doc senses where things are going even before Findley answers. Johnny Doc recognizes the tone and inflection of loss.

Everything is getting away from him. The sure thing that suddenly isn't. The reprieve that is anything but. Johnny Doc sitting back in his seat and chasing his breath. An overdose of fight or flight and his nerve endings running on both and neither.

I am a long way from myself, he thinks.

He listens to Andrew Findley talk about end stages and hospice and explain how nothing Eric does can touch Kyra now. He listens to Andrew Findley talk about blessings in disguise. He listens to Andrew Findley talk about a newfound acceptance of limits that is the equivalent to a default morality.

Johnny Doc looks out the east window of the Hook and Line Club. The sky and ocean are the same shade of blue, and the thin windblown smear of clouds and the white icing the crest of the waves seem to overlap.

Everything, everything, is getting away from him.

He hears Raychard Balen say, "You understand, you don't pay up, it's not just your reputation. At bottom, you're signing your son's death warrant. The Bowen Brothers will put out a contract."

Eric Findley doesn't say anything to that.

The Bowen Brothers will not stop after killing Eric Findley. Johnny Doc knows that. They will still expect restitution for the dead girls, and they will come after him.

He looks at Andrew Findley. He looks at Raychard Balen. He looks out the east window of the Hook and Line at a sky and sea that have disappeared into each other.

THE LENGTH OF DAYS

Johnny Doc Nowell needs a still point.

Because everything is getting away from him.

It feels as if time itself has become braided. 1975 and 2009 are throwing each other's shadow.

He knows he is sitting with Andrew Findley and Raychard Balen, but if he looks to his left, he can see John Sloane, the closest thing he's ever known as a Father and the owner of the Colorado on Tu Do Street, tending bar at the Hook and Line, and if he looks to his right, it's not their waitress but Colonel Le Van Thu from the reeducation camp who's bringing over their lunch check.

Except it's not the check but the photo taken in the doorway of the Colorado Bar after the fall of Saigon with Colonel Thu holding up John Sloane's severed head.

Colonel Thu sets the photo in front of Johnny Doc.

Without thinking, Johnny Doc lifts his hand and touches the shirt button in the middle of his chest.

And he hears the jukebox at the Colorado Bar on Tu Do Street begin to play B-10.

It's the Beach boys singing "Help Me, Rhonda."

Last Call, John Sloane says.

Help, help me Rhonda / Help me Rhonda yeah / Get her out of my heart.

Last Call, John Sloane says. *When it comes to the heart and what lives there, there is no Rhonda, Johnny Doc. There never was or will be a Rhonda. That's the truth no one wants to admit. We're all on our own. There's no help when it comes to our hearts and what lives there.*

Then Johnny Doc Nowell is sitting back in the Hook and Line Club.

"Enough," Andrew Findley says. "That's all. Enough."

THE LENGTH OF DAYS – THIRTY-SIX

Arturo Morales has been digging up dead girls in his sleep. Even working double shifts at the Bayview complex has not been enough to keep shovels and corpses out of his dreams, so when the two a.m. knocking starts, Arturo is pulled from shallow sleep with something approaching a backhanded relief.

Billy Jo, his next door neighbor, steps inside, looks around, and asks about coffee. His blonde wig is askew, canting left of center, and he's missing an earring. The nails on the fingers holding closed the neck of a kimono covered in orchids and hummingbirds are painted a shiny vermillion.

"Coffee?" Arturo asks. "Do you have any idea what time it is?" When Billy Jo's fingers slip and the kimono opens, Arturo is hit with waves of alcohol mixed with perfume whose combination ends up smelling like overripe peaches.

"I'm in a situation," Billy Jo says. "I need coffee and your help."

Arturo points toward the cupboard and then slips on a pair of jeans and his shoes. "How serious?" he asks.

"You'll see," Billy Jo says. "I should have known better."

Billy Jo's shoebox efficiency is the same size as Arturo's, but unlike the spartan and stoic lines of Arturo's, Billy Jo's is filled with dozens of overstuffed pillows, enough scented candles to give any fire marshal pause, and strategically placed low-watt lighting. There's a boom box in one corner and a haphazard pile of Billy Holliday CDs. Taped to the wall above the daybed is a black and white Life magazine photo of Ava Gardner who's as lushly curved as Billy Jo is anorexically thin.

There's a pinwheel comforter covering the daybed, and underneath the comforter is someone who is racking up some world-class snoring.

Billy Jo gets the coffee going and then moves close to Arturo and whispers, "He's a goat. Every time I think he's finally out for the night, he wakes up again. Then it's like he's got an extra set of hands. I want to get him out of here and in a cab." Billy Jo stops and adjusts the cant of his wig. "I didn't think someone his age could drink and go at it as much as he did."

"His age?" Arturo asks.

Then as if on cue, there's a moan, and the comforter shifts, and Weldon

THE LENGTH OF DAYS

Trulane III rolls over and sits on the edge of the bed. "I need boots on the ground," he says, tapping his feet on the linoleum. "Got a bad case of the Whirlies here."

He looks up. "Arturo? Is that you? Where am I? Back at Bayview? Not sure how I got back there exactly."

Billy Jo is setting out coffee cups. "You know him, Arturo?"

Arturo nods. "You're at the Drake Hotel, Mr. Weldon, not Bayview. I live next door."

Weldon shakes his head and buries his face in his cupped hands. "Last thing I remember was drinking at the Horizon."

Billy Jo rolls his eyes and sets out cream and sugar.

"Where have you been staying, Mr. Weldon? I mean, since you and Mr. Samuel had the falling out."

"I think I'm looking at an End-Times-sized hangover." Weldon slows lifts his head. "Where? At the Mimosa Bay Marina. One of my ex-wives has a boat and enough mercy in her heart to let me crash there for a while."

"I'll bet you take yours black," Billy Jo says, handing a cup to Weldon. Arturo waves his off.

Weldon takes a sip and grimaces, then seems to notice Billy Jo for the first time. "Wait a minute," he says.

"That's my line," Billy Jo says.

"Oh man," Weldon says. "I think, no scratch that. I'm afraid I'm remembering something else here." He looks down. "My clothes. Where are the rest of my clothes?"

Billy Jo sweeps his arm, taking in the room. "You were in a big hurry to get them off, Sugar."

"I don't believe this," Weldon says. "I thought you were a woman."

Billy Jo sets down his coffee cup. "And I thought you were a gentleman, Honey."

Weldon locates his shoes and starts scouting out his shirt. "I thought you were a woman," he says again. "I was sure of it."

"That's enough, Mr. Weldon," Arturo says. "Billy Jo is a friend and neighbor."

"There's such a thing as truth in advertising," Weldon says. He picks up his shirt. "Shit. Lipstick stains and I'm missing buttons."

"You should have slowed down some then and not been in such a hurry to sample the goods." Billy Jo crosses his arms across his chest.

"That's enough, Billy Jo," Arturo says. "It's late, and that's not helping either." He turns to Weldon and says, "When you're dressed, you can crash at my place for the rest of the night. I'll drop you off at the Marina on my way to work tomorrow morning."

"FYI," Weldon says, slipping on his shoes. "And this is for both of you. I, Weldon Trulane III, know what a woman is."

"Oh Honey," Billy Jo says, "so do I."

Weldon steps over and taps the magazine photo of Ava Gardner. "That is a woman. Look at those lips, tits, and hips and what they did to Frank Sinatra's life."

Then he turns to Billy Jo's refrigerator and points to the photo of Connie Fuentes that's clipped to and held in place by a butterfly magnet. "That is a woman," he says. "Or at least on her way to becoming one. She's still a little young, but my oh my, you ought to see that ass in a pair of tight jeans. It's a sight to behold."

Arturo steps up next to Weldon. "Her?" he says. "You've seen her?"

"With both eyes," Weldon Trulane III says.

THE LENGTH OF DAYS – THIRTY-SEVEN

A cardboard box. 32 x 25 x 30 inches. It does not seem right that someone's life, or at least his professional life, should fit in one.

And even then, with room to spare.

Carl Adkin's in the Department locker room. He's come in early on shift to clean out Truman Cooke's locker and box everything up. Later, he'll drop it off during lunch break with Denisha, Truman's wife. No, he thinks, scratch that. Truman's widow.

Truman's locker. No surprises. But that was Truman. No surprises because a good man held none. Or at least none that carried fine print.

Taped inside the locker door, at eye level, an index card and Truman's handwriting: Isaiah 1:17. *Learn to do right. Seek Justice. Defend the oppressed. Take up the cause of the fatherless. Plead the case of the widow.*

Below that, a family photo of Denisha and the kids.

Inside the locker proper: a University of South Carolina Gamecock sweatshirt, the sleeves cut off. A pair of gray sweatpants. Athletic shoes, size 11. A pair of jeans. A black and white striped ref shirt for YMCA youth basketball league. A blue cap with Mac Jones Fish Camp on its face.

On the locker's top two shelves: a wristwatch, a good one Truman never wore on patrol. A pack of Lifesavers with one piece missing. A book of stamps. Deodorant, toothpaste, and mouthwash. A toothbrush with its head wrapped in cellophane. A plastic cup containing loose change. A pair of sunglasses. Three granola bars. A hand-sized Bible with T. C. C embossed along its lower edges. An expensive pen with T. C. C running down both sides. Two white handkerchiefs with T. C. C stitched in the upper left corners.

Truman Carlton Cooke. Denisha's penchant for monograms. It had been a running joke between Truman and Carl.

He takes down the family photo and slips it inside the small Bible. He starts to read the quote from Isaiah again, stops halfway, and takes down the index card, folding it in half and dropping it in the box with the other stuff.

No surprises. Carl keeps trying to resurrect Truman's expression at Pinewood Bowling when he'd discovered Carl standing over the bodies of Wayne Summer and Gary Lidd. Had it simply held surprise? Or regret? Sadness? Resignation? Or something else entirely just before Carl turned and shot him through the neck with the Walther?

The placement of the shot had at least spared Carl from having to hear Truman's last words.

Each night, though, his thoughts have been an endless loop of him doctoring the crime scene afterward, methodically erasing his presence and choreographing the placement of the bodies, everything in place as each loop came to a close except for one detail that Carl would not find out about until it was too late to fix, the fact that Carl had put the Walther in the wrong hand when he was finishing up with the trajectory of the crime scene.

The detail stuck in his throat. He can't and couldn't believe he'd made a mistake that basic.

That, of course, led to worries about other mistakes he may have made.

And those long nights of restless sleep and the worries that threatened to spill into Carl's waking hours, it was there that Carl knew he had to be careful and vigilant because that combination could end up undoing him.

He could, for example, start thinking he was being set up. That he had in fact placed the Glock in the correct hand, but that the detectives in Homicide had circulated the opposite scenario in hopes of tripping him up.

And if that was the case, then all the vows and oaths to avenge Truman's death from McKelvey and Williams and the rest of the rank and file were just so much smoke, a way of getting Carl to let his guard down.

Maybe he was getting played. Maybe everyone was waiting for him to admit to a mistake he hadn't made.

Carl tells himself he needs to be careful. He needs to stay focused. He needs to keep his thoughts in line.

He needs to find his Slot again.

He's taking steps to do that.

Johnny Doc Nowell, for example. At bottom, he still owed Carl serious money. Johnny Doc had managed to front a third of Carl's fee for coming up with the name of the guy who set the fire at 805 Jefferson. Carl had delivered, but whenever Carl pressed for the rest of the money, Johnny Doc Nowell kept putting him off and floating promises tied to some future loan that he was waiting to clear.

THE LENGTH OF DAYS 167

So Carl figured it was time to cut his losses. He didn't want to end up as collateral damage if things went sideways with the Bowen Brothers over Johnny Doc and Eric Findley. Carl's made a couple preemptive phone calls and established bona fides and fees for keeping tabs on Johnny Doc in case he decides to rabbit.

The next step then to Carl finding his footing again was a little more sleep and a little less drinking. Carl needs to stay focused. Ever since Truman's funeral, his thoughts have a tendency to bunch and gather, clogging his concentration or stray off in unexpected and unwelcome directions.

He's afraid one day he won't be able to recognize himself.

He doesn't want to let that happen. He's arrested enough people over the years who have eaten their own shadows. He's looked into their eyes and seen everything they've given up on or lost.

Carl isn't planning to join their ranks.

He finally was able, yesterday, to get ahold of Arturo Morales. Up until then, Arturo had been ducking him. Arturo might deny that, but it was true. He'd called in sick for work at the Bayview Complex, and he hadn't been anywhere near his apartment. Carl's calls over close to three days had gone straight to voicemail.

Carl had explained to Arturo that he needed to forget that Wayne Summer had been Carl's snitch and to forget that Carl had enlisted Arturo in the first place to help set up Wayne for that.

Arturo had said okay. Carl intends to keep it that way.

Which is why on his way to Denisha Cooke's to drop off the contents of her husband's locker, Carl Adkin takes a detour.

A small detour. Hunch-driven.

Carl takes the blue and white through Garrison Park. It's noon. The air is full of pollen. There are people riding bicycles. Jogging. Flying kites. Walking dogs.

He parks along the curb in sight of the lake. Its edges have yet to be latticed by algae. Mallards bob in a loose cluster in the middle. The surrounding surface is a reflected churn of spring clouds.

Under a trio of live oaks, there's an impromptu camp of the homeless at the crest of the slope leading to the lake. They're Regulars. Carl knows most of them by name, and they know Carl, and all of them, Carl included, know the routine.

Carl rousts them. They leave. They eventually come back, and Carl, or someone else on Patrol, rousts them again.

Carl pulls the box with Truman's possessions over and starts going

168 LYNN KOSTOFF

through it again, taking one of the monogramed handkerchiefs, the pen, and the Bible out. He double-checks that the photo of Denisha and the kids is still tucked in the middle of the Old Testament. Then he gets out of the blue and white and starts toward the impromptu camp.

Once he's spotted, the homeless begin to disperse.

Carl's counting on Mitch to be one of the last to leave, and Mitch doesn't disappoint.

He's scanning the sky over the lake.

Carl asks when the next landing is scheduled.

Mitch looks back over his shoulder. "Truth tell, Officer Carl, I'm worried. The landings are starting to be few and far between. I'm afraid Jesus is wrapping things up. There's room on the saucer. Always has been. But there are less and less who have earned a seat." Mitch takes in a breath and shakes his head. "I'm starting to get afraid, Officer Carl. I'm afraid Jesus has already picked up most of the Worthy, and the rest of us, well, I'm afraid He's going to leave us here alone."

"Mitch," Carl says, "you know Jesus is not going to leave you behind. There will always be a seat on the saucer for you."

"Not all the Pharisees were aware that they were Pharisees," Mitch says. "Who can know his own heart?"

"Look," Carl says, "you need to move along, Mitch. I don't think the world's going to end any time soon."

"We can think what we want," Mitch says, "but not always want what we think."

"Let's set aside thinking and wanting for a while, okay?" Carl points to the east. "Time to move it along, Mitch."

"Hand me my jacket, okay?" Mitch says, "and I'll be on my way then."

The jacket is Goodwill corduroy. Carl picks it up and shakes it out. Mitch's back is to him, and Carl slips the monogramed handkerchief, pen, and Bible into available pockets and then hands the jacket over to Mitch.

Mitch puts it on, shakes Carl's hand, and cuts across the park at a diagonal. To the southeast, where the trees are starting to thicken with spring foliage, Carl can just make out the claws and snout of the dead rat on the billboard advertising Maxwell's Pest Service.

THE LENGTH OF DAYS — THIRTY-EIGHT

Earlier in the day, Arturo Morales rented a shiny black Explorer with tinted windows and oversized tires, and then with some misgivings, he had gone clothes shopping with Weldon Trulane III. Weldon picked out various combinations of shirts, pants, and shoes until Arturo resembled a made-for-television cliché—an upwardly mobile Mexican drug dealer with too much money in his pocket, nothing resembling good in his heart, and no fashion sense whatsoever: snakeskin cowboy boots, tight black jeans, and a neon blue shirt with collars folded open to display the thicket of gold chains and the oversized crucifix nesting in the middle of Arturo's clean-shaven chest.

Arturo pulls the Explorer up to the security checkpoint at the Mimosa Bay Yacht Club and powers down the window.

Weldon Trulane III unbuckles his seat belt and leans over, giving the guard a friendly wave. "Gonna need a guest parking pass for the day, Jimmy."

Jimmy hesitates a moment, taking in Arturo, but passes a yellow card with A-18 on it. "Good until tomorrow morning, Mr. Weldon."

Weldon tosses out a salute. "Thanks, Jimmy. Next time I see you, I'll let you buy me a beer."

Arturo takes the Explorer down Windjammer Drive. Weldon hands him a pair of wraparounds. "You can put these back on now, Arturo. And leave them on. From this point on, you need to look Predatory."

"I don't know," Arturo says. "This outfit and everything, Mr. Weldon."

"We're not chasing nuance here," Weldon says. He holds up his index finger. "Keep the glasses on." He studies Arturo again. "No offense, but it wouldn't have hurt to use a little more hair gel."

Windjammer Drive passes through two mirror-image condo complexes and the home of a half dozen tennis courts and four Olympic-sized pools and an open-field driving range before funneling between overarching oaks bearded in Spanish Moss and bromeliads clinging to the trunks. Surrounding them are single-family homes starting at a million-plus.

Arturo follows Windjammer until the traffic circle where he takes a right on Bougainvillea. It's a stretch of high-end shops and restaurants, a landscape fueled on leisure and privilege that left no room for anything but itself.

The Mimosa Beach Yacht Clubhouse is Low Country architecture on steroids. Columns everywhere. A massive multi-angled tin roof. Verandas cubed. Gazebos and cupulas like wedding cake decorations. Forest-green hurricane shutters and glassed-in oceanfront views above a pristine stretch of private beach.

Arturo parks the Explorer. Weldon Trulane leans over and knocks open the glove box. He takes out the Bersa 380 and hands it to Arturo who then slips it against the small of his back and makes sure the shirt covers it. Earlier he had asked Weldon where he'd gotten the gun, but all he would say was that it was clean and not to worry about it.

Weldon Trulane holds up his hand. "At a slant and slow. That's how we need to take this. You fit the image, but first we need to get Eric to let his guard down. And then make sure the girl's on the boat."

"I thought you were sure. That's what you said."

Weldon explains that his ex-wife's and her new husband's yacht where he's been staying is a dock and three slips over from Eric's. "I spotted the girl a couple times," he adds. "She looked like the one in the photo."

"Okay," Arturo says. "I guess now there's only one way to find out."

"At a slant and slow," Weldon says. "Let me handle the intros."

They cross the parking lot to the entrance of the marina. Weldon punches in the security code, and when the gate opens, they move down a sidewalk through carefully manicured grounds. They're familiar, more than familiar, but Arturo does not mention that to Weldon Trulane. For the first ten months after he moved to Magnolia Beach from Burlington, North Carolina, Arturo had worked as part of the landscaping crew for Mimosa Bay. He knows the layout.

The Clubhouse sits in the middle of the arc defining the bay, and the marina lies to its north. There are six floating docks jutting from the shoreline with slips of varying sizes on either side. The farther north, the bigger the slip. Weldon points out the various yachts that aren't out in the bay this afternoon, everything from Express Cruisers to Sedan Bridges, Skylounges and Express Sportsfish to a couple Trideckers.

When they get to the third dock, Weldon points to the eighth slip on its east side. "That's the *Glass Ceiling*, the one I've been staying on." He points to the fourth dock and the fifth slip on its west side. "That's our boy's." It's a white Hatteras 80 with upper and lower helms and an open bridge under a hardtop.

THE LENGTH OF DAYS

Weldon takes out his cell. "My friend and me," he says, "we're here." He listens for a moment and nods. "We have liftoff," he says to Arturo. Eric Findley's waiting for them on the foreshortened bow of the *No Questions*. From a distance he looks almost boyish, clean-shaven and All-American, but the closer Weldon and Arturo get, the more those features turn overripe and florid, something that makes the floppy locks, white-band-collar shirt, tan khakis, and deck shoes seem more like camouflage than fashion statement.

"Weldon," Eric says. "Have to admit I was surprised to get your call." He tilts his head, looking past Weldon. "That your friend?"

"His name's Arturo," Weldon says, "and he has needs."

"Why are you here then?"

"I like to watch," Weldon says.

"Another surprise." Eric smiles. "Duly noted. And added to the tab."

They step on board the *No Questions* and follow Eric Findley to the upper deck and take seats. Around them Mimosa Bay gathers itself. The wind's on its own clock. Four pelicans follow the line of the horizon and then drop one by one into the waves to get their share of a running school of fish.

"You speak English?" Eric asks.

Arturo nods.

"How about take the glasses off for a moment?"

Arturo does. Eric tilts his head again, studying him, and then asks if he is a cop. Arturo tells him no and puts the glasses back on.

"You still look familiar," Eric says. "You sure we haven't met?"

Arturo shakes his head no.

"Okay, then." Findley reaches back over his shoulder and brings out two embossed ledgers and hands one each to Arturo and Weldon. He then gets up and brings back three Coronas, passing them out, before sitting back in his deck chair and crossing his legs at the ankles.

Arturo opens the book and starts reading. His stomach lurches. He's glad he's got the sunglasses on.

"Today's Menu," Eric Findley says.

It's a grouping of sex acts and prices that mimic the typical structure—Appetizers, Entrees, Desserts, and Side Dishes—of a menu. There's everything from Lap, Shower, and Bed Dances to Golden Showers, BJ's, Around the World, Half and Half, Bareback, and Hardcore.

Arturo tries to erase the thought of any of them being done by and to a fifteen-year-old girl.

He tries but can't. And that makes it worse.

"Weldon, you change your mind about Watching, there's a special today on Fisting." Eric tips his bottle and smiles.

"I think you've outdone yourself here," Weldon says.

It sounds to Arturo that Weldon Trulane is struggling to keep his voice even.

"Not like you to suddenly go shy on me," Eric says.

"I was just wondering," Weldon says. "Why all this? Our families go back a couple generations. I know you don't need the money."

"You're right. I don't need the money. Never have."

"Then why?" Weldon clears his throat once and then once more. "I mean it. I don't understand."

"The answer requires another round." Eric gets three more Coronas.

Arturo looks over at Weldon. He's puzzled and more and more quietly disconcerted. Weldon Trulane is going off-script, and Arturo is not sure why.

Eric sits back down and tilts a fresh beer in Weldon's direction. "I don't need the money I make on this enterprise, so I donate it anonymously to various charities." He lifts his hand and ticks off some examples finger by finger. "Saint Jude's Children's Hospital. Alzheimer's research. American Cancer Society. Salvation Army. Humane Society."

"I still don't get it," Weldon says, shaking his head. "The point. I don't."

"The point's simple. It's frisson." Eric drops his head back and faces the sky. "Frisson. Listen to the word itself. What it intends. Where it leads."

Arturo starts to say something about getting down to the business at hand, but Findley cuts him off.

"There is no center," he says, "to us or anything. That's the truth of it all." He stops. "No, not that. It's simply the art of it all. I make money selling flesh. I give all the proceeds to charities anonymously. In doing so, I am simultaneously Pimp and Saint. It's like holding hands with yourself and not being afraid to admit how satisfying that is."

Findley points his beer at Weldon, then Arturo. "I don't have to do any of this, but I do anyway. That makes it the purest form of Free Will. I never feel closer to God and creation than when I'm putting a price tag on flesh."

Weldon finishes his beer and looks down at the deck of *No Questions*.

Arturo leans over and points to the fourth Entrée on the menu. "With handcuffs," he says, tapping Side Orders.

"Seems we have a connoisseur on the premises," Eric says. He stands and says, "Follow me, Gents." They leave the bridge and move to the

THE LENGTH OF DAYS

main deck and then through the hatch to the cabin and rooms below. Along the way, Eric Findley picks up the handcuffs.

"I'll make the intros," he says, "and then take *No Questions* out while you remain below deck and have yourselves some fun. You've bought yourself an hour's worth."

They're almost to the galley when Arturo rushes things. The Bersa 380 is out before he thinks about it. He grabs Eric Findley by the shoulder and spins him around.

"Connie Fuentes," he says. "Take us to her."

"Whoa, Friend. What's this about?"

"We're taking her with us," Arturo says. "Now." He takes the handcuffs from Findley and hands them to Weldon Trulane.

"Let's make this simple for all concerned," Findley says. "You want her? She's yours." He shrugs. "This Connie? She's a filly that's now a couple of furloughs from dog food. She's been stretched and broken. You can have her. There's a lot more like her out there."

Arturo points the Bersa at Findley's chest. "Take us to her."

"Starboard side. Door Number Two," Findley says, "but the key to the room is in the galley cupboard."

He turns and starts toward it. "Watch your head." He points up at the doorframe. "It's lower than you think. Don't want you shooting me by accident."

Eric Findley long-arms the move, placing his hand along the top of the doorframe and shifting to accommodate the extra step down to the galley.

Arturo lets his attention wander one second too long. He'd been thinking about getting Connie out of there, and he doesn't see until it's too late Eric Findley swing his free arm in his direction or the hand holding the knife he'd taped above the doorframe.

Arturo turns his head and throws up his forearm at the last moment. Findley buries the knife deep in his side.

Arturo drops the Bersa 380.

Weldon Trulane is yelling something.

Arturo chases his breath. He's dizzy and feels like he's going to throw up. There's blood blooming in the folds of his shirt.

Weldon Trulane is still yelling. Arturo can't find the words.

Findley stabs Arturo a second time. The knife hits bone.

Weldon Trulane stops yelling. He's grabbed the Bersa Arturo dropped. Eric Findley drops the knife and backs deeper into the galley.

"Get the key," Weldon says to Findley.

174   LYNN KOSTOFF

Arturo works on keeping his breathing even. His side feels wet and hot. He leans against the doorframe. He tells himself he's not going to pass out.

Eric Findley tosses Weldon Trulane the keys. Weldon tosses Findley the handcuffs and tells him to cuff himself to the refrigerator door handle.

Eric Findley does. He's smiling though.

Arturo points toward the second door starboard.

Weldon follows his lead and brings out Connie Fuentes. She looks like she's on a hard-line fast-track from fifteen to fifty. She's in bra and panties and barefoot. Her pupils are pin-pricks, her movements slow and syrupy. She looks at Weldon Trulane and Arturo and asks which one she's supposed to blow first.

Eric Findley starts laughing. "No Center," he says, rattling the cuffs.

Weldon Trulane hands Arturo a dish towel from the galley and tells him to put some pressure on the wounds.

"No hospital," Arturo says. "Someplace else. Safe." He waits a moment before adding, "For all three of us."

Arturo then brings up a name. Nancy McKenzie. He explains she's a nurse at the Bayview Complex. She can take care of him and the wounds. She owes him a favor.

"Let me think," Weldon says.

"Someplace safe," Arturo says again. "For all three of us." He has come to doubt, though, that such a place exists.

Weldon takes out his cell, punches in a number, and explains what's needed. He has to explain it more than once.

"Samuel Fulton's going to put us up at the townhouse," he says after pocketing the cellphone. "You can call the McKenzie woman to meet us there."

Arturo's ears are ringing. Every one of Weldon Trulane's words sound like pebbles shaken in a tin can. His pulse is sending him its own version of morse code.

"Him?" Arturo asks. He tries to point in Eric Findley's direction.

Weldon Trulane starts opening cabinets. Behind a set near the sink are four propane tanks clustered together.

He looks at Eric Findley handcuffed to the handle of the refrigerator, then at the four propane tanks.

Weldon Trulane takes out a book of matches from his pants pocket.

Eric Findley quits laughing.

Weldon Trulane III hits Eric Findley twice hard in the head with the

THE LENGTH OF DAYS

butt of the Bersa 380, uncuffs him, and pulls the body closer to the sink and propane tanks.

"What say you get Connie some clothes and then you two go topside and meet me in the parking lot in a few minutes?"

"What are you going to do?"

Weldon slips the handcuffs in his pants front pocket. He points at the propane tanks, then holds up the book of matches.

"Boom," he says.

THE LENGTH OF DAYS — THIRTY-NINE

In the middle of the night, as has been happening more and more lately, Pam Graves finds herself wide awake and staring at the ceiling after Daren Lowe immediately dropped off into a postcoital sleep that was a couple heartbeats shy of a coma.

And as has been happening more and more lately, Pam Graves gets up, dresses, and drives back to her place.

Daren Lowe has yet to say anything to her about this practice. Pam is not even sure he's noticed.

Tonight, though, on the drive home, Pam Graves on impulse takes a detour.

She has no idea why.

Except a part of her does.

Which is why edging one a.m. when the sky breaks and the rain starts in earnest, Pam Graves pulls to the curb outside the Farmers Market on Sheridan and calls her mother.

Her mother gives her an address. *Call me again when you get there,* she says.

It isn't the home address.

Twenty minutes later, Pam Graves pulls into the drive at 1125 White Pine Lane. Her mother is waiting on the front porch.

Pam Graves watches her make her way down the sidewalk, a newspaper held over her head and tented against the rain.

Her mother slides into the front seat. She tosses the rain-soaked newspaper into the back, and says, "You called. I'm here."

"You said when I was ready to hear the truth," Pam says. "I am. That's why I called."

Her mother drops her hand on the inside door handle and shakes her head. "My terms then. You can stop me at any point, and I'm gone. I'll tell you going in, you aren't going to like what I'll tell you. I'll stop when you say so."

Pam Graves nods yes.

The rain drives in from the east. It's hard and at a slant. The windshield runs and swarms.

"Okay," her mother says, "before you ask." She points at the house, an old money mansion among a street of old money mansions. "His name

THE LENGTH OF DAYS 177

is Andrew Findley."

Her mother taps the door handle and looks over at Pam. "The last time we talked, you asked how I could live with myself. He's part of the answer, Andrew Findley is. A large part."

And before Pam can respond, her mother adds, "Your father too."

Pam drops her hands from the steering wheel into her lap. She waits.

She waits, and then she listens to a story about a young college student named Catherine Conolly who met and fell in love with another college student two years her senior named Andrew Findley, their ensuing relationship, an unwieldy mix of infatuation, lust, passion, and love leavened by an abiding friendship.

"The total package," her mother says.

There had been only one problem. Andrew Findley's engagement to one Kyra Newsome, the daughter of old Magnolia Beach money and family friends of the Findleys who were old Magnolia Beach but whose money had all but disappeared.

In lovemaking after lovemaking session, Andrew Findley promised Catherine Connolly that he was going to break the engagement.

Then Andrew Findley's father died.

Andrew Findley's mother went Blanche DuBois.

He married Kyra Newsome during Christmas break his senior year.

Catherine Connolly continued fucking Andrew Findley. Neither of them knew how or when to stop.

Kyra and her family continued to control the purse strings. Andrew Findley's mother continued to privately cry Chapter Eleven. Andrew Findley stayed married.

Kyra and Andrew Findley eventually had a son. They named him Eric.

During her senior year, Catherine Connolly met a man named David Graves. He was the quintessential Nice Guy. He was funny and decent and well-intentioned and didn't ask too many questions.

Catherine Connolly and David Graves got married. They eventually had twins named Peter and Pamela.

Throughout it all, Catherine Connolly-Graves and Andrew Findley continued to sleep with each other.

"And still do," her mother says. She drops her right hand on the door handle and looks at Pam. "No apologies. No judgments. If there's any judging, I'll do it myself. My life. My terms. That's how I live with myself."

Pam thinks of the pantheon of feminist photos on the walls of the

Second Wave and remembers the mnemonic device she'd developed as a young girl when her mother used to quiz her on their names. *Best save good karma. Go back and arrive* and Betty Friedan, Simone de Beauvoir. Gloria Steinem, Kate Millet, Germaine Greer, Bell Hooks, Alice Walker, and Adrienne Rich.

The sound of rain drumming on the roof of the car and Pam slowly turning her head and meeting her mother's eyes.

"Enough truth for you?" her mother asks. "We can stop right here if you want. I'll get out of the car. You drive away."

"You mean there's more?"

"I'll be the first to admit I'm not the mother you wanted. Never was. Never have been. But I loved you, both you and your brother."

"But not my father. Not with this setup."

"Of course I love your father. You just could never see that because you're just like him in too many ways."

Pam doesn't say anything. Her mother tells her goodnight and starts to get out of the car.

"Okay," Pam says quietly. "The rest."

Her mother sits back in her seat. "You remember growing up how much you liked looking through the family photo album? How often, growing up, you did that?"

Pam nods. Her father used to half-joke that he was the official Family Photographer. The album was fat with family history.

"You never noticed any of them. The gaps, I mean. You never asked. They were right there."

Then Pam's mother begins to itemize those gaps in the chronology of the album and what came to be known as temporary setbacks in Dave Graves's holding a job as well as his off-and-on visits to a sick aunt in Ryland, Ohio.

Her mother runs through some of the jobs her husband held and lost during their marriage, everything from selling insurance to working as a realtor, to a produce manager at the local Food Lion. As far as the sick aunt in Ohio, she tells Pam she was a pure fiction and a stand-in for Dave Graves's stints in a psychiatric ward.

Dave Graves was a good man, she says. Dave Graves was also a very fragile man. He got up every morning and loved his son and daughter and wife until sooner or later he ran into his life. Or maybe, it was his life which ran into him.

Difficult times, then finally a redemption and reprieve of sorts.

Andrew Findley, while initially bankrolled by the Newsome family,

THE LENGTH OF DAYS

started to make money on his own. A lot of it.

And David Graves discovered sandwiches.

Catherine Connolly-Graves didn't see her place as inhabiting the kitchen. She hated to cook and wasn't good at it to boot. She left that up to Dave Graves.

Who loved sandwiches. And was good at making them. Very good, in fact.

Witness the genesis of Dave's Deli.

Pam's mother taps the door handle. "We can stop here and let things rest. It'll be close enough both to a happy ending and answer to your question."

Pam is tempted to agree but remains silent. She watches the rain sheet and sweep across the windshield like someone trying to turn a page in a book.

Her mother takes her silence as assent and starts to get out of the car.

Pam stops her.

And wishes she'd hadn't because over the next fifteen minutes, Pam Graves listens to her mother as she dismantles Pam Graves's world.

It comes down to love and money. To passion and duty.

To a husband who couldn't hold a job. To a wife and mother of twins who'd tried to keep the family finances afloat on two part-time jobs.

To a long-term lover who married old Magnolia Beach money.

The dots had been there to connect. Pam hadn't noticed. She'd been too busy putting the best face on the face of things and being the family peacemaker.

It all came down to Andrew Findley who'd become an official and unofficial mover and shaker in local Magnolia Beach politics and tourism.

To Andrew Findley who was ethically ambidextrous.

To Andrew Findley who quietly bankrolled Dave's Deli, the Second Wave Bookshop, and Pam's college education. Her twin brother's too, up until he died.

It all came down to what Pam Graves had never questioned. To what she had taken at face value.

Andrew Findley had left his fingerprints all over their lives.

The irony, her mother tells her, is that Dave's Deli turned out to be a moneymaker and the Second Wave was perpetually in the red.

Pam looks up at the house on 1125 White Pine Lane, but the night and rain erase it. It's as if she's looking into the center of an immense

Black Hole.

"I wish I could say I was sorry," her mother says, "but I can't. I know it's hard for you to accept. But where it all started, the '70s, it was a different time. I wanted my own life on my own terms, but I couldn't leave your father. It wasn't finally in me. I couldn't do that to him. I'm Second Wave, and I accept that."

There's another dot.

One that Pam Graves is afraid to connect. She's noticing things now.

Finally, this: Pam asks about her paternity.

"Okay," her mother says, slowly letting out her breath. "Maybe. I'll admit it. Andrew Findley, me, we weren't too careful in those days."

"You've never been careful," Pam Graves says. "Never."

"I don't know whether to take that as a compliment or a criticism."

Pam Graves won't let her mother see her crying. She starts the car and hits the wipers and keeps her face pointed at the front windshield and the clear swath of night the wipers leave.

Pam drops her hands at 10 and 2 on the steering wheel and says, "Ever think not being able to tell the difference might be your and your generation's problem, Mother?"

The only answer tonight is the sound of the door handle lifting.

THE LENGTH OF DAYS — FORTY

Johnny Doc Nowell is in the glassed-in room at the rear of the house on Danvers when his cell rings. He checks caller ID and hesitates a moment before answering. Outside, the Inlet is running high tide, and the morning is empty of birds.

"The news, the last couple days?" Raychard Balen asks. "The explosion and fire over at the Mimosa Bay Marina?"

Johnny Doc nods, then catches himself and says that he's watched the news.

"You have anything to do with that?" Raychard asks. "Anything with helping our friend Eric Findley check out in what the local media called 'a ball of fire'?"

Johnny Doc says no.

"You didn't have Carl Adkin over there playing with matches?"

Johnny Doc again says no.

"Carl's been ducking my phone calls," Balen says, "and I'm trying to figure out why. Have you talked to him lately?"

Once again, Johnny Doc says no.

"Not happy to hear that, but okay," Balen says. "Next item. The Bank of the South, Rhodes Woodbury, the status of the loan you had him working on?"

Johnny Doc doesn't say anything. The sky is empty of clouds, but in the distance is a small plane traveling south to north, moving like a stray pencil mark on an otherwise clean sheet of paper.

"Am I talking to myself here?" Balen says.

"I've got money set aside," Johnny Doc says. "You'll get paid for your services, Raychard."

"That's not what I asked."

"It fell through," Johnny Doc finally says. "The loan did."

"Didn't you have something on our friend, Rhodes Woodbury?"

"Evidently not enough to scare him into delivering," Johnny Doc says. "I was counting on Rhodes being weak or scared or both. It turns out he was neither."

"Hey, we're talking Bankers," Balen says. "The thing is, at this juncture, even with Eric Findley in extra-crispy mode, the bottom line hasn't changed, and you don't have the money. Bottom line, the Bowen Brothers expect restitution. So I'd have to say you're fucked, friend."

Johnny Doc knows how the Bowen Brothers' three-tiered model for dealing with business problems plays out. Phase One, setting the terms and a warning. Phase Two, a serious beatdown to encourage and expedite on those terms. Phase Three, well, there was no reason to spell that one out.

"How much time?" Johnny Doc asks finally.

It's Raychard Balen's turn to wait a long moment before responding.

"Laine gave me the heads-up but not the specifics," Raychard says, "but the word that comes to mind is *imminent*. Two days, maybe three, tops. That's the usual time frame with the Bowens." He clears his throat, then adds, "The next words that come to mind are *Run* as in *Soon*."

"Why?" Johnny Doc says. "Why this call?"

"Hey, I can read tone," Balen says. "I told you. It was a heads-up. I didn't have to make the call."

"That's what I mean. You didn't have to warn me."

Raychard Balen starts laughing. "Once in a while I surprise myself and do something decent, and your response is a solid reminder why it's in my best interests not to. Nathaniel Laine called me as a professional courtesy. He wasn't and isn't interested in warning or saving you. He called to tell me to make sure I'd already collected on what you owed me."

Johnny Doc starts to apologize, but Balen drops the call. He hits redial, but Balen won't pick up until the third attempt. He lets Johnny Doc run through his apology once more.

"Okay, okay. Don't overdo it," Balen says. "It'd be better if you see this call more as a general PSA."

"I don't understand."

"All I did is tell you that the hit is being contracted out. What I didn't tell you is odds are you won't see it coming. Phase Three, that's the way the Bowen Brothers like it." Raychard seems on the verge of adding something, but leaves things there.

Johnny Doc hunts down an ashtray. He's trying to find a *Where* to append to Balen's *Run* and *Soon*, but his pulse is running hard and high and erasing destinations before he can settle on one and think clearly about it.

He counts the number of cigarette butts in the ashtray, then hesitates, counting again, before shaking out a new cigarette and lighting up.

THE LENGTH OF DAYS – FORTY-ONE

The moon's up, edging full, and hangs in the top right corner of the windshield like a small smudge. Daylight savings started five days ago, and the extra hour is bleeding out into a softly-lit evening. Pam Graves leaves Old Market Boulevard at the Doral Street exit and drives south and then heads west toward the Bayview Assisted Living Complex.

She takes a left at the entrance of the Bayview Complex and drives into the adjoining Bayview Townhouse neighborhood, eventually parking curbside at 4-B.

It takes Samuel Fulton a long time to open the door. Pam smiles and holds up a bag from Dave's Deli. "I brought supper," she says. "Enough for Mr. Weldon, you, and me."

Pam's smile dissolves. Samuel Fulton's appearance is more than a couple beats off from what Pam's accustomed to. Overdue haircut. Thumbprint-sized dark circles under his eyes. Skin pale tending toward sallow. A broken posture. Shirt and pants cross-hatched with deep wrinkles. His demeanor reminds Pam of someone who has misplaced his keys and spent much too long searching for them and then forgets why he needed them in the first place.

"Are you okay, Mr. Fulton? I stopped by Bayview earlier with some flowers for Ms. Glenda and noticed from the sign-in log you hadn't been by to see her for a day or so." Pam tries to resurrect her smile. "I was worried you might be sick or not feeling well."

Samuel Fulton turns and walks back into the townhouse. Pam hesitates for a moment, then follows.

The place is a mess. Any sense of the order she'd always previously found is missing.

Samuel Fulton walks into the living room and slowly levers himself onto the couch, each of his actions, however small, self-conscious as if carefully thought-out beforehand.

The television is on with the sound muted, and the screen holds a commercial with two overweight men in brown and green bowling shirts and the logo for *Floor to Ceiling* and *Coming Your Way Soon!* running across the bottom of the screen.

The kitchen counter and sink are covered in dirty dishes, food-

184   LYNN KOSTOFF

encrusted pots and pans, and ranks of smudged glasses, and Pam gives up and pulls a handful of paper towels and detours for two sodas and returns to the living room.

"I just noticed something," she says. "It's quiet. No Professor Longhair soundtrack tonight."

"For the time being, Weldon is staying on one of his ex-wife's boats," Fulton says. "We needed his room."

"We?"

"Someone's staying in it for a while," Samuel Fulton says. "Weldon's room, I mean." He unwraps his Club sandwich and carefully smooths the wrapper across his lap, then pulls the tab on his soda.

Pam sits down in a plaid upholstered chair across from him. "Please tell me what's going on," she says. "Something is obviously wrong."

Samuel Fulton won't meet her eyes. "The less said the better." He takes a bite of the sandwich, the adds, "And safer too for everyone, myself included."

"Better? Safer? I don't understand."

"There's a kind of trouble that's both simple and complicated," Fulton says.

Pam waits. Samuel Fulton finishes his sandwich.

"What if we talked, just you and me?"

"You mean, like off the record?"

"Something like that," Pam says, hoping Samuel Fulton will leave it at that and not press her further.

"I guess so," Samuel Fulton says after a moment. "It's not like you weren't part of it too."

"Part of what, Mr. Fulton?"

He's up, however, and heading for the kitchen, substituting the soda for a cold beer.

Pam looks around the living room. She's beginning to see and hear Madison Hopewell's admonition—*You need to own your ambition*—in a new light.

There's a story here, she can feel it, and she needs to be ready. Ready, this time, not to put the best face on the face of things, but to chase down the face of things itself, unadorned.

And over the next half hour, she teases out the details of that story from Samuel Fulton, asking leading question after leading question, going through the back door when necessary to get where and what she needed.

And the story she ended up with *was* both simple and complicated:

THE LENGTH OF DAYS

Weldon Trulane III and Arturo Morales rescuing a girl named Connie, one of the two that had been missing, Arturo seriously wounded in the process and Weldon calling Samuel and Samuel agreeing to let him recuperate at the townhouse, a nurse from Bayview taking care of him off the books, Connie's uncle eventually coming for her and taking her home, Weldon Trulane again moving temporarily onto one of his ex-wife's boats, all of them holding their breath and waiting for things to settle down again.

Pam waits a long moment before asking, "That means the man who started the fire at 805 Jefferson and trafficked the girl named Connie is dead, doesn't it?"

Samuel Fulton nods yes and adds that the man had also killed the second missing girl. Then he excuses himself and says he needs to use the bathroom.

Pam waits until he makes the hallway, and then she grabs her phone and moves quickly upstairs. She finds Arturo Morales in the second bedroom, one whose east wall is a makeshift homage to New Orleans. Posters of Jackson Square and Preservation Hall. Between them a framed album cover of Professor Longhair's *Crawfish Fiesta*. A street artist's faded caricature with a smudged date. A Mardi Gras mask.

Pam stands at the foot of the bed and runs a short video of Arturo Morales asleep, his head propped on two pillows, the bedcovers pulled up as far as his waist, his lower torso wrapped in a wide swath of white bandages. There's a large bloodstain on his left side just below the ribcage, the blood dried a rusty brown on the outside edges and holding a wet red in its center.

The face of things, unadorned. Pam Graves coming to own her ambition.

One piece left, though, that she still needs.

She just makes it back to the living room and her chair when Samuel Fulton emerges from the hallway.

"A name, the name," Pam says, "of the one who started it all with the fire."

"I told you what happened. That should be enough. The girl's safe. Her uncle took her home. Things should end there. That's what we all agreed on."

"A name, the name," Pam says. "Then the story's complete."

"Complete's not the same as finished," he says. "If you live long enough, you'll understand that."

One piece.

A name. She could work backwards from a name. A name, the name, that's all Pam Graves needs.

"The thing is," Samuel Fulton says, "I met him one time and talked with him."

"You mean the one behind the death of all the girls?"

Samuel Fulton nods yeas and tells her about a face-to-face encounter at the Mission Field Pier that moved to the In Your Cups coffee shop.

"We sat across from each other," Samuel Fulton says, "and he told me what would happen to my wife if I said anything." Samuel closes his eyes for a moment. "He told me he wanted to stay *At Large*."

"He's dead though, right? He can't do anything to Ms. Glenda or you now."

"I know he's dead," Samuel Fulton says, "but it doesn't feel that way. It feels instead like he'll always be around."

"Please, his name," Pam says. "You said yourself, I was a part of what happened."

Samuel Fulton hesitates.

Pam pushes harder. "Please. To be this close. It's hard not to know."

Her last words seem finally to unlock something in Samuel Fulton, and for a moment, Pam is afraid he's about to cry, but in the end, Samuel Fulton bows his head and gives up the name.

And that's what she's left with. She's starting to understand where it will take her.

Eric Findley.

Dead, according to the media, in a yacht fire. Killed, according to Samuel Fulton, by Arturo Morales or Weldon Trulane.

Eric Findley, a monster, who had locked twelve young women in a room and then set fire to the house after he'd murdered another in the front lawn by snapping and breaking her neck.

Eric Findley who went on to track down the two women who managed to escape the house fire, killing one and conscripting the other in his personal version of the sex trade.

Samuel Fulton gave Pam Graves the name, and the story followed.

Except for one thing.

The story that followed the name wasn't the only story.

There was another.

One with Pam Graves's mother and her long-term lover, Andrew Findley.

One that ended with Pam Graves' mother saying, *Look, all I'm saying is there's a chance Andrew Findley could be your father. We weren't too careful in those days.*

Leaving Pam Graves a putative sister to a monster.

Leaving Pam Graves having to find a way to live with both its truth and uncertainty.

She's now afraid truth and uncertainty have become one and the same.

A DNA test won't change anything because, whatever the results, Pam Graves knows, on one level, it doesn't matter.

Eric Findley and she are joined in either case. He is part of her life now and, without her realizing it, has been a part of her life from the moment she stood in the back yard of 805 Jefferson amidst the smell of burnt flesh and broke down crying while the camera ran and she delivered the news.

The news that now has delivered her to a place she'd never seen coming and abandoned her there.

PART THREE

WHEN THINGS END
WHERE THINGS END
HOW THINGS END

THE LENGTH OF DAYS – FORTY-TWO

8:24 p.m. 512 Houston Street

The sky bleeding out dusk. The employee parking lot of the Bayview Assisted Living Center. A dark blue Mercedes parked next to Arturo Morales's Chevy Impala.

Arturo just coming off shift and four hours overtime.

The window of the Mercedes powering down. A headshot of Felina Fuentes-Sorbano framed in the open window. She is beyond lovely.

"Passenger door is unlocked," she says.

He gets in. She holds up a small canvas bag. Arturo waves it off. "Not here," he says.

Felina hesitates, then follows his directions through Magnolia Beach, south to 512 Houston Street. The drive takes twenty-five minutes.

"It's an empty lot," Felina says once they've parked.

"Not quite," Arturo says, "you'll see."

There's a quarter moon, thin and high-watt, in the center of the windshield, a smear of clouds, and banks of half-hidden stars. Felina smells like rose petals.

She sets the canvas bag between them and then replaces both hands on the steering wheel. She keeps her face pointed forward, and the streetlights outline her profile. The black hair in a thick braid that's draped over her right shoulder. The smooth plane of forehead. The nose that's small and delicately proportioned. Lips which are slightly parted.

She's wearing a soft blue sweater and a jeans skirt and tan sandals. Looking at her, Arturo feels an ache that runs deeper than any kind of knife wound Eric Findley had managed to inflict.

"Connie said to thank you," Felina says. "You and the other man."

"His name's Mr. Weldon. Weldon Trulane."

Felina Sorbano lifts her right hand from the steering wheel, points at the canvas bag, and then returns her hand to its original position. "You can count it if you wish."

Arturo holds up his hand and waves off the offer.

"Luis might have picked Connie up to take home, but I told him I wanted to deliver the money myself," Felina says. "I needed to thank you."

"That was part of the deal," Arturo says, "Luis picking up Connie and delivering her to you. He wanted to be a hero in your eyes."

Felina glances over at Arturo and then away. She measures her words out carefully. "The world doesn't need any more heroes. It needs more good men."

Right now, Arturo doesn't care about good men or heroes, but rather the woman sitting across from him. "That could be a bag full of dreams if we let it," Arturo says.

"Don't talk like that, Arturo. I'm a married woman."

"Wrong answer," Arturo says. "You should have said, 'I love Luis Sorbano.'"

"That bag, it's a little pretend, that's all," she says. "A little pretend. Not real." She looks over at Arturo, then down and away. "Just like us sitting here. It's nice, but we're not teenagers anymore." She brings up a small tentative smile. "Those dreams you talk about, they're a lifetime ago."

Arturo reaches over and rests his hand atop Felina's on the steering wheel. She doesn't move her hand away. "I don't believe you, the pretend."

"You should," Felina says, spacing out each word, "because I am pregnant." Arturo can feel her hand beneath his tighten on the steering wheel. "We have been trying for a long time. Everyone, especially my Madre and Padre, says it's a blessing."

"What do you say it is?"

"Don't talk like that, Arturo." Felina pulls her hand out from under his. "It's life. I mean, a life. That's what it is."

Right then, Arturo Morales is twenty-two years old again and working construction in Burlington, North Carolina. He is in love with a young woman named Felina Fuentes. She is in love with him. Their love makes every breath feel equally necessary and reckless. Luis Sorbano with his Wings, Beer, and Burgers franchises and his old school manners with Felina's parents is not yet on the horizon.

But the moment is only a moment.

"I still don't understand," Felina says.

"What?"

"This. The empty lot," Felina says. "Why you asked me to drive here."

"I wanted you to see it."

"It's empty. Nothing more than cinders and ash and chain-link fence. There's nothing here."

THE LENGTH OF DAYS 193

"Yes there is," Arturo says.

"What then?"

"Life," Arturo says. "A life."

Felina frowns and shakes her head. "I don't see what you mean. Any of it."

Arturo asks her to close her eyes and then asks again, and when she does, he begins to conjure up A.M. Motors, describing the shiny rows of used cars, windshields running the price of each, the colored pennants snapping in the wind, the moonglow of the lot's halogen lights, the cinderblock office and Arturo himself standing on the top step and wearing a pair of pressed pants and a crisp white shirt open at the collar. His shoes are new and so is his watch.

He lays out every detail.

"There it is, Felina," he says. "Can you see it?"

Felina's shoulders are shaking. Her eyes are closed. Her hands still resting on the steering wheel.

"Can you see it?" Arturo asks again.

"I wish," Felina says. Her cheeks are wet. "I wish I could."

9:37 p.m. Charlotte Douglas International Airport

Evacuation and Exile. Johnny Doc Nowell understood the contours of each. He'd lived inside them before, and he has now started to once again. He feels like he's moving through a long tunnel with no light at the end, just an end in itself that he will eventually step into, an end that's provisional and smaller than the life he's in the process of leaving.

It's called Survival, he tells himself. Survival passing as an Exit Strategy.

Of course, he needed more time. Who didn't? Wasn't that the point of everything? Time in the face of Exit Strategies.

He's made it as far as Charlotte, North Carolina and the Charlotte Douglas airport. He's passed through TSA and is sitting in the Tic-Tac-Toe Lounge six gates away from the one for Delta Flight 2039 for Cleveland, Ohio.

The flight's an hour and a half from boarding. The bartender at the Tic-Tac-Toe delivers up a Scotch and Soda. Turner Classics playing *The Asphalt Jungle* on the set over the bar. The volume's low, but set for closed captions.

Cleveland to Baltimore to Buffalo to Rochester to Niagara Falls. The point was to keep moving but moving without a schedule that fit a pattern. He'd done his best to confuse the Bowen Brothers and whoever they sent after him.

His ultimate goal, once June and the summer get here and the new law of required passports to cross into Canada takes effect, is to get to Toronto. Once there, he'll disappear into the Vietnamese community clustered on Spadina Avenue and Dundas Street, maybe eventually moving west to Mississauga if circumstances warranted.

He intends to cross into Canada with a passport and documentation identifying himself with his given name: Nguyen Duc Xuan.

In the meantime, Johnny Doc Nowell has sent Johnny Doc Nowell West in a hopscotching series of flight and hotel reservations that eventually culminate in San Diego. A trail of breadcrumbs he hopes the Bowen Brothers will follow while Nguyen Duc Xuan heads east and north.

Johnny Doc turns back to the television. He estimates he's watched John Huston's *The Asphalt Jungle* probably three, maybe four, times. A jewelry heist film full of greed, violence, lies, corruption on every level of society, double-crosses, sabotaged plans, and layers of dark irony in a world too small and mean for tragedy.

Across from him, closed captioned, Sam Jaffe as Doc Riedenschneider, the master-mind behind the heist, says, *One way or another, we all work for our vice.* In Doc's case, it was girls. Young girls.

To Johnny Doc's left is a young man working hard to impress the woman sitting next to him. He's sporting an overly-symmetrical goatee and a full head of hair gelled in a throwback nod to Michael Douglas in *Wall Street.* He's gym and personal trainer fit and is wearing an expensive suit that moves in a blue sheen each time he does.

"I'm in Software," he says.

"And I'm not Mrs. Robinson," the woman says.

"Okay, but who's that?" he says. "Anyway, no wedding ring. I checked."

"Married to my job. I'm a Claims Adjustor."

"Software's the future," the young man says, "and I have both feet in each."

"Maybe," she says, "but I'll put my money on claims adjustment. There's always a disaster around any corner."

"Hard to get," he says. "I totally understand that. You like the thrill of the chase. Old-school moves."

"I'll let you buy me one more drink," she says, "and then I think you should disappear."

"Is this some kind of test?"

THE LENGTH OF DAYS

"No," she says. "In the meantime, I'll have another gin and tonic." For a brief moment, Johnny Doc and she meet eyes over the young man's padded suit shoulder.

Johnny Doc is not sure he'd call the woman beautiful, but she is striking, no denying that. He's drawn to the lips and the bright red lipstick that imprints the edge of the glass she's lifted to them. He likes her eyes, a deep clear brown and bracketed by fine lines she doesn't try to hide. He likes her hair, shoulder-length and a luxurious confusion of brown and red tones. He likes the black one-piece dress and shadowy cleavage.

Maybe, most of all, he likes her voice. It's slow and smoky and her own.

"I'm into mature women," the young man says. "Totally."

"No," she says. "You're into desperate women. And I'm not."

"I am more than capable." He holds up both hands. "You don't know what you're missing."

"No, you're wrong." The woman lifts her glass in his direction. "I know exactly what I'm missing, believe me."

She gets up and moves to the vacant seat to Johnny Doc's right.

"My name's Anna," she tells Johnny Doc. "It's a palindrome."

"Pardon me?"

"A palindrome," she says. "Spelled the same way forward and backward." She rests the gin and tonic against her lower lip, waits a long moment, and takes a slow sip.

"Please tell me you're not in Software," she says, setting down the glass.

"No," Johnny Doc says. "Tires. Not very exciting, I'm afraid. American Wheels, that's the name of the chain. Home base, Atlanta."

She reaches over and touches the ticket sticking out of the breast pocket of Johnny Doc's suit. "Cleveland?"

He smiles. "Exploring business opportunities."

She takes a sip of her drink and returns the smile. "Thank God you said business. If you'd said vacation, I'd be worried." She lifts the glass in Johnny Doc's direction. "Of course, only native Clevelanders get to make jokes like that. They've earned the right. All those lake effect snowstorms."

"So you're from there. A Claims Adjustor, right?"

"Someone's been eavesdropping." She wags her finger and leans closer. "Something happens. Something goes wrong. People put in a claim. I investigate. I take care of what's wrong. I adjust consequences." She

196   **LYNN KOSTOFF**

gives Johnny Doc a slow smile. "I'm good at what I do."

"I'm not surprised," Johnny Doc says.

"Someone once said surprise is the last refuge of the innocent."

Johnny Doc turns his head. "Pardon me? I didn't catch that. Something about a prize?"

"Let's call it a backhanded request for another drink." She touches Johnny Doc's forearm. "Okay? I'll be back in a moment." She heads in the direction of the women's bathroom.

When Anna returns and takes her seat, she sets her right hand on Johnny Doc's forearm again and nods at the gin and tonic. She knocks that smoky voice up into breathy falsetto range and says, *"Thanks, Uncle Lon."*

Johnny Doc pulls his arm away.

"Take it easy," Anna says. "You're not the only one that loves Turner Classics. That was my best shot at Marilyn Monroe doing Angela Phinlay playing up to her sugar daddy, Alonzo Emmerich who's Uncle Lon, the one who tried to double-cross everyone connected to the heist."

Johnny Doc leaves his arm where it is. "How do you know I'm a fan of Turner Classics?"

Anna shakes her head. "I told you I'm a Claims Adjustor. It's my job to notice things. While Mr. Software was trying to get in my pants, I noticed how intently you were watching *Asphalt Jungle*. Most men would have asked the bartender to change the channel to ESPN."

Johnny Doc slowly nods, picks up his glass, and touches it against Anna's.

She smiles. "To Cleveland."

They watch the rest of the film, trading comments on the characters and their fates.

They eventually end up with Doc Riedenschneider carrying a briefcase full of hot jewels and getting into a taxi. He's making his getaway.

"Where's he going?" Anna smiles again.

"Cleveland."

"Doc Riedenschneider's going to Cleveland. I'm from Cleveland. You're on your way to Cleveland."

"A coincidence," Johnny Doc says and codas with a small shrug.

"You know," Anna says, "there's a school of thought that says coincidences are anything but."

Doc Riedenschneider is free and clear. But then, a small detour. The taxi driver and he stop at a roadhouse. There's cold beer, cigars, food, a jukebox, and a teenage girl hanging out with teenage boys. A teenage

THE LENGTH OF DAYS

girl in a tight sweater and with sweet hips that's she auditioning on the dance floor.

Doc Riedenschneider's gaze zeroes in on her and holds.

The music stops,

None of the teenage boys have the green to restart the jukebox.

Doc Riedenschneider offers to fix that. He passes over a handful of change.

The taxi driver reminds Doc that they should get going because they have a long drive ahead of them.

Doc Riedenschneider holds up his hand. The girl starts dancing again, all torpedo bra and tight sweater and gyrating hips. Doc's eyes absorb every move.

Two cops appear at the roadhouse window. They recognize Doc Riedenschneider.

Anna looks over at Johnny Doc and shakes her head. "Doc almost made it. That's at the heart of everything. He had gotten away. In the end, though, he's like a lot of people."

Johnny Doc takes a sip of his drink and waits for her to finish.

"They should know better," she says, "but they never see it coming until it's too late."

10:33 p.m. 435 Chestnut Lane, Delmar Woods Subdivision

Carl Adkin is full.

He's a husband at the tail end of what his wife, Linda, calls a Date Night. The two of them are sitting together on the living room couch, the picture window in front of them holding a quarter moon and a handful of stars. The lights in the room are low. Carl's opened a second bottle of wine and poured each of them a glass.

Off to their right is the dining room and the table still holding the detritus of their meal. The bones from the steaks Carl had grilled on the deck behind the house. The buttery skins of the baked potatoes. The stray sautéed green bean. A depleted basket of dinner rolls. Empty salad bowls in drying sienna swaths of French dressing. The dessert dishes crumbed with Red Velvet cake. The first round of wine glasses ghosted with their fingerprints.

Each of the kids has been farmed out to a friend's for the night.

It had taken a while before Linda and he could move the evening to candlelit and romantic. They talked about a new refrigerator for Linda's mother. Carl Jr.'s cavalier attitude toward quadratic equations and

Algebra II test scores. Their daughter Savannah's stubborn belief in the Tooth Fairy and the six-dollar tab said Fairy was owed. The middle child, Richard, and his deepening retreat into hiding in plain sight. And what bills were due, and pressing, and which ones could be put on hold for now. Linda talked about some of the neighborhood gossip. Carl gave carefully edited anecdotes about work. They cleared their plates and went back for seconds. They finished the first bottle of wine, opened another, and moved to the living room.

Where Linda is resting her head against his shoulder. Her perfume smells like a cross between lemons and apples. Her skin is flushed and warm. Carl has known Linda since they were five years old. The arc of their lives had blurred together at some point he's now unable to remember. She's always been there. They've thrown each other's shadows for over thirty years.

Carl's full, and Linda's cuddled next to him, and he finds himself thinking of his father and can't say exactly why. His father had fucked up his life and his family's because he was decent and ambitious. He'd never been able to reconcile the two, each working against the other. He jumped from job to job, career to career, and was just successful enough in each to be dissatisfied and want more, but he then was too decent to do what was necessary to get it. His life had been the equivalent of trying to drive seventy mph in second gear.

Linda runs her hand along the inside of Carl's thigh. He forgets about fathers. He kisses the top of Linda's head.

Carl closes his eyes for a moment. He brings up the Linda of Date Night. The one with the new haircut, shorter with blonde highlights, that follows the contour of her jawline. His favorite dress, cleavage-friendly, and the bright lipstick and the lines that define and redefine what Carl has always thought her best feature: a set of cobalt blue eyes.

"John McKelvey called here earlier in the day looking for you," Linda says.

"He found me."

"I thought so." Linda lifts his right hand and kisses each knuckle.

Carl had been on break when McKelvey caught up with him. "1209 Hanover," he said. "Mario's Pizza, the one that closed down a few months ago. Come in the back door."

"What's this about?" Carl had asked.

"I found Truman Cooke's murderer," McKelvey said, "and I thought you'd like to meet him. See you in twenty."

THE LENGTH OF DAYS

When he got to Mario's, McKelvey handed him a small Bible bookmarked with a family photo, a pen with TCC running down each side, and a crumpled handkerchief holding the same monogram. "Lifted them off one of those homeless guys over in Garrison Park," he said. He pointed toward the next room. "I got him warmed up."

Mitch sat in a small room whose corners were filled with empty pizza boxes. He was handcuffed and studying something between his feet that turned out to be three of his teeth lying in thumbnail puddles of blood.

"Officer Carl," he said, "that policeman said I killed another policeman."

Carl realized he didn't know Mitch's last name. Mitch was Mitch. It had never gone further than that.

"I don't think I killed anyone, Officer Carl."

"You sure? Maybe you just forgot."

"Nobody forgets a sin, Officer Carl."

Carl waited, rubbing his jawline, and then said, "Best I can do, Mitch." He looked over his shoulder at the closed door. "Closest thing to mercy and forgiveness at hand, so listen up. When I tell you to yell, you do it. Okay? Every time I tell you, you yell."

Mitch nodded and did as he was told. Carl punched the wall, and Mitch yelled. They repeated the sequence a half dozen times. Carl then threw in two more for good measure.

By the time Carl rejoined McKelvey, the knuckles on his right hand were distended and bleeding. He nodded to McKelvey and went on to finish his shift. McKelvey went on to book Mitch.

"Let Mama make things right." Linda leans over and kisses the knuckles on Carl's right hand again. "There's Justice done. God bless you and John McKelvey."

Carl pulls Linda close and settles back against the couch. She's a cop wife, and it is Date Night, and he is full. He is slowly acknowledging and accommodating the one truth that nobody likes to admit: that given enough time, you can get used to anything.

It's that everyday truth that is the most profound and runs deepest. You set your alarm, and then you get up. You move through your days, and those days move through you.

There's no room, finally, for a dead Truman Cooke or room, as far as Carl can see, for forgiveness or atonement or hope. The everyday is everything. It has no room for anything but itself. Not even the space between stars or breath.

Carl Adkin kisses his wife. He's full. His heart is beating. He's counting on that to let him know he's alive.

11:53 p.m. 1607 Dalton Street

Pam Graves's dreams have always unfolded along familiar lines. They're fueled on and by the quotidian. She's usually riding a bus with rain-streaked windows, sitting in an empty church, standing in an exceedingly long line at the grocery store, watching an empty screen and waiting for a computer to boot up, navigating serpentine lines to get gas for her car, or setting the timer again and again for a meal that never is fully cooked.

Tonight's dream starts out no differently.

She's sitting in the back seat of the WTKW van. Dave Preston is driving, and Paul Westbrook, the cameraman, is in the passenger seat. Pam is scrolling through her phone for candidates for this afternoon's segment of *Rescue Me!* She knows, therefore, it's a Wednesday, and they're headed for the animal shelter on Cornelius Street.

When she looks up from the phone, though, the van is headed in the wrong direction, and Dave Preston and Paul Westbrook have disappeared. Instead, it's Pam's mother behind the wheel and her father in the passenger seat.

Her mother and father are talking, but Pam can only hear half the conversation because her mother's signing. Pam tries to read her mother's lips, but can't tease out anything. Her mother keeps lifting both hands from the wheel in order to sign, and both Pam and her father try to keep the worry and unease from their faces.

When Pam starts waving to get their attention, her parents disappear, and then it's Pam's dead twin brother Pete driving, and the passenger side is empty.

He winks at her from the rearview mirror and holds up a cold beer. She calls out his name. He hunches his shoulders as if he'd just been struck. He's driving faster than he should.

Pam closes her eyes and tries to wake up.

She looks back to the front of the van. Her brother's gone, and Madison Hopewell is now driving. There's a suitcase sitting upright in the passenger seat. Madison Hopewell keeps running red lights.

Outside the windows is a string of familiar landmarks—Saint Matthew's Lutheran Church, John C. Calhoun High School, the public library, the Laughing Zebra convenience store, the burned remains of the house at 805 Jefferson, the Lowe Tide, the home office of WTKW, the Second Wave bookstore, Dave's Deli, the Mercy General Hospital

THE LENGTH OF DAYS 201

complex, the Bayview Assisted Living Center, and the Mission Field Pier. The places are familiar, a part of Pam Graves's life, but they are now torn free of maps, GPS, or topography. None are where they should be.

The van picks up speed.

Then Madison Hopewell is gone, and Daren Lowe is behind the wheel.

Daren takes a photo of Pam from his pocket and props it on the dash. When he moves his hand, Pam can see that the fuel gauge is wavering on E.

She tries to get Daren's attention, leaning forward and reaching over to touch his shoulder, but he doesn't notice because he's talking to Pam's photo.

I'm back here, Pam says, but then like the others in her dream, Daren is suddenly gone.

This time Eric Findley's behind the wheel.

Buckle up, he says and winks into the rearview mirror.

Pam reaches for her seat belt. Her fingers find air. The belt's missing.

Please, she says, *Please,* but there's no one behind the wheel now.

The van's still moving fast. Pam Graves braces herself for the inevitable crash.

Except that doesn't happen either.

The van stalls out curbside at 1607 Dalton Street.

Pam frowns. The carriage house looks familiar. More than familiar.

The drapes are partially open, and there's a light on in the front room.

Pam Graves gets out of the van. She starts down the flagstone path toward the front door of the carriage house. The lawn and everything around her are moon-smeared.

Someone clears his throat.

Paul Westbrook, WTKW's cameraman, is standing in the front lawn. He lifts and readies his camera.

"Hey, it's Wednesday and *Rescue Me!,*" he says and begins filming. "Who is it this time?"

Pam Graves stops walking. She looks over at Paul Westbrook, then at the front window and the pale slice of light bisecting it.

Pam Graves wants to believe she's ready to rescue the woman who lives at 1607 Dalton Street, but as she walks to the front door, she's suddenly afraid there's nobody home, and she stands at the front door counting her breaths until she's ready.

Then she lifts her hand and knocks.

12:07 a.m. Bayview Manor Townhouses, 4-B.

Insomnia-driven, Samuel Fulton is in a small room off his kitchen trying to work out the logistics of sorting through an unwieldy pile of laundry when someone begins alternately knocking on the front door and ringing the doorbell.

The knocking and ringing double up.

"You going to let me in?" Weldon Trulane III says. He's cradling a brown paper bag against his chest.

Samuel Fulton opens the door the rest of the way, and Weldon steps into the foyer. He looks around, carefully taking in the downstairs, and says, "Didn't take you long, did it? Everything clean and in place. You erased any sign I'd ever been here." He looks around again. "Bet you've boxed and packed up all my stuff upstairs too."

Samuel Fulton doesn't say anything.

"Roger that." Weldon heads off to the kitchen. He drops into a chair at the table and sets the paper bag in front of him.

Samuel Fulton reluctantly follows and sits down across from him.

Weldon makes a show of holding up the bag and setting it down again.

He then takes out two six-packs of Abita Amber. "New Orleans finest," he says.

"You sure you need any more?" Samuel recognizes the early warning signs of one of Weldon's binges.

"Did it ever occur to you, Samuel, that you've spent your life being the spokesperson for the Self-Evident?" Weldon shakes his head and slides an Abita across the table.

"Why exactly are you here, Weldon?"

Weldon points at the six-packs. "Consider them a stand-in apology and reparations."

Samuel Fulton remains silent. He leaves the beer in front of him untouched.

"Hey, I'm trying here," Weldon says. "As usual, you're not making this easy."

"Most things in life aren't."

"Look, I'm talking apology here. I'm sorry I took the keys and your car and the Bersa, okay? I'm sorry I read that letter to Glenda you've been hanging onto." Weldon stops and slowly lets out his breath. "And I appreciate too that you helped out and took Arturo in until he healed."

THE LENGTH OF DAYS

"I did that for Arturo, and as far as anything else goes, apology accepted," Samuel says.

"A couple quarts low on the sincerity there, friend." Weldon shakes his head and takes a hit on the Abita.

Samuel starts to get up from the table, but Weldon holds up his hand, palm out. "Come on, share one beer. We'll call it a peace offering." Samuel sighs and sits back down.

Weldon's all smiles and nods.

They can't hide, though, what Samuel sees when he looks across the table at the small unshaven man in a battered and wrinkled seersucker suit.

Desperate and *ungroomed* come to mind. That's what the smiles and nods can't hide. Samuel's not sure the last one's even a word, but it seems to fit Weldon on any number of levels.

Samuel takes a sip of beer, then another. In between, he connects a couple dots.

"Didn't take that long, did it?" he asks Weldon.

Weldon frowns. "For what?"

It's Samuel's turn to nod and smile. "To get kicked off your ex-wife's boat and out of the Mimosa Bay Marina."

Weldon opens another beer. "The circumstances were extenuating."

"With you, they always are."

Weldon sits back in his chair. "You're enjoying this, aren't you?" He points at Samuel with his beer, then adds, "I'm sure I'm not the first person, Samuel, to point out that there's a definite Pharisaical cast to your character."

Weldon sits back in his chair. "Don't make me beg, okay? I need a place to crash. I know Jesus decided to take a pass on me as one of His Sunbeams. I didn't make the cut. My friend HT didn't either."

"HT?" Samuel asks. Weldon going off-topic, Samuel has never fully gotten used to it.

"Five days," Weldon says. "Five days and a lifetime."

Weldon then adds something Samuel doesn't catch at first.

"Love," Weldon says. "I said love, okay?"

Before Samuel can respond, Weldon launches into a customary monologue. He's back in New Orleans, and it's five days in 1968, June 28th through July 2cd to be exact, five days or 120 hours that Weldon claims came to define the arc of the rest of his life. Weldon in New Orleans on some trust fund bankrolled partying and running into his childhood friend, HT Rowe, in town for a convention of lawyers, and the two of them agreeing to get together for a drink later that over the course of the evening became drinks that in turn provided the means and opportunity for one thing leading to another, HT moving in and sharing Weldon's room and the cocoon-like privacy of the Gilmore Hotel for the next five days.

Then HT went back to Magnolia Beach, South Carolina and never again mentioned or acknowledged in any way the reality of those five days. He expunged, denied, and erased them, and completely cut Weldon out of his life, leaving no room for anything connected to those 120 hours in the summer of 1968.

"New Orleans, those five days, they should have made some kind of difference. You have any idea where that leaves you when it all dead-ends like that? When you lose everything you never had?"

Once again, before Samuel can say anything, Weldon plows on.

"I'll tell you where that leaves you," he says. "It leaves you an Old Homo who loved one man who couldn't love or admit to loving him. An Old Homo who lives in South Carolina where the only Stonewall anyone admitted to or knew was named Jackson. It leaves you me, an Old Homo with a heart full of painful memories and curdled regrets and a couple six packs of Abita Amber."

"Okay, okay," Samuel says. "You can stay here for a while, okay? Just calm down."

The thanks Samuel expected doesn't materialize.

"HT and I missed everything," Weldon says. "No one *celebrated* us. No one wore Rainbow Ribbons. No parades or rallies. We missed it all. We were cheated. HT stayed in the closet. I drank too much and hid behind Rhetorical Questions. We got old and missed it all." He abruptly stops and points his beer at Samuel again. "So don't talk to me about calming down. Cheated is *cheated*."

"Did you hear me?" Samuel says. "I said you could stay."

"You don't see it, do you?" Weldon asks softly. "You're more lost than I am."

Samuel frowns. "What are you talking about now?"

"Everyone thinks there's always enough time," Weldon says. "The thing is, there isn't. I wasn't gone that long," he says. "A couple drinks, that's all, and I didn't hear them."

"What?"

Weldon waits a long moment before answering. "HT's last words. I didn't hear them. I wasn't there. I should have been, but I wasn't. I'd been in his room sitting bedside all day, and then I went out for a quick

THE LENGTH OF DAYS

drink, and I missed them. His last words. HT was dead when I got back."

Weldon looks at Samuel and starts nodding, then suddenly gets up from the table and moves to the living room. A moment later, Samuel hears him opening and closing drawers.

Then he's back in the kitchen and at Samuel's shoulder. Weldon leans over and sets a pen and piece of paper in front of him.

Samuel looks at them, then at Weldon. "Why? I don't get it."

"A chance. Yours. HT and I missed everything. You don't have to." Weldon straightens the piece of paper and leans closer. "A letter to Glenda. From you. You owe her."

"That doesn't make any sense," Samuel says. "Glenda can't read it."

"Write the letter, Samuel. Ask her forgiveness."

"Forgiveness? Why?

Weldon moves back to his seat and picks up his beer. "I know you, Samuel. I know what you're thinking. Glenda cheated on you, and you were faithful to her, right?"

Samuel gives a small reluctant nod.

"Fuck your Faithful. We're talking about what matters. What holds. I only had five days. You've had forty-nine years with Glenda to figure that out."

Weldon points at the pen. "Pick it up, Samuel."

If the pen were an electrode holder and he was back at Ryland Iron and Steel welding railroad car frames and tankers, Samuel would know what to do with it. MIG, TIG, Stick or Flux-cored welding, at work or around the neighborhood, if something had weakened or cracked or broken, Samuel could fix it. He knew what to do. He had the eye. He had the hands. But now when he looks down at the blank sheet of paper, he doesn't have any idea how or where to begin.

"Jesus Christ, Samuel. Imagine I have a gun to your head," Weldon says, "and I'm not afraid to pull the trigger."

Samuel slowly pens in the date and Dear Glenda and then shuts down. The rest of the page looms and intimidates. "I don't have the words," he says. "I don't."

"Imagine the Bersa pressed against your temple. My finger on the trigger. We're talking Glenda and what matters and what's left and what you can do about it."

Samuel waits.

He eventually picks up the pen and starts hunting words, but then to his surprise, the words he's been hunting find him instead. It's like they were waiting for him. They come slowly and laboriously at first, but still there, appearing on the sheet of paper like images slowly developing in a photograph and gradually coming into focus, Samuel starting where everything does, at the beginning, when through the chance dynamics of alphabetical order, Glenda McGuire came to sit in the seat to the right of Samuel Fulton in middle school, and that moment tipped like the first domino in a line that stretched and snaked close to a half century, two lives that became a life, and with each word Samuel found, the length of those days returned and returned Samuel to himself and in doing so returned Glenda to him.

When he's done, Samuel Fulton sets down the pen and closes his eyes.

MISSION FIELD PIER 3:00 a.m. THE DEAD

Step up to the railing.
We're here.
There are many of us.
We've been waiting.
We have things to tell you.
Things that run through your dreams
and your days
and your grief and your fears
and the need that feeds upon itself
late at night.
Listen.
We're here.
We've always been here.
Don't be afraid.
There's truth in the Tides.
That's where everything starts
and ends.
We're here to tell you that
and other things
that shadow your breath.
But first you have to listen.
When you're ready,
this is what you must do.
Take your index
and middle fingers.

THE LENGTH OF DAYS

Put them together
and lift them.
Set them against the side of your neck
and press.
Listen to what you feel.
That is where we live.
You're ready now.
Listen.

Crime fiction fans should also enjoy....

Charlie Stella

Johnny Porno $15.95
"Psycho cops, bent cops, straight cops, Feds, wiseguys, good women, bad women, really bad women, guys on the make, gamblers, dumbasses, good guys, bad guys. This book's got 'em all (and more)."
—Bill Crider, author of the Sheriff Dan Rhodes series

Rough Riders $15.95
"Stella cares about his characters and he made me care about them too. Close to a masterpiece, *Rough Riders* is number one with a bullet."
—Mike Parker, *Crime Fiction Lover*

Eddie's World $9.99
"Stella is carving himself a niche in crime literature somewhere between the late Eugene Izzi's street noir and Elmore Leonard's ironic tragicomedies."—*Booklist*

Tommy Red $15.95
"Stella serves up a tasty goombah stew with a splash of Guiness, and no one can make this recipe simmer better than he does."
—*Publishers Weekly*

The Voices in My Head $17.95
"A masterful, stunning creation from Charlie Stella, as he tells the powerful story of his life. Once started, hell to put down."
—Marvin Minkler, *Bookseller*

Joey Piss Pot $15.95
Joseph Gallo is worried that his grandson is in with the mob, and nothing will stop him from preventing this from happening. "...the dialogue dances while the bodies fall."—Kevin Burton Smith, *Deadly Pleasures*

Rapino/Amato $15.95
In this sequel to *Joey Piss Pot*, mob hitman Giovanni Rapino is released from prison by the CIA and recruited to deal with the Mexican cartels operating in Bozeman, Montana.

In trade paperback from:
Stark House Press, 1315 H Street, Eureka, CA 95501
griffinskye3@sbcglobal.net / StarkHousePress.com
Available from your local bookstore, or order direct from our website.

Made in the USA
Monee, IL
02 July 2025